GETTING PAST PI[...] WAS THE EASIEST [...] OF GATHER MORSE'S JOB

Gather had to try to win ballgames with the most inept team ever to disgrace a major league uniform.

He had to get out from under a club owner who made George Steinbrenner look like a boy scout.

He had to survive the murderous wrath of black fans after his cocksure plan to get traded exploded in his face.

He had to break down the resistance of a fantastic beauty whose previous lovers had turned her off America's #1 indoor sport.

He had to satisfy the most ravenous groupie ever to hunt sexual souvenirs.

But fortunately for himself and his fans, Gather was always ready to rise to the occasion. . . .

BREAKING BALLS

SIGNET Sports Books You'll Want to Read

BREAKING BALLS

by

Marty Bell

A SIGNET BOOK
NEW AMERICAN LIBRARY
TIMES MIRROR

PUBLISHED BY
THE NEW AMERICAN LIBRARY
OF CANADA LIMITED

NAL BOOKS ARE ALSO AVAILABLE AT DISCOUNTS IN BULK
QUANTITY FOR INDUSTRIAL OR SALES-PROMOTIONAL USE.
FOR DETAILS, WRITE TO PREMIUM MARKETING DIVISION,
NEW AMERICAN LIBRARY, INC., 1301 AVENUE OF THE
AMERICAS, NEW YORK, NEW YORK 10019.

First Signet Printing, March, 1979
1 2 3 4 5 6 7 8 9

SIGNET, SIGNET CLASSICS, MENTOR, PLUME and
MERIDIAN BOOKS are published in Canada by The New
American Library of Canada Limited, Scarborough, Ontario

PRINTED IN CANADA
COVER PRINTED IN U.S.A.

For Peter Bell
and
Vida Blue

Prologue

This ain't just another one of those wisecracking, quick-buck, jock-type autobiographies. I swear it.

I was first asked to tell my side of this tragic story by an editor at *Sports Illustrated* I once got paired up with at the Garcia Aurora Memorial Golf Tournament in Hollywood. The Hollywood in Florida, that is.

I'm sure you remember Garcia, poor bastard. He was that shortstop for the Cardinals whose wife caught him in the sack with her sister, got near-hysterical, pulled out a pistol, and ended his career—and his life—prematurely. Garcia's teammates then took it upon themselves to see that the widow was provided for and started this annual fund-raiser, which just goes to show you that there are still some athletes who are concerned with more than what the other guy's making. 'Course, some folks kid about this and call it the Gotcha Aurora Memorial Golf Tournament, which I think is downright disrespectful.

Anyway, I entered last year's event and got teamed up with this editor I was telling you about. Guy turned out to be one of those journalists who leaves his integrity behind at the office. Fact is, he took just one putt on every green, picked up his ball, and said, "That's a gimme." Even when he rolled it fifteen feet past the cup, he still said, "That's a gimme." Then he got into our golf cart, asked me some real personal-type questions, and insisted I be honest with him.

I hadn't heard from the screwball since that tournament when he tracked me down here yesterday at my honeymoon suite in the Plaza Hotel in New York City. He called to offer me ten thousand dollars if I would put my version of my famous feud with August A. August, my former boss and the former owner of the Washington Dudes Baseball Club, into this here Sony tape recorder. (Just so happens, this tape recorder is a memento of the golf tournament where I met the man who made the offer, which I think is kind of fitting.)

Anyway, it seemed like the respectable thing to do, telling my side. Especially since anyone who ever pulled on a jock seems to be writing a book or making a movie these days. And besides, I gotta admit, I've been real troubled since Augie was found dead last Friday in his Washington home. Lot of those chipmunks writing for the newspapers keep implying that I'm somehow responsible for the old man's death. And that's ridiculous.

Sure, Augie and I spent the four years that I pitched for his team calling each other names that don't get printed in the papers. And there were times when I wanted to make the tip of his big ugly nose parallel with his cheekbones. I did do some crazy-ass things the last few weeks to force him to trade me. And, okay, I do happen to be honeymooning at this very minute with the lady he loved. That's all true. But does that make me a killer?

I know in spring training this year, Augie called one of the chipmunks over and quoted me as saying, "I hope the old man kicks the bucket." I guess that quote's appeared in just about every paper in the country in the last week. But it's just a whole lot of unpasteurized bulltwang. I never said it. Someone like me, who's scared he's gonna get himself killed every time he walks to the mound, doesn't joke about things like that. I did tell one writer that I wouldn't be upset if Augie got polio, but that's the meanest thing I ever said.

Other folks have pointed out my spending the first part of this season telling anyone who would listen that I was willing to do whatever it takes to get myself traded. And the record proves I did just that. But when I said "whatever it takes," I didn't include murder.

If you know me at all, you know that with all the hollering and squawking and name-calling and threatening, I still had some feeling for the old man. Not much, mind you, but some. There was a short time there, back about four years ago, when he treated me kinder than anyone else ever had, and I never forgot that. I always hoped, till the day he died, that our troubles with each other would evaporate, just like the stickum on my pitches does before the ump gets a look at the ball.

All I wanted, all I ever asked for, was that Augie show me he knew there was a person inside uniform number 13. But he always treated baseball players as if we were no different from the hamburgers he used to sell before he got into the game. That's all I was to him the last few years, a hamburger with a good curve. No one knows yet about the horrible things he did to me.

Maybe it's not fair for me to be telling these things now behind his back. But I've been anxious to get them off my chest. So when the editor from *Sports Illustrated* called me, I thought it would be a good idea for me to have my say once and for all. And the pin money he offered made it an even better idea. But before I committed myself to the magazine, I wanted to make sure that they were willing to print the whole truth. So, as long as I had the screwball on the phone, I asked him, "How much fucking and sucking you looking for?"

Guess he didn't expect that, 'cause there was this long silence. Then he cleared his throat and said, "Well, Gather. We're just a sports magazine and our readers don't take kindly to that sort of thing."

So here's this guy who cheats at golf, insists that I be honest with him, then offers me ten thousand dollars to tell my story, provided I leave out some of the most important parts. See what I mean about integrity? In good conscience, I couldn't take the man's money.

'Course, I was awake much of last night, listening to Melinda breathing in her sleep, thinking all about the nice things we could do with the extra cash. I was even tempted to call the editor in the middle of the night and tell him I changed my mind. But I got up this morning and decided that money is not the important thing. Not this time, anyway. I have to be able to tell the whole, honest truth.

Deceiving people doesn't sit right with me, except of course, when those people are standing up at home plate. Fact is, deceit has been the cause of all the problems in my life, especially my feud with Augie. So I forgot about the offer—for the time being—and decided to tell my story into this Sony just like I remember it, fucking and sucking and all.

I know this won't make things any better between me and Augie now that he's left us. You can't expect an apology from a dead man. But it will make it easier for Gather Morse to live with Gather Morse.

And maybe the fans and the chipmunks will get a chance to listen to what I have to say and stop accusing me of killing the old man.

Part I

The Trade-Me-Now-and-Get-What-You-Can-Or-I'm-Leaving-at-the-End-of-the-Season-for-Nothing Blues

1

I guess the best place to begin this story is back on June 1. That was the day I was first introduced to Melinda Towers, which makes it the beginning of the end of my career with the Washington Dudes.

I was scheduled to pitch that evening against the world-champion Cincinnati Reds, so I spent the afternoon at home, relaxing, in my apartment in Southwest Washington. Just about every baseball player I know has his own peculiar habits to get himself mentally and physically prepared for a game. And I'm no different. Some guys go in for TM or yoga or one of those other weird-type exercises. But all I need is a good, hearty pregame meal. So, round about one o'clock that afternoon, I received a visit from a little lady friend name of Laura Lacy. She was my pregame meal that particular day.

Now, I don't want you to start right off with the wrong impression of me. I'm not just another one of those jock pigs who has no respect for women and goes through them fast as he goes through a wad of tobacco. Really I'm not.

They say behind every good man there's a good woman, and I second that emotion. Fact is, before I hooked up with Melinda, there were thirteen good women behind me—one in each National League city. These ladies were largely responsible for my success, and that's not just a lot of bulltwang.

You see, even though I've been pitching since I was six years old, I still get pitiful nervous every time my turn comes up. Once the game begins, I can focus my mind on the hitters and my concentration becomes so intense that there's no room in my head for any worries. But if I have too much time by myself to think before a game, I get so sick and scared that a truckload of quaaludes wouldn't calm me down.

When I was in high school, this problem almost ruined my baseball career. But one lucky day at the end of my senior year, I fell upon a solution.

I grew up in this small farming town called Mantua, Ohio, about thirty miles south of Cleveland. I know I don't exactly talk like I came from Ohio anymore, but after hanging around the clubhouse for a short time, all baseball players start to talk alike. We all start tossing around the currently popular phrases. And since the majority of players are either good ol' boys or black folk, we all pick up a kind of Southern drawl. First time I went home to Mantua after my rookie season, Mom listened to me talk with horror in her eyes and said, "My God, Gather. You're starting to talk like a colored."

That's when I knew I couldn't be mistaken for anything but a major-league ballplayer.

Anyway, all week long during practice, I was the best pitcher on the Crestwood Heights High Red Devils. But on game day, I became a mental case and my stomach started in tumbling like a clothes dryer. Any food I tried to force down came right back up, and even though I was already six feet tall, I only weighed 135 pounds. My family doctor insisted that I quit the team for the sake of my health. But in order to be popular with the young ladies, you had to be a jock. So I was willing to live with my stomach problems and stick it out.

All my classmates knew when there was a game 'cause I spent the whole afternoon farting in class. It was embarrassing as hell. I spent more time in the boys' room than in the classroom.

By game time I was too nervous to concentrate on the mound, so Coach had to keep me on the bench. I was only on the squad for emergency situations.

We had a pretty fair team my senior year, but every other team in our league stunk. So we went undefeated and into the state championships. The day of the final game, against Elder High from Cincinnati, our history teacher caught Joey Fox, our number-one pitcher, jerking off under his desk. The old biddy made him stay after school and sit with his arms above his head until it got dark. This was an emergency situation and Coach had no choice but to let me pitch. I found out about this at lunch hour and I sat in the cafeteria shaking like an epileptic.

At the time, I was going out with this skinny little blond thing name of Susie Trees and had already asked her to the senior prom. We had touched each other in just about every place there is to touch, but we decided to leave the final plunge for prom night. At least, Susie decided. She said that way it would be something I always remembered. Shoot, we could have done it in McCluskey's barn on Arbor Day and I would have remembered it. But I respected Susie, so I went along with her. I even went to a pay phone and made a reservation for prom night at the Valley View Motel in Cleveland.

Susie spent the whole year charting her cycle. She wanted to make sure that when we did it (she never used the words; she always said "do it"), she wouldn't have to worry about getting herself pregnant. I really appreciated that. The other guys I knew all had to go to Claussen's, the only drugstore in Mantua, and pretend they were buying rubbers for their older brothers. But Mr. Claussen was a friend of my folks and knew I didn't have any brothers, so Susie was saving me some genuine embarrassment.

Susie saw how upset I was at lunch the day of the

championship game, so she suggested we take ourselves a little walk. We walked along the road outside the school for a few miles, holding hands, not saying a word to each other. It was a clear spring day in northern Ohio and the sky was streaked with white brushstrokes. The corn stalks along the road were nearly chin-high already. We walked into one cornfield and sat down together. A breeze was whistling through the stalks, but that was the only sound we heard. It was as if we were alone in our own little world. If my stomach wasn't aching, I could have enjoyed just being there with her.

We kissed a little bit, but my mind wasn't really on it. Then Susie said to me, "Come on, Gather. Let's do it."

"Do it?" I shrieked. "Are you crazy, Susie? Here? Now?"

"I wanna feel you inside me," she said. Just hearing her say that made me as hard as a Louisville Slugger.

"But, Susie," I said. "I already got that motel reservation."

"We're not gonna be able to do nothing on prom night," she said. And she looked like she was about to cry. "I figured it out. Just ain't gonna be possible. 'Less, of course, you cover yourself up with something."

Well, I tell you, I was struck plumb dumb. Here I was counting on this the entire senior year. I had spent plenty of nights in my bedroom with the door closed practicing up, pretending my pillow was Susie. "You sure," I said.

She just shook her head.

As you can see, I had no choice. So we took off our clothes and started rolling in the corn. Wasn't the most comfortable place to *do it*. And I was just this dumb hick then and didn't know much about loving yet. I didn't know that, just like in pitching, to be at your best when the action gets hot, you gotta warm up first. So I just tried to force my way on into Susie. She was as tight as a closed car hood and dry as your mouth after you smoke grass. I figured the only way I was getting in was with a pick and shovel. But I kept pushing, and before either of us knew what happened, I shot my load.

Well, both of us said it was the greatest thing that ever happened to us in our lives. And even if it wasn't, we certainly weren't going to admit it to each other, or to anyone else for that matter.

We walked back to school, holding hands, with smiles on our faces as wide as Lake Erie. And as I pulled on my uniform in the locker room, I wasn't worrying about those Elder High hitters. No sir. All I could think about was lying there naked in the cornfield with all of my skin pressed against all of Susie's. I was never so relaxed as I was going into that game that beautiful afternoon.

I'm not a smoke thrower, but I have big hands and I can make the ball do a boogaloo. Even now, on my better days, it usually takes me a few innings to get complete control of my breaking balls. But that afternoon, everything I threw from my first pitch on caught the corners. I was calm and controlled from the minute I took the mound, and I had those Elder hitters swinging where the ball wasn't. When it was all over, I had thrown a perfect game and we were state champions.

As chance would have it, there was this scout from the Washington Senators sitting in the stands that day with a contract intended for Joey Fox folded in his pocket. When the game was over, he erased Joey's name from the dotted line and put "Gather Morse" there instead. And a few months later, I left Mantua, Ohio, and Susie Trees behind forever and went off to Iowa City to play minor-league ball. I guess I should have split my first year's salary with Susie. Without her, I wouldn't be where I am today.

Needless to say, I have made sure to fuck my brains out the day of every game I've pitched since then. And I'm much better at it now.

After traveling for four years in the major leagues, I had ladies waiting for me in each town we visited. I dropped them each a little note before we got to town in-

forming them which day I'd be pitching. And before this
thing with Melinda got going, Laura Lacy was my main
lady in Washington. She had a Dudes' schedule in her
wallet with the days I was supposed to pitch marked off.
The whole arrangement got screwed up occasionally when
we had a rain-out or when Skip messed around with the
rotation. Sometimes I had to see the same lady two days
in a row. But that wasn't so bad. It all worked out well
enough to make me a twenty-game winner each of my first
two full years in the bigs, and the winner of my first eight
decisions this season.

Anyway, like I started to say, on June 1, Laura
came over to be my pregame meal. And I was just finishing up the appetizer when my telephone started ringing
away.

Just like a lot of folks, Laura doesn't like to be dis-
turbed while being eaten. With the first ring, I felt her
hand touch the back of my head and her legs rise up off
the mattress and onto my shoulders. The phone didn't
care and kept on ringing. But Laura had me clamped in
place where she wanted me. I was at her mercy, and so
was the caller.

I ignored the phone and kept slurping away at her. I'd
been at it for half an hour already but her pussy just
wouldn't stop. Fluid gushed from her soft, slimy skin till I
thought I had a waterfall running down my chin. My
tongue and her breathing kept getting faster and faster
and neither of us had any intention of stopping. But neither did the phone.

Must have rung a dozen times when Laura pressed
even harder on my head and my back and lifted the receiver with her one available limb. She's not the kind of
lady who's ashamed of anything, so she just panted right
into the phone and managed to say, "Yeah," between
breaths. I figured she had things under control, so I kept
at it. But then I heard her say, "He's eating now."

That remark startled me. I was agape in her groin. But

she dug her heels into my back, begging me to go on. So I did.

"Wait. . . . Wait. . . . Wait. . . ." she said into the phone, and I heard the receiver fall to the wood bedroom floor.

She was huffing and puffing and moaning now. And then she let out this screechy wail. It was a sound that only meant one thing, and it must have had my neighbors as well as whoever was on the other end of that phone call drooling with envy.

Her legs fell off my back and onto the bed like she had lost control of her muscles. I lifted my head up from between her thighs, wiped my mouth with the back of my hand, and reached for the dangling receiver. "Yeah," I muttered, hoping like hell it wasn't my mom who had been eavesdropping on us.

It wasn't. But it was almost as bad. It was the Skip.

"Gather, what the fuck are you doing there, you dumb sumbitch?" he growled in his familiar baritone, which was grainy from too much chewing tobacco. His voice was so loud it startled me and I shook my head to try to clear it out. Skip kept shouting. "You dumb sumbitch, you gotta pitch against the Reds tonight. You're gonna use up your legs on some dumb cunt. What are you gonna have left for the hitters?"

I just sat there dumbfounded waiting for my head to clear. I took a deep breath and still had the smell of Laura's pussy lingering in my nostrils. I shook my head again, then said, "Hey, Skip. What's up?"

He started right in shouting some more and I had to move the receiver away from my ear. "You're crazy, Morse. You're supposed to be getting yourself psyched up for the game, preparing yourself mentally."

I thought of telling him that that was exactly what I was doing, in my own fashion. If every pitcher on our club had the same pregame meal as I did, maybe we wouldn't have been a perennial last-place ball club.

But I didn't tell the Skip any of that. If I did, he would

have run right on into Augie August's office and reported
it to the old man, just like he reported anything the players ever told him in confidence. Skip was nothing more
than Augie's Sony tape recorder. And if the old man
knew about my pregame routine, he would have pulled
out the scorebooks, added up all the games I'd started
over the past four years, and fined me for breaking training before every one. I could just hear him saying,
"That's not what I have in mind when I give you meal
money, son."

I don't usually lie, but this time I didn't have much
choice. "I don't know what the lady was doing in here,
Skip," I said. "But I was out in the kitchen eating a big
juicy steak and drinking some milk."

"Just because you're a dumb shit," Skip screeched,
"you think I'm a dumb shit? Now, I know, Gather Morse,
that you were not out in the kitchen while some bitch lay
in your bedroom massaging herself into delirium. And if
you were, you're even a dumber sumbitch than I
thought."

This was one time I wanted to be a dumb sumbitch.
"Well, that's just what was happening, Skip," I said.

"You're crazy, Morse," Skip said. "You guys are all
crazy. Only way to win in this league is to find yourself a
team full of eunuchs."

"Are the Cincinnati Reds eunuchs?" I asked.

He didn't touch that one. "Now, look, Gather, my
boy," he said in a suddenly calmer tone of voice. "I'm
calling you to ease your mind a little before you pitch
against the world champions tonight. I know how upset
you've been about this contract hassle. Well, I just came
out of Augie's office and he's agreed to sit down again
with you and your agent tomorrow morning to try to
work things out once and for all. Between you and me, I
have a feeling he's ready to bend just a little bit."

That got me pissed off. Skip was deceiving me and he
was probably deceiving himself. He wasn't trying to ease
my mind, not with that news. I was pitching just fine

without a contract and I intended to continue that way until the end of the season. then put myself up for grabs on the open market. But Skip was trying to ease his own mind. He refused to believe that I really wanted to be a free agent. Without me, his team would be the underdogs in the Little League World Series.

"Hey, Skip," I said calmly but forcefully. "Like I've been telling you all season. I'm not gonna sign a new contract with the old man. We've got this free-agent business now, and I don't have to be Augie's slave anymore. Either he trades me or I'm playing out my option."

"Ah, come on, Gather." he said. "Just go to the meeting tomorrow. Listen to what the man has to say. Okay?"

"I don't wanna think about any meetings now," I said. "That'll just get me aggravated. And you know when I'm aggravated I don't pitch well. If this call goes on much longer, Skip, I'm gonna get hit hard tonight. Guarantee you that. And it's all gonna be your fault."

"Hey, Gather, my boy," he said, trying his damnedest to be gentle, "I didn't mean to razz you. You know I'm only thinking of you 'cause you're important to me."

"I sure am," I said. "That's the first sincere thing you've said."

"Now, you just go back into the kitchen and finish that steak," Skip said. "And come to the ball park tonight ready to beat the world champions. You hear me?"

I hung up the phone and sat there on the edge of the bed mad that Skip had called and bothered me. He knew I had to relax on days I pitched. And when I thought about Augie August, I couldn't relax. Just hearing the man's name started my stomach tumbling again.

I had to calm down. I had to be at my best that night. I wasn't just pitching for the team anymore. I was pitching for myself, for my freedom from Augie August. I was determined to win twenty-five or thirty games and make myself such a valuable property that any owner would give up his wife and kids if that's what it took to get me.

I turned and looked at Laura lying on my bed, her nipples standing straight up like two Washington Monuments side by side. Her tongue was circling her lips, begging me to come to her. "Give me, Fellini," she said in a soft, sexy voice.

I guess it's time I introduced Fellini right about here, since he's an important character in this story. Fellini is what everyone I know calls my cock. It was a name given to the big fella by the guys on my junior-high baseball team. One day they went around the locker room with a ruler measuring everybody. Without even getting excited, I measured 8½. So this one real smart kid named me Fellini, since a man by that name directed some movie called 8½. I never did see the film 'cause the smart kid told me I wouldn't understand it.

Anyway, I moved Fellini to Laura's lips. She had him standing up faster than a soldier when the sarge calls "Attention!" And in no time at all, she had my mind off baseballs and on my own.

At around five o'clock, Laura and me got in the yellow Stingray Augie had given me as a gift when I pitched a no-hitter in my rookie year and headed for her apartment up in the Northwest part of town. The sky over Washington that evening was the same gray color as most of the government buildings downtown. It was another one of those uncomfortably sticky June evenings and I could tell I had pit stains on my shirt five minutes after walking outside. Those kind of days ain't much good for anything except for pitching. At least, for my kind of pitching. Everything's so full of sweat that the umpire's not surprised to find a little moisture dripping off my ball as it travels toward the plate.

I dropped Laura off in front of her building on P Street, kissed her good-bye, and said I'd look forward to seeing her in five days. We were in town for a two-week homestand, our longest stay of the season, which meant I'd have three pitching turns and see Laura three times.

I would have seen her more often if she would have let me. She was one of the few ladies I knew that I even enjoyed talking with. We had a lot of things in common. Like the fact that she called herself a junk artist, which was exactly what some of the newspaper guys called me. She made erotic sculpture out of garbage she collected from junkyards. I had one of her pieces in my living room, a baseball player made of automobile parts. The whole thing couldn't have been more than a foot high, but she used two Rawlings baseballs for the cubes and a Louisville Slugger for the pecker. She called the piece *Gather Morse: Up for the Game.*

As you can see, she was a lady with a sense of humor, and that was one of the many things that I found so attractive. She said she was only attracted to me for my body, which both flattered me and offended me. She was pretty serious with this Panamanian art dealer. He was real dull, she said, but at least she could have a stable relationship with him, which was something she couldn't have with me. So I had to settle for seeing her on the days I pitched.

I could understand how she felt. If I was a lady, I sure wouldn't get myself involved in any kind of steady relationship with a baseball player, or any athlete for that matter. Messing around is, after all, as much a part of an athlete's life as Gatorade and Desenex.

I guess that's something that starts back in high school, where the jocks can have any lady they want just for the asking, and sometimes even without asking. I don't know of any high school in the whole country where the best-looking ladies don't hang out with the jocks. They just go together naturally like corned beef and cream soda. Back at Crestwood Heights, if you didn't play ball, you waited till the athletes picked their honeys, then chose yours from the leftovers. A lot of the guys who spent their time debating or building science projects didn't think that was fair. But those are the breaks.

It just seems like sports and sex are connected. The

classroom was for doodling, the lunchroom was for copying homework, and the locker room was for talking about pussy. Everyone knew that. If a teacher overheard you using a word that had something to do with sex, she'd say, "Save that for the locker room." Even she knew. Maybe it had something to do with the fact that there were all these guys standing around naked together, but if you didn't brag about what you were doing to whom, people thought you were some kind of faggot.

Well, the major-league clubhouse ain't much different from the high-school locker room. High-school jocks talk about trying to get pussy, and major-leaguers talk about how much they're getting. The only thing besides ladies that major-leaguers talk to each other about is money. But what do you expect? On any ball club you have a collection of white folk, black folk, and Latinos, country bumpkins and city slickers, teenage rookies and burned-out vets. These people don't have much in common except for the fact that they all get paid and they all get laid.

So sex is almost always on our tongues. And there's usually some foxes waiting outside the clubhouse door to show us it's on theirs too. For a jock, it seems like getting laid is as easy as taking a dump. For some of the older guys, it's easier. And once you've become accustomed to such things, it takes an unusual guy to give it up. I haven't met too many athletes who are that unusual.

Every athlete's aware of this, but some of them go off and get married anyway. Fact is, we have a joke in the clubhouse that rookies marry their hometown honeys and vets marry stewardesses. (Actually, stewardesses are usually hometown honeys who got left behind.) But any lady who thinks that getting a jock to marry her is gonna change his ways is one dumb mother. And she'll probably end up a lonely, unhappy mother, too.

I guess every lady who hitches up with a jock thinks it's gonna be different for her. Most of these ladies were the prettiest girls in town their whole young lives and are used to being treated like princesses. But the men they marry usually end up treating the prettiest girls in every other town like princesses instead of their wives.

Personally, I find this all kind of sad. But the record proves I'm right. Now, you say to me, "But, Gather, you went out and got yourself married."

And I say to you, "Buddy, when you fall madly in love with somebody, you think you can throw out the record book."

'Course, I never intended that it would end up this way between me and Melinda. She was just a means to an end. But I'll get to all that.

So I dropped off Laura, drove to the stadium, left my Stingray in the players' parking lot, and walked through the gray concrete tunnel under the stands to the clubhouse. I could tell I was near the clubhouse even if I was blindfolded, 'cause the smell of Ben-Gay seeped out into the hall.

I was usually one of the last guys to arrive before a game, but I always knew just what to expect when I walked in. Disco music was blaring from a radio, and Chi Chi Blanco, our center fielder, was standing in the middle of the room wearing nothing more than his Dudes' cap, sweat socks, and spikes, doing the Latin hustle with himself.

"Ooh, ah, ooh, yeah," he sang to the music. Every song that he sang had the same lyrics. "Ooh, ah, ooh, yeah."

"Gasser, Gasser," Chi Chi shouted when I walked in. "Want to learn to hustle, Gasser? Ooh, ah, ooh, yeah. Ooh, ah, ooh, yeah."

Gotta admit, Chi Chi sure could dance. Now, if he could only field as well, he would've made my life a lot easier.

Chatsworth Chung, our right fielder, rushed over and offered me a taste of his wife's latest concoction. Chatsworth is a soul chink, half black, half Chinese. Gabby Smith always said that on December 7 Chatsworth bombs

Pearl Bailey. Chatsworth shoved a little grits foo yung in my face, but I told him my stomach couldn't handle it.

Most of the other guys were just sitting quietly in front of their cubicles watching Chi Chi dance. Baseball's not a real emotional-type game like football, and you don't find any of those wild pep rallies going on in the clubhouse. You don't see any guys working themselves into a rage and punching out lockers or water coolers. 'Course, if our players did anything like that, Augie would charge them for the damage.

Most of the guys just come in, strip down to their Jockey shorts, and sit on their stools thinking by themselves till just before we have to go out and hit. I never have understood why everyone takes off their civvies soon as they arrive. Sometimes I think it's just because they want to show off their new Jockeys. I'm serious. You see, no major-leaguer would be caught dead wearing plain white underpants anymore. No sir. You gotta wear either pastels or patterns these days. Stars and stripes, rainbows, even polka dots. Pinky Potts, our left fielder, had the best Jockey-shorts collection on our team. He knew every boutique in every town we visited and checked out the latest models every trip we made. He even found this one pair in a boutique in L.A. that was flesh-colored and had pubic hair painted on the front. Only trouble was, when he went to take a leak, he forgot to pull them down.

I greeted a bunch of the jocks in Jockeys as I walked across the "August-auburn" carpet to my locker. The carpet was actually a common shade of cherry red, our team color, but like everything else, the old man had renamed the color after himself. Before he was finished, I hear he planned to have the name of the town changed from Washington to August. Probably would have succeeded if he'd lived long enough.

Right beside my locker, our starting infielders were already into their daily game of team dominoes. The teams were always the same—the right side of the infield, third baseman Rod Smith and shortstop Gabby Smith, against the left side, second baseman Tony Smith and first baseman Aurelio Smith. Actually, only Gabby and Rod were born with the name Smith. Tony's real name is Santucci and Aurelio's is Dominguez. But Augie gave them each a bonus to change their names to Smith. Old man thought it would be a good promotional gimmick. I guess it is. But it's very confusing trying to read our box scores. And neither Tony nor Aurelio can pronounce the *th* at the end of his new name.

I took off my civvies and hung them in my locker (I was wearing light blue Jockeys that day), then sat on my stool watching the Smiths play dominoes. Both teams cheated. The partners communicated across the table with hand signals that would have made a third-base coach proud. The Smiths all missed the signals when they were on the base paths, but they never missed one at the domino table.

"Hey, Gathermorse," Gabby said to me. He always ran my two names together as if they were one. "I hope you had some good ass today, 'cause we got a tough one tonight."

I had roomed with Gabby a few years back so he knew all about my regular pregame meal. And since Gabby knew, all the other guys knew too.

"Don't worry about me, Gabby," I said. "I spent the afternoon with one of the finest creations I ever did meet. Lady made me happier than you can imagine."

Gabby turned his attention away from the dominoes and toward me. "Yeah," he said, holding back from drooling. "Who was she?"

"Your wife," I said.

Gabby just sat there chewing on his wad of tobacco a little bit, then spit a long trail of tobacco juice at me. I ducked, and the juice hit Bubba Bassoon, who was sitting next to me, on the back of the neck. Bubba touched his neck with his hand, then looked at his hand. He stood up slowly, still looking at his hand.

Bubba's our catcher and he's built solid as the Capitol

Building. He's so strong that once he tried to swat a fly off his nose and broke three bones. He's six-foot-six and when he goes into his crouch behind the plate, he's still as tall as most of the hitters standing beside him. No one messes with Big Bubba.

Gabby was back at his game, pretending like it wasn't him who decorated the big fella's neck. But Bubba knew. He stood beside Gabby, dropped his pink-and-blue-striped Jockeys, scratched his cubes a little, then used our shortstop's thigh as a latrine. Gabby had no choice but to sit there and enjoy being violated. The other Smiths sat by biting their lower lips to hold back their laughter.

I laughed, then took some fan mail out of my locker and opened a few letters. They were all the same. Fans pleading with me to sign a new contract and stay with the Dudes. I appreciated their concern. Made me feel good that there were people out there who cared enough to write. But they weren't going to change my mind. If they knew what had gone down between Augie and me, I'm confident they would have understood my position. Fact is, I hope everyone who ever wrote to me gets a chance to hear this here tape in some form or another.

Just before we had to go out to hit, I ducked into the trainer's room so Benny the Nip could rub me down. Lying on the table there, I got my mind tuned up for the game by trying not to think about it. Instead, I closed my eyes and went over the videotape-replay-in-my-mind of my afternoon with lovely Laura Lacy. Benny the Nip knew my routine so he just massaged my muscles and didn't interrupt my thoughts.

I started right at the beginning with the kissing, then went through the whole shebang just like it happened. I moved my lips down her naked body, heading for the promised land. But when I got there, Skip interrupted, just like he had earlier in the afternoon.

"Gather, my boy," he growled. "Hope you're ready for the big one tonight."

I could smell his tobacco breath over me. I opened my

eyes and saw his chubby cheeks turned upward in a fatherly sort of grin. Skip's name was Jack Shaw, but the guys who didn't call him Skip called him Stubby because he looked just like Stubby Kaye. He was round as a baseball. His dome was bald and looked like a batting helmet with hair sticking out of the sides. The man was always smiling. I don't know what he smiled about. He was the fourth manager employed by Augie August in four years, and even though our sixteen and nineteen start was better than usual, we were still in last place and his pink slip was due to arrive any day.

I sat up on the table to get out of the direct path of his breath. "This isn't a big game, Skip," I said. "There are no big games when you're in last place."

"Come on, my boy," Skip said. "It's only June. We're not out of it yet. And besides, tonight we have a chance to knock off the world champions. We can beat 'em good with you out there."

"We haven't beaten anybody good in four years," I said.

He put his hand on my shoulder and looked me in the eye. I turned my head so I wouldn't have to smell his breath. "Gather, my boy," he said. "Why can't you be a happy fellow?"

"I was perfectly content before you walked in here," I said.

"I don't just mean right now," Skip said. "I mean in general. You don't get full enjoyment out of your life."

I didn't know what he was getting at, but whatever it was, I didn't want to hear it. "Look, Skip," I said, "you want me to be happy? Tell the old man to trade me, and I'll laugh my way through the rest of the season." I tried to get up off the table, but he pushed me back down.

"You see," he said, raising a finger in the air. "You're not a happy person. And why are you not a happy person? I'll tell you why. Because you're living in limbo. No one's happy when they're living in limbo."

"I'm not living in limbo, Skip," I said. "I'm living over

on R Street Southwest. You gotta come over sometime
and bother me there. But not now. I gotta hit."

The man wouldn't let me leave. "Hold it, my boy," he
said. "I'm trying to help you, and you won't let me. I care
about you, Gather. You're a fine boy and a talented boy.
Playing baseball is every kid's dream. It's a great game.
It's a great life. Boy, you've got the world by the balls."
He held his hand out in front of me with his palm up and
slowly made a fist. "Your only problem is you're living
with uncertainty. Your future is a dark room and you're
walking around carefully so you don't trip over anything.
But you have the power to turn on the light. Then you
can see your way. You can run through the room. You'll
be happy."

"Skip, just get out of the way before I put your lights
out," I said.

He took his hands off my shoulder and stepped back.
He pointed at me like I was a naughty little boy. "Okay,
you dumb sumbitch," he said. "Don't sign your fucking
contract. You think those fucking free agents are going to
get as much money next year as they did this year? No
way, boy. No way in hell. The owners made a mistake
and they know it. Next year you'll be playing somewhere
else and making dogshit."

"At least I'll be somewhere else," I said. "The money
don't mean a thing."

I walked out of the trainer's room and back to my
locker. On the way, I practically tripped over Chi Chi and
Aurelio, who were sitting on the floor doing their TM.

I couldn't get real mad at Skip. He was just carrying
out the orders Augie had given him, begging me to sign
like that. And he was trying to save his own ass, which is
all anybody ever tries to do. Skip was actually a pretty de-
cent guy. And I felt kind of sorry for him. He had no
brains, no talent, and was so ugly that the hookers on
Capitol Hill ran away when his car pulled up.

But that fucking Augie August. After the shit he pulled
on me, he still really believed that he could connive me

into staying with his team. I might as well tell you now that the problem wasn't money. I gotta say that because anytime an athlete's unhappy today, the fans think it's over money. Augie was already offering me about $200,-000 a year for three years, which was more money than I knew what to do with. No, money wasn't the problem at all. It was respect. Augie had wronged me, he had humiliated me, and I could never forgive him for it.

Now, I know a lot of folks have no sympathy for any athlete who cries the blues, because we're all getting paid so well. The money's supposed to make up for everything else. I get letters all the time that say, "Gather, keep your mouth shut and pitch."

But the money isn't the only important thing. You gotta get some joy out of what you're doing. And how can you get any joy when you have to come in every day and face a boss whose guts you hate? I hear stories all the time about people in normal jobs who quit because they can't stand their bosses. Those people just go off and look for another job in the same field. Well, that's all I wanted to do. I wanted to be just like the average Joe. In the past, baseball players couldn't think about things like that. They were the property of their owners. But the Messersmith-McNally decision changed all that. It eliminated baseball's reserve clause. It gave us the chance to quit and find work elsewhere. I'll bet if that decision had been made before 1973, if we had the chance then to become free agents and move around as we pleased, then Augie would have made damn sure he treated me a whole lot differently. But it was too late for that. For the first time, I had Augie August by the balls. Least, I thought I did.

I pulled on my August-auburn uniform with the yellow trim and the yellow number 13 on the back. Bubba called our uniforms "clown suits" and suggested we all wear clown makeup on our faces. He meant it as a joke, but Augie probably would've liked it and insisted we do it all the time. I can just hear the old man saying, "The kids love it and we need those little bastards."

I walked down the runway to the dugout and out onto the field to take some batting practice. We were the home team, so we hit first, but a lot of the Reds were already out there standing around the batting cage, making fun of our players' swings. I looked forward to that hour out on the field before the action began. Gave me an opportunity to shoot the shit with the opponents and find out if their GM's might be in the market for an all-star pitcher like myself. 'Course, baseball players never know what's really going on in the front office. The chipmunks from the newspapers all know more than we do. But we still stand around dreaming up deals. Then we pass them on to the chipmunks, hope they print it, and hope the front-office folk read it. It might give them some ideas they never thought of.

When it was my turn, I walked into the cage and took some cuts. Even when my mind is on it, I'm not much of a hitter. Fact is, I keep hoping the National League will adopt the designated-hitter rule to save me some embarrassment. That day, my mind wasn't even on my hitting. I was struggling to concentrate on Laura and not on the Reds. I swung at a few of the meatballs our batting-practice pitcher was dishing out. I managed to bounce a few around the infield, but whiffed at most of them.

"My grandma swings a better stick and she's eighty-seven years old," said a voice behind the cage.

"Yeah, but your grandma can't make her pitches dance," said another voice.

" 'Course she can't," said the first voice. "She don't wet them up."

I finished my ten cuts, turned around, and saw who the two wisecrackers were. I should have known all along. Pete Rose and Joe Morgan were standing with their noses in the cage, chattering away as always. I had gotten to know those two guys a little bit by playing on a few all-star teams with them. Shoot, they were always chattering away about something.

Only time they stopped chattering was when they were standing up at the plate, and I wished they'd talked some then. Might ruin their concentration a bit. I'd say concentration, along with quickness, is what separates the professional athletes from the guys who never make it. You gotta have that ability to wipe all your other worries out of your head and just think about what's happening at that very instant. I hear tennis players call it tunnel vision sometimes, which I never understood, 'cause I can't see nothing when I'm driving through a tunnel.

The guys with the best concentration are the most consistent major-leaguers. And you don't find too many who are more consistent than Pete Rose and Joe Morgan. Record speaks for itself. 'Course, when they're not concentrating, they're always chattering.

I walked out of the cage and over to talk with the two little wiseacres. I shook hands with Rose and he started wiping his paw on his pants. "He's got his palms greased up already," Rose said to Morgan, and we all started to laugh. They always kidded me about doctoring up the ball, and while I never admitted that I did, I never said that I didn't. I wanted them to be looking for greasers up at the plate. It gave them a little something extra to worry about and gave me a psychological edge. I'd do anything to get the edge on the hitters. If they were afraid to hit against a fairy pitcher, I'd spread a rumor that I was one of them too. And you know there aren't too many things I'd less like to be.

"Hey, Gather. You signed yet?" Morgan asked me. Like everyone else, they were always talking about money.

"Nah," I said.

"Well, don't sell yourself short," Rose said. "You hear me? You ain't got too many good years in this game, so you gotta get what you can while you can."

"Nah, I'm not gonna sign here," I said. "It's too late for that."

"Augie's crazy to let a pitcher good as you go over

money," Rose said. "A guy with your stuff don't come along every Christmas." One thing I like about both those guys is that, with all their joshing, they have a whole lot of respect for people with talent.

"Oh, he's offering me good money, Pete," I said. "More than I ever dreamed of making."

"What's good money?" Morgan asked.

"I don't think I should say," I said.

"More than Reggie Jackson's making?" Rose asked.

"Nah, not nearly that much," I said.

"More than Tom Seaver?" Rose asked.

"Yeah, I guess it's more than Seaver," I said.

"More than I'm making?" Rose asked.

"A little less, I think," I said.

Rose smiled a little at that one. "Well, a pitcher only works every five days," he said. "Shouldn't make as much as a regular."

Morgan spit some tobacco juice on the grass, leaned on his bat, and said, "Papers say he's not offering enough."

"Hey," I said. "Don't believe what you read in the papers. Those writers don't know about my troubles with the old man. Soon as they know something's wrong, they think money. Make it sound like all that matters to us is money."

"I hear ya," Morgan said.

"Yeah," said Rose. "I don't care about money. Long as they pay me what I think I deserve, I don't care about it."

"Well, he's offering me what I deserve," I said.

"So sign, man," Morgan said.

"Nah, I'm not gonna," I said. "Man's done a lot of things to me I'll never forgive him for. Money won't change that."

"What'd he do to ya, Gather?" Morgan asked.

"Well, it's a long story," I said. "I'll tell you about it sometime, but not now. I gotta pitch against you, and talking about it gets me upset and hurts my concentration."

"Tell us about it, then," Morgan said, spitting out some more tobacco juice.

We all laughed.

"Well, I sure wish we could get you over our side," Rose said.

That started me off daydreaming a little bit. I would have loved to pitch for the Reds. What pitcher wouldn't? They score so much that a pitcher can afford to make a mistake or two without it costing him the ball game. And they have so much speed and intelligence in the field that they cover up a lot of the pitcher's mistakes. Sometimes I think they've intentionally maintained a mediocre pitching staff to let the opposing hitters make contact and provide their fielders with a chance to show off their skills. But the best thing about pitching for the Reds is that you don't have to pitch against them. "Boy, I'd give anything to pitch for you guys," I said. "Why don't you put a bug in your GM's ear?"

"Tell him yourself," Rose said. "Dick Wagner's here in town with us. He'll be sitting in Augie's box tonight."

My first thought was that maybe I was the reason Dick Wagner had come to Washington. It was no secret that I wasn't planning on signing a new contract with the Dudes. So maybe Wagner was in town to try to pry me loose.

I said good-bye to Rose and Morgan and strutted confidently back to the clubhouse, twirling my bat like it was a baton. I was glad I had talked with them, 'cause they had given me a little extra motivation. Baseball folk like to call motivation the X factor, the unknown quantity. I found this out when a guy named Shep Stinson, an Oriole scout, came to our high school and spent a day following all the seniors on our baseball team around. He trailed me into one class and said he was just checking up on my X-factor. "How can you check on it if it's an unknown quantity?" I asked him. I guess he didn't like that, 'cause the Orioles never drafted me.

Well, that night my motivation was a known quantity. I was determined to convince Dick Wagner, if he wasn't already convinced, that I was just what the Reds needed to win a third straight world-championship. And the best way to convince him was to prove that his boys couldn't hit me. 'Cause if the Cincinnati Reds can't get to you with their loaded lineup, then there ain't any other team in existence that can.

At about 7:15 our guys headed for the dugout to begin the game. I waited until everyone was out of the clubhouse, like I always do when I pitch. I had some last-minute business to attend to.

When the room was empty, I reached into the inner pocket of my sport coat and took out a spray can. I hid the can in my jersey and walked into the john to make sure Benny the Nip didn't see what I was up to.

I'm gonna let you in on a little secret now that I never even let my teammates know about. It's the kind of thing pitchers just don't talk about. But I said right from the start that I was gonna put the whole story down on tape, and if this doesn't prove that, then nothing will.

'Course, I may just be joshing you. This may all be a lot of bulltwang. You'll never know. And neither will the guys around the league. I might be making this whole thing up just to give the hitters who face me something else to think about. And then again, I might not. Eat your heart out, Pete Rose!

Now, like I told you, I'm what the press calls a junk-ball artist, and what I like to call a breaking-ball pitcher. I'm just not capable of throwing major-league smoke.

Fact is, if I try to throw a fastball, my catcher could go out for coffee while I'm in my windup and get back behind the plate in time to catch my pitch.

Sure I wish I had a hummer like Tom Seaver or Nolan Ryan. It would make my job a whole lot easier. If a pitcher knows he can just rear back and burn one by a hitter anytime he wants to, he doesn't have to be as careful with every single pitch. He can have a few lapses in his concentration and still get by.

But I can't do that. So instead of intimidating hitters, I have to deceive them. Like I told you, pitching is the only time I believe in deceiving people. Every pitch I throw looks like it's going one place but ends up someplace else. I can make the ball break right, left, up, down, sometimes all four on the same pitch. If you were hitting against me, you'd be standing up there, watching the ball coming at you, trying to guess where it was going to break. And most of the time you'd guess wrong. Guarantee you that.

No hitter is in control of the entire strike zone. The better hitters just control more of it than the others. But even the best hitters have spots where they see the ball best and make their best contact. My skill is keeping it away from those spots. Some players say my skill is boring the hitter to death. They say it takes so long for my ball to reach the plate that by the time it gets there, they're too bored to swing. If that's true, it's fine with me. I'm not proud, I'm just successful.

Okay. Here's my secret.

In high school and in the low minors, I was able to fool the hitters just by using the legal breaking pitches—curve, screwball, and an occasional slider. Most young pitchers only throw smoke, and so a kid with my stuff was as rare as black folk who don't know how to dance. I had and still have what they call a street-corner curve, which means you can stand around the corner and I can still throw the ball to you. But when I got near the top of the minors, even that pitch wasn't enough to get all the hitters out.

We had this pitching coach on the Charleston Comanches, my Double A ball club, guy named Winnie Turkel, who you may know, since he spent a few years in the bigs with the Chicago Cubs. Winnie was a breaking-ball pitcher too, so we understood each other.

One day, after I got banged around pretty hard, Winnie took me aside and said, "Gather, you don't have no drop pitch. If you're gonna make it without smoke in the bigs, you gotta get yourself a drop pitch."

"Okay, Winnie," I said. "Teach me to throw a drop pitch."

"Don't you know what I'm saying, boy?" He said. I was real embarrassed, but I didn't.

So that night, Winnie took me out to a local hamburger joint to get some eats. We were sitting at a table downing some greasy hamburgers when Winnie said, "Wait here a minute." He got up, went out to his car, and came back with a baseball. It was after eleven and there was no one else in the place to witness what happened next.

Winnie told me to stand up, and he walked to the other end of the restaurant carrying the baseball and a bottle of ketchup. He stuck his finger in the ketchup bottle, wound up, and threw the ball at me. I held out my hands to catch it, but just before it reached me, it dropped to my feet and hit the toe of my Weejun.

"Now, that's a drop pitch, boy," he said.

"Oh, you mean a greaser," I said.

"Boy," he said. "In the bigs, there ain't no such thing as a greaser. There ain't no such thing as a spitter. There's only a drop pitch. Got it?"

As we were driving back home, I asked Winnie what he used to doctor up the ball. "Only natural stickum," he said.

"What kind of natural stickum?" I asked.

"Well, boy," he said. "In between innings, I would go down the runway outside the dugout, where no one could see me, and whack off."

"Nah," I said.

"Swear to God," Winnie said. "Gave me just enough stickum to get through the next inning. Only trouble was, I was never able to pitch more than three innings a night. That's why I was always a relief pitcher."

I swore the man was joshing me, but he swore he wasn't. Even said his wife eventually divorced him on grounds of lack of affection. "But it was worth it," he said. "Got me a shot at the bigs. They should have a plaque in the Hall of Fame for me. I'm the only player in baseball history who had to retire because of impotence."

I didn't know whether to laugh or cry at that one. "Now, you're a starter, boy," he said. "And unless you're the world's biggest stud, you just ain't gonna have enough natural stickum in you to go a full nine innings. So you gotta find your own magic solution.

"But take a little tip from me. Whatever you use, always hide it in your crotch. Baseball players are always scratching their balls out there, so the ump won't think you're doing anything unnatural. And even if he does, he ain't gonna come out to the mound and rub his hand in your crotch in front of all those people."

Now, I'm not the kind of guy who likes to do anything illegal, except of course when it's absolutely necessary, which is the way most folks are, I guess. And I was determined to make it to the bigs, so this time it seemed absolutely necessary. I started working on my drop pitch, experimenting with Vaseline, marmalade, K-Y jelly, all the things you hear about. But one thing Winnie didn't warn me about is that if you throw a drop pitch, you need a catcher who rubs the ball good in his mitt before he lets the ump take a peek. And at Charleston, I was stuck with this catcher named Luther Davis who I couldn't depend on. Luther was one of those born-again Christian folk and he insisted that if he wiped off my ball, he was deceiving the Lord and he'd be struck down dead right there at home plate. So I not only had to hide the stuff from the ump, but also from my own catcher.

One day I went down to Joe's Department Store and shared my little problem with Joe Stankovitz, who owned the place. Joe was a real Comanche fan and he was glad to help me out. Me and him, we took every spray can on the shelves into the yard and tried all the contents out. Sure enough, I found my foolproof magic solution, which I've been using to this very day. Scrubble Bubbles Bathroom Cleaner. Greatest stuff in the world. It's as if they invented it for pitching. It's there when you release the ball and gone by the time the catcher catches it. Now I have a great drop pitch and the cleanest bathrooms in town.

So that day before I took the mound against the Reds, I squirted a good glob of the stuff in my crotch, enough to get me through the first inning. Then I headed to the dugout, stopping along the way to hide my can behind the water cooler, ready to beat the world champions.

At 7:30, my teammates ran out onto the field and I walked slowly to the mound. I'm not bow-legged like a lot of jocks, but I walked like I was so I wouldn't rub out the Scrubble Bubbles between my legs.

I picked up the ball and looked around the stands. On an average weekday night, our stadium usually looks like a crossword puzzle before anyone starts filling in the spaces. But that evening, the fifty-five-thousand seats were more than half filled. Part of the reason for the crowd was that me pitching against the Reds was as good an attraction as the Washington fans were gonna get. But most of the credit should go to the clever advertising campaign Augie thought up for the Reds' visit.

Like every other owner, Augie ran little one-column teaser ads in the local papers the day of every game. In most cities, those ads just stated the date, the starting time, and the teams involved. Occasionally they might also name a few of the star players on the visiting team. But Augie's ads were more creative. He realized that the one thing Americans are most interested in is gossip, and so he filled his ads with juicy lines that sounded as if they came right off the pages of the *National Enquirer.* For this game, the ad read, "Tonight. Dudes vs. Cincinnati Reds. Come out and see Johnny Bench, a great baseball star currently involved in a sensational divorce case. A man whose wife accuses him of having spent his entire honeymoon playing Ping-Pong. Will he take his anger and frustration out on our Dudes?"

Well, the fans sure responded. And when there's a sizable crowd, major-league ball parks are sure pretty places. More colorful, even than Pinky Potts's underpants. And RFK is even prettier than most of the new parks, because it still has real grass. The screaming fans and the sheer beauty of the setting sent a chill running from my ears to my toes every time I took the mound. I liked to tell ladies that I met in bars in Washington, especially ladies who worked in those fluorescent-lighted gray cubicles in the government buildings, which is where most everybody in town worked, that I had the prettiest office in the city.

I turned toward center field to listen to the National Anthem and I had to laugh, 'cause Chi Chi was standing in center field scratching his ass through the whole song. But I guess he don't know nothing about respect for our country, since he's only a Latino.

When the song ended, I turned back toward home plate to complete my warm-ups. I glanced over at Augie's box beside our dugout to make sure that Dick Wagner, the Reds' vice-president, was sitting there like he was supposed to. Wagner was there, all right, sitting behind the old man. But I didn't look at him too long. 'Cause, much to my surprise, sitting in the seat next to our dear old owner, was just about the most beautiful creature these eyes have ever had the pleasure of staring at. This lady had hair the color of daffodils and so shiny that the stadium lights formed a glow around her head. She was wearing these dark glasses, like she was some kind of movie star or something, so I couldn't get a real good look at her face. But that didn't matter. What I could see was fine. She was dressed appropriately for that muggy night in this blue halter top that covered her speakers about as successfully as a quilt would cover the Rocky Mountains. Boy, would I love to spend my vacation camping out in those hills, I said to myself. And I never considered myself much of an outdoors type. I felt Fellini pushing himself up out of my jock strap. Anyone in the stands with a pair of binoculars could see my mind wasn't on the game.

Augie August wasn't exactly what you'd call a ladies' man. He wasn't queer or nothing, but he was a little uneasy around women. He never had time for women because he was always working so hard. Or maybe he had so much time to work because he never had women. Whichever, he had managed to stay unmarried for all of his fifty-six years, which is quite an accomplishment with all the money he had. You'd figure some gold-digging bitch would have found the way to his wallet via his fly. But he avoided that, probably because he was so cheap.

So I wondered what this artistic creation was doing with the old man. I wondered where he'd found her. But wherever he'd found her, I wished he'd left her there for the night. I was sure gonna have trouble looking at Pete Rose standing at home plate with her sitting beside the dugout. I once heard Tommy LaSorda, then the Dodgers' third-base coach, tell Rose, "Congratulations, Pete. You came in second in the voting for the best-looking guy on your team. Everyone else tied for first." Well, far as I was concerned, that night everyone else at RFK tied for second behind that lady.

I couldn't take my eyes off her. Bubba came running out to the mound and told me that the home-plate ump had called "Play ball" five times already. But I hadn't heard him. I apologized to Bubba and got ready to throw my first pitch. Since I'm a lefty, I always had a good view of Augie's box when I was on the mound. It usually bothered me, since I hated even looking at the guy. But that night, with that lady beside him, I had the best view in the house. It was too bad I had to waste my time pitching.

Pete Rose stepped into the right-hander's batter's box and flashed a wise-ass grin at me. Sumbitch was daring me to get him out. Rose is a spray hitter who will take any pitch you give him and slap it into an open space on the field. I just have to keep moving the ball around on him and hope he doesn't get good wood on it. The drop pitch comes in handy, because if he does hit it, at least it will be on the ground.

Sure enough, Bubba flashed a fist, calling for a drop pitch right off the bat. The only problem was, I was inhibited about scratching my balls. The lady sitting next to Augie might think I was showing off for her. So I ignored the signal and threw what was supposed to be a curve. But I wasn't concentrating real good and I didn't snap my wrist down hard enough. The ball headed right for the middle of the plate. I prayed for it to break someplace, but it didn't. Rose's eyes opened real wide like a waiter had just put a juicy steak down in front of him. He whipped his bat at the ball.

He made solid contact, and the next thing I knew, a line drive was heading at my skull. I hit the dirt. I was amazed that it didn't hit me. I was even more amazed to discover that Gabby Smith had made a lunging grab behind second base.

Bubba came running out to the mound to make sure I was all right. He was real comforting. "You dumb fuck," he said. "Why didn't you throw what I asked for?"

"Sorry, Bubba," I said. "I was a little distracted by the scenery." I moved my eyes toward Augie's box, and he looked over there, then back at me.

"Look, asshole," he said. "I don't give a fuck if Charlie's Angels are sitting there with their feet on the rail and their beavers hanging out. Get in the game, man. You coulda got yourself killed."

I knew Bubba was right. Standing on the pitcher's mound can be like standing on the wrong end of a shooting gallery. You can get killed out there. Fact is, first baseball game I ever saw live was the one where Herb Score damn near got his head knocked off. And that game affected my whole life.

It was May 7, 1956, my seventh birthday. And my Dad had gotten two box-seat tickets from Mr. Catchings, the man who owned the truck Dad drove. It started out to be a real exciting day for me. Since we lived just south of Cleveland, the Indians were my favorite team and Herb Score was my favorite player. I was going to grow up to be him, even though I couldn't throw smoke. Herb Score pitched that day against World-Champion Yankees, and it was as if they had arranged the match-up for me.

I remember that game as well as I remember that day with Susie Trees in the cornfield. I was sitting in a box right behind the Indians' dugout, eating some peanuts, when the game began. Hank Bauer, the Yankees' right fielder, was the first batter. Herb Score threw a little smoke past him, then fooled him with an off-speed pitch. Bauer got some wood on the ball and bounced it to third-baseman Al Smith. Smith fielded it with ease and tossed it to first baseman Vic Wertz for an easy out.

Gil McDougald came up next. Herb Score went into his windup and McDougald seemed to be swinging before the pitcher even released the ball. Then I heard two cracks. Like two gun shots. The first crack was the sound of McDougald's bat against the ball. The second crack was the sound of the ball against Herb Score's head. The pitcher fell to the ground. The ball ricocheted to Al Smith, who grabbed it and threw McDougald out.

After throwing, Smith ran to the mound. Players were rushing out of the dugouts and in from the field. And my favorite player, Herb Score, was lying there motionless on the clay, blood flowing from his head. I was horrified. I felt tears crawling down my cheeks and peanuts tumbling in my stomach. As I think of it now, I still feel like crying.

A stretcher was brought out and Herb Score was carried off the field right in front of me. The blood had dripped down his face and all over his white flannel uniform.

"Is he dead, Dad?" I asked.

"Dead? He's not dead, son," Dad said. "It's just a game."

But I didn't believe Dad. Herb Score sure looked dead to me. I had gone to see my first live baseball game and thought I had seen my first dead man. I couldn't keep myself from crying. Snot ran down my lip and into my mouth. I gagged a few times, then barfed my peanuts all over this fat lady sitting in front of me. Before the Indians even came to bat, me and Dad were in his car heading back home.

I couldn't get that picture of Herb Score lying there covered with blood out of my mind. Every time I closed my eyes, I saw this baseball the size of a medicine ball coming at my skull. I didn't sleep. I didn't eat. And I sure as hell didn't play baseball. You could get killed playing that game.

I must have spent the whole summer lying in bed with my door closed. When school started again in September, I had to leave my room for part of the day. But as soon as the last bell rang, I got right on the first bus and headed for my bedroom. The other kids all stayed around to play baseball in the schoolyard. But not me.

One day, must've been late September, I got off the school bus and saw Dad's red Mack truck parked on our dirt driveway. I never remembered Dad getting home from work before I got home from school, so I figured something was wrong.

I walked through the screen door in back of the house and into the kitchen. Dad was sitting there at the table, wearing my Indians' cap, holding a bat, a glove, and a hardball.

"Come on, son," he said. "We're going to have ourselves a catch."

My eyes opened wide as the O's on an electric scoreboard. I told Dad I had too much homework to do.

He stood up, walked over to me, and put his hairy hands on both my shoulders. "Look at me, son," he said in a gentle voice, which wasn't like him. "This is the first time in the fifteen years I've been driving for Mr. Catchings that I've come home from work early. I don't even come home early when I'm feeling sick. But I came home today to play ball with you."

I could tell this was real important to him, so I had no choice. I left my schoolbooks on the table and followed him out into the yard. He threw me my glove and I walked through the brown weeds that came up to my ankles until he told me to stop. I put my glove on my right hand. The leather was stiff and dry, since I hadn't used it in a long time. It felt strange against my skin, like it didn't belong.

Dad started by hitting me grounders. Slow ones at first, then faster ones. I fielded the first few with my head turned away from the ball. But as I got more confident, I started looking down.

After an hour or so of grounders, Dad hit me a pop-up. One of those slow, lazy flies that seems like it's never coming down. I put my glove out in front of my body with the palm up and stretched my arm out as far as it would go. The ball still fell a foot in front of my glove. Dad yelled, "You look like a sissy, son. Hold that there glove up in front of your face like I showed ya."

He hit another pop-up and I held the glove up in front of my face. It blocked my eyes so I didn't have to see the ball. But the ball must've seen me 'cause it fell right into my glove. I was surprised by how easy it was, and it got easier as we went along.

The sun was already starting to disappear behind McCluskey's barn down the road when Dad yelled to me, "Okay, son. This is too easy. Get yourself ready for a real major-league pop-up."

I spread my legs apart under me, opened my eyes wide,

and looked at Dad. He tossed the ball up with his left hand and whipped his bat. But he didn't hit a pop-up. He hit a line drive. Right at my head. In panic I threw the glove up in front of my face. I felt the ball smack against the leather, and I fell backward to the ground.

"Stand up, you sissy," Dad yelled.

I jumped up. I ran into the kitchen, through the living room, into the bathroom. And I deposited my school lunch in the john. Then I went into my room, jumped on my bed, took my hand out of my glove, and wrapped my arms around my pillow. I started crying. My stomach was churning away.

I got up to walk back to the bathroom, but Dad was standing there blocking my doorway. His hefty frame seemed to fill the whole space. I couldn't possibly get by him.

His chest was pumping up and down. His skin was stretched so tight across his face that if there was a seam it would have split. His fists were clenched and his muscles were bulging. I don't ever remember seeing him that mad.

"Now, listen here, you little sissy-ass," he said, straining to get the words out. "You don't eat, you don't sleep, you don't go out of this house. All you ever do is throw up. You're making yourself sick, you're making your mother sick, and you're making me sick. I'm not putting up with this sissy crap from you anymore.

"You come back out there to the yard or I'm going to whip your butt. You're going to stand up there and catch anything I hit at you, just like a man."

He stood there waiting for me and looked bigger and meaner than he had ever looked before. His breathing got heavier and heavier. I didn't know what to do.

I couldn't see Mom come up behind him, but I heard her voice. It was cracking and worried. "John, John," she pleaded. "Please calm down. You're going to give yourself a heart attack."

She took him by the shoulders and led him away. She

reached inside my room to close the door and said, "My God, Gather. You're going to kill your father."

Well, that made me feel even more miserable. I didn't want Dad to die. I didn't want Mom to hate me. I had to play baseball, even if I was going to get killed doing it. It was either me or Dad.

I reached on the bed and picked up my glove. The ball fell out of it and rolled on the floor. I was stunned. I had caught the ball. I had caught the line drive.

I walked out of my room and into the kitchen. When Dad saw me, he didn't say word. He just picked up the bat and led me back out into the yard. And he hit line drives at me until the crickets were screeching and we couldn't see the ball in the darkness.

We played like that every evening for months. After a while we started using two balls. When I was throwing one, he was hitting the other. I still hadn't forgotten about Herb Score, so I made sure I was ready for everything he hit at me. That's how I learned about concentration. Fact is, without that experience, I might not be in the majors today.

I don't think I forgot about concentration for even one pitch I threw over the next twenty years. Not until that game against the Reds when I let that lady in Augie's box take my mind off the curve I threw to Pete Rose. And sure enough, just like he knew about me and Herb Score, Rose slammed it back at my head. So after Bubba yelled at me and ran back behind the plate, I stepped off the back of the mound to collect my thoughts. I had to get into the game. I waved at Gabby to thank him for making the grab. I rubbed up the ball and thought about the importance of this game with Dick Wagner sitting by waiting to trade for me. Then I walked back to the rubber, ignored the lady, and focused my attention on Ken Griffey, the Reds' second hitter.

Griffey's mostly a line-drive hitter, but he also bunts a lot to take advantage of his speed. The drop pitch is real effective against a good bunter, and Bubba called for it.

But I figured Griffey would be looking for that, so I shook it off and waited for the sign for a screwball. I got it, wound up, threw, and, sure enough, Griffey squared around to bunt. He was looking for the ball to drop, but instead it broke in on him and hit off his bat handle for a strike. Since he had bunting on his mind, I figured I'd try to get him to go after a bad pitch next. Bubba called for a curve ball, which was just what I was thinking.

When you have a greaser in your repertoire, even if you're not throwing it, you still have to go through your fidgety motions on every pitch, so when you do throw it, it doesn't look as if you're doing anything unusual. I touched my ear, scratched my nose, wiped my forehead, scratched my balls, and went into my windup. Griffey squared around again, but my pitch broke away outside, as I had intended, and he pulled his bat away in time. The count was one and one.

I wasn't sure if he'd try bunting again or if it was just a decoy to pull the infielders in and open up the field a bit. But just in case he still wanted to bunt, I thought I better show him a drop pitch. I went through my motions, making sure I reached far enough into my crotch to get some Scrubble Bubbles, and threw him the greaser. He swung as the ball dropped, topped it, and it came back to me on two hops. I threw him out easily.

Joe Morgan stepped in next, flapping his left arm like a bird with one wing. There isn't a more difficult out in the league than Little Joe. He's got a good eye for the strike zone. And he's got wrists quick as flippers on a pinball machine, so he can wait until the ball breaks, then lash out at it if it's a pitch he fancies. You can't mess with him, because he doesn't swing a bad pitches, and you never want to walk him. Give him a free pass and he'll dance around the bases, distract you, and take your mind off the hitter.

Bubba called for a drop pitch, which Joe let go by for a ball. I threw him a good screwball next, which almost fooled him. He swung late and hit it off the handle. But it was just a soft liner that glided right into third-baseman Rod Smith's glove.

I sighed with relief and swaggered off the mound, happy to have survived the inning. As I entered the dugout, I glanced up at Augie's box and was glad to see his lady friend clapping for me. As she clapped, her speakers rolled like waves in the ocean. I tipped my cap to her, which prompted Augie to put his arm around her bare shoulders, a move clearly intended to let me know that she belonged to him. For the time being, anyway.

Our guys went down in order against Fred Norman in the bottom of the first. Before I had time to sneeze, I was back on the mound facing George Foster. Foster got some good wood on my first pitch, a screwball, and hit a sinking liner to center field. Chi Chi came charging in, dived for the ball, and went into a somersault. He came to his feet and held his glove high in the air, which was real dramatic. Only thing was, the ball was still lying on the grass. When Chi Chi realized this, Foster was already standing on second base. The official scorer, a chipmunk from the Washington *Star* named Bobby Ward, called it an error, which was just about the dumbest thing I ever heard. A jackrabbit couldn't have caught up with that ball. Not even a Latino jackrabbit.

I got through the inning without letting Foster score, and through the next six without letting another Red reach base. So, because of Bobby Ward's dumb-ass call, I walked out to the mound in the top of the ninth, three outs away from my second no-hitter.

We had managed to scrape up a run in the seventh when Toby Smith walked, took second on a fielder's choice, tagged up on a fly ball, and scored on a wild pitch. It wasn't a real artistic run, but it was the only run of the game so far.

By the sixth inning the crowd was sensing a no-hitter and celebrating every out. Every pitch took on greater importance, and every play in the field became more exciting. As soon as our team scored, the fans lost interest in our halves of the innings. They just wanted to see me get back out on the mound and try to finish up this no-hitter.

Actually, I gotta admit, when you throw a no-hitter you're usually not pitching any better than any other day. The hitters are just hitting worse. It's a matter of luck. The Reds were making some contact against me, as they always did. Luckily, the ball just happened to keep falling where the fielders were standing. What was even luckier was that our fielders were making the plays.

There's an old baseball myth that no one in the dugout mentions the no-hitter while it's still in progress. It's supposed to be bad luck. But not on our team. From the fifth inning on, Chi Chi ran up and down the bench yelling, "No one tell Gasser he has no-hitter. No one tell him nothing."

And, of course, Rose and Morgan were shouting at me from their dugout on every pitch I threw. "We're just playing with you, Gather," Rose yelled. "You ain't gonna no-hit this team."

"We're gonna cream you yet, Morse," Morgan yelled. "You can count on that."

But standing there on the mound ready to begin the ninth inning, I was one cocky sumbitch. With Dick Wagner present, with the lady with the quadraphonic speakers watching me, and with the trade deadline just around the bend, it seemed like it was in the stars for me to no-hit the world champions and make all twelve National League GM's offer their best players to get me.

Dave Concepcion, the Reds' shortstop, was the first batter I faced in the ninth. He hits eighth for the Reds, but he's good enough to be in the top half of the lineup on any other team. Davey's a lanky guy—he looks like a capital I at the plate—and he likes the ball where he can reach for it. So I jammed him with a screwball and got him to bounce to Toby Smith at second for an easy out.

Then, Sparky Anderson put Bob Bailey up to pinch-hit for Fred Norman. You don't usually remove a pitcher from a 1–0 ballgame, particularly with the hitters the Reds have coming up following him. But having a no-hitter thrown against you is an embarrassment to any manager, and Sparky was gonna try anything to break it up. Bailey's got some power, so I had to work him carefully. I missed with a few curves and went to a full count. I had Rose coming up next, which was enough of a problem. So I had no intention of walking Bailey and having to face Griffey too.

I figured Bailey wouldn't be expecting another curve since I had already missed with three. But I had confidence that I'd get the next one over. Bubba was surprised when I shook off the drop pitch and waited for the curve sign. But I threw a good curve that broke over the inside corner. Bailey got out in front of it and lifted a lazy fly to left field. Pinky stood there waiting for the ball to drop, and I held my breath. Pinky catches a cold more often than he catches a fly ball. But this ball fell into the webbing of his glove. There was a lot of white showing, but he caught it, which is all that counts.

So now I was just one out away, and Pete Rose came up to hit. He's a proud little bugger, and I knew he would do anything to get on base and end my glory. His face was tight as a fist, and if he opened his mouth, he would have spit fire.

I started him off with a drop pitch, and he let it go by for a ball. I was behind already, which is just where he wanted me. I decided that I better make him hit the ball instead of fooling around. So I snapped my wrist down hard, throwing him my biggest curve ball. He swung down on the ball and bounced it toward third-baseman Rod Smith. It was a high chopper and Rod stood there waiting for it to fall. Rose chugged down the line toward first. Rod grabbed the ball and hurried his throw. Everyone in the ball park held their breath. The ball and Rose arrived at first at almost the same instant. It was all up to umpire Bernie Bechenheim. My no-hitter was in his hands. And his hands gave the safe sign. Dumb kraut!

Well, I tell you, the place broke out in pandemonium. My team came charging out of our dugout. The Reds came charging across the field. Fans came pouring out of the stands. Everybody was after Bernie Bechenheim.

"You Nazi bastard," Skip yelled. "They shoulda put you in the ovens."

One kid jumped in the air and landed on Bechenheim's back. And then the whole thing broke out into a barroom brawl. Fists were flying all over the place. There must have been two thousand people around first base flailing away. No one knew who they were hitting or why. Later on, Bubba told me that he punched out his father-in-law by mistake. "But I've been meaning to do it for years," he said.

During all this commotion, I just stood by myself on the pitcher's mound, stunned by the call. I wanted the brawl to end so I could finish the game and go home by myself to brood. It must've been a half hour before the umps restored order.

Finally the field was cleared, Bechenheim was helped off, and we went about finishing the game with three umpires. By then I felt as if all the air had been let out of my balloon. Losing a no-hitter is always disappointing, though a lot of pitchers won't admit it. But losing it under those circumstances, on a bad call, just makes you want to dig a hole in the mound and crawl in. The delay had given me extra time to think about how miserable I was. Dumb kraut!

I could have just dished up a few meatballs and given the game away right there. But Dick Wagner was still sitting by observing me, and this was my opportunity to show him how tough I was.

Ken Griffey stepped in, but I walked around the mound for a few minutes trying to psych myself up. I thought about how much I hated Augie August and how desperate I was to get away from him. Then I was ready to protect my one-run lead and come out a winner.

I had fooled Griffey with a drop pitch in each of his

first three at-bats and retired him without trouble. I knew he'd be looking for the drop pitch again, so I messed with his mind a little. I threw a screwball inside and a curve outside. Then I had him set up for the greaser.

Bubba knew just how I was thinking and flashed the fist. I touched my ear, scratched my nose, ran my hand through my hair, straightened my cap, and reached down into my crotch. But I got nothing on my hand. I went through all the motions again. This time I reached even deeper between my legs. Still nothing. My Scrubble Bubbles had dried up during the delay. I had to throw a greaser, but I had no grease. I felt panicky. But I couldn't let Griffey know that. So, without further delay, I went into my stretch, checked Rose close to the bag, and threw to the plate. I didn't really concentrate on the pitch. I didn't decide where I wanted it to go before I released it. The ball sailed in waist-high over the center of the plate. It was as if I had put the ball on a hitting tee for Griffey.

As he swung, I started walking off the mound. And by the time the ball landed in the right-field stands, I was already walking through the tunnel to the clubhouse, a 2–1 loser.

The only sound in the clubhouse was that of players pulling tape off their ankles. Even Chi Chi knew enough to keep his mouth shut this time.

I peeled off my uniform and left it in a pile in front of my locker. And I thought about what a strange business I'm in. If Bechenheim had only called Rose out—which he could have done without much of an argument—our guys would have been celebrating like we had just won the World Series. But instead, because of one pitch out of eighty-nine, because of one call out of twenty-seven, they were all mourning as if their best friend had just kicked off.

Our clubhouse was not usually so quiet after a loss. After all, losing came as naturally to us as walking. But in this game, we were like the guy who gets shot down by women his whole life, finally gets a beautiful lady all revved up in his hotel room, and discovers that she's got the clap. So close and yet so far.

I knew the press would be stampeding into the clubhouse any minute, crowding around my locker as if I was the pope giving out blessings and asking all those dumb questions.

How do you feel, Gather? What were you thinking when the kraut made that call? Is this the biggest disappointment of your life? Are you going home to commit suicide? Is this the end of the world? What's the capital of Nebraska? What's the square root of 697? Does a bear shit in the woods? What's the meaning of death? Tell us, Gather. Tell us something. Tell us anything. But hurry up. We've got deadlines.

I was in no mood to play expert. So I stripped down naked, grabbed a towel, and headed for the showers where I could hide. But as I got to the entrance of the shower room, I heard that froggy voice of August A. August announcing proudly, "Fellas, I want you all to meet my good friend Miss Melinda Towers."

I turned around. There, in his August-auburn blazer, flashing his dentures like he was doing a Crest commercial, was the bald eagle himself. And holding his arm, which was at his side and not too far away from his wallet, was the blond with the quadraphonic speaker system. The lady who almost got me killed in the first inning.

I sure didn't expect to see her in the clubhouse. Augie always brought friends down there and showed off his ball club like parents show off their newborn babies. All owners do that. Sometimes I think it's the only reason rich folk buy baseball teams. But even Augie had never escorted a lady into the jock-strap jungle before.

Most of the guys were naked when she walked in, and they grabbed for towels, which was the proper thing to do, I guess. But the chick announced, "You don't have to do that, boys. I'm not interested in what *you've* got." And she just stood there, with no expression on her face, like she was waiting for a bus.

Well, I knew right away that behind those speakers the wiring was loose. Lady was big on looks but short on manners. That didn't seem to bother Augie none. Fact is, this time he wasn't showing his ball club off to his friend. He was showing his friend off to his ball club. *Look what I got, fellas. And you can't have her.*

There was no way I was going to flatter the old man with interest, so I managed to remove my eyes from our visitor and headed for the showers.

I turned the water on real cold and just stood under the nozzle letting it run on my head and cool my body. We were the only major-league team with shower massages in our clubhouse. Not because Augie had bought them, mind you, but because he was given them by some company we all did appearances for. I took one off the wall and started moving it around my arm and my shoulder. Even though I don't throw much harder than a kid pitching pennies, my shoulder and wrist still ache after a game from all the twisting I have to do to make the ball dance. When the arm started to feel a little looser, I moved the shower massage down to my stomach, which was real relaxing, and then I did something I had never done in the clubhouse before. Or at home, for that matter. I put the shower massage to Fellini. I don't know what made me do it, except that I felt bad and wanted to feel good. I stood there with my eyes closed getting real excited from the cold water on my head and the vibrations on my cock. Gotta try this more often, I thought to myself. And then I heard someone clearing his throat.

I opened my eyes, and there, standing in front of me, watching me pulling off, were Augie and his lady friend.

"Wha . . . Wha . . . Wha . . . What the fuck are you doing in here?" I said. I tell you, I was mortified, standing there like that.

"Gather my boy," Augie said, "my friend Miss Towers was anxious to meet you."

"She must be real anxious if you had to bring her in here," I said.

"Oh, come on, Mr. Morse," she said in a voice so sultry she must have practiced with a tape recorder to get it right. "I think we're all a little bit beyond the childish embarrassment of seeing each other's bodies by now. Aren't we?"

I didn't know whether to be embarrassed or angry or amused. I mean, I'd been seen by my share of ladies in my time, but this was a little bit different from anything I'd ever experienced. "The least you could have done was taken your clothes off before you came in here," I said, which I thought was a good line.

Augie's face turned August auburn. I didn't know if he was embarrassed or angry, but I can assure you he wasn't amused. His lady friend was, though. She opened her mouth wide and let out one of those breathless laughs. "You're cute," she said. "And very well hung."

I looked down at Fellini, then up at her, and let out kind of a squeaky giggle that I wished I had kept inside.

"Well, we just wanted to let you know how much we enjoyed your performance today, son," Augie said. "You showed a lot of guts out there. Didn't he, Melinda?"

She stood there with her eyes focused on Fellini and said, "Terrific!"

"We got ourselves a little meeting tomorrow, son," Augie said. "I'm looking forward to it. I think I may have a surprise for you."

"You're just full of surprises," I said. And I turned to remove Fellini from her sight and Augie from mine.

"Come on, Melinda," Augie said.

"Very nice meeting you, Mr. Morse," she said. "Hope I see more of you soon."

"Ain't much left to see," I said. She laughed again and they walked out of the shower room.

Well, that was sure the strangest introduction to a lady I ever did experience in my life. As I look back now, it all seems kind of funny. But I didn't think so at the time. I remember thinking she was a crazy, ballsy bitch and I wouldn't want to spend five minutes with her, lovely as she happened to be. I certainly had no idea that me and her would soon be husband and wife.

3

Before I go on and tell you all about my meeting with the old man the next day—which is the turning point of this story and of my whole major-league career—I gotta take a little time right here to talk about something that's real painful for me to discuss. I already said that no one, not even the chipmunks, really know what went down between me and the old man. No one knows what he did to make me hate his guts. But in order for you to appreciate what's coming up, you gotta know the whole story of my background with August A. August. I know it's gonna be hard for you to believe some of this, but it's the whole truth. I swear it.

Let's see now.

Even though I didn't know Augie August until 1973, when I came up to the Dudes, he was an important part of my childhood. Yours too, I bet. I guess just about everybody in the United States grew up on the famous Augie Burgers, which he invented. Greased hockey pucks, we used to call them. They were so greasy I feel like washing my face just talking about them. The reason they served them on buns was 'cause they would have slid right off the plate. But that didn't stop me and my friends from downing them regularly.

When I was in high school, a big Friday night out meant cruising around the parking lot of Augie's Burger Bin in Mantua trying to get the cheerleaders into the back seat of Mike Matson's Chevy. If it wasn't for Augie, kids in the Midwest wouldn't have had no kind of social life.

Augie started out in the burger business after the world war. He grew up in Cincinnati and his dad died of leukemia when Augie was thirteen. So Augie helped support his family by working the grease grill at Crosley Field (where the Reds used to play) on weekends, after school, and during the summers. He was at the University of Cincinnati—studying business, of course—when the war broke out. He joined the Army and was stationed in Hawaii, where he ran a mess hall. When the war ended, he came back home and, with the money he had saved from his grease-grill days and his Army days, he built the first Augie's Burger Bin. It was just a tiny white wood shack, with a green asphalt roof, on Reading Road, about fifteen minutes from downtown Cincinnati. Whole place was no bigger than a dugout. The reason I know all this is 'cause in my rookie year, Augie made a road trip with the Dudes to his hometown, rented a school bus, and took the whole team by the site. He stood up in front of the bus with a bullhorn telling us the story of his rise to fame and fortune.

Augie always had this genius for promotion, and his shack soon became the most popular eating place in town. "I just gave the people what they wanted," he said that day on the bus. "That's always the key to success. People in Cincinnati didn't go for none of that fancy-Dan, raised-pinky-type eating. Just give them a good old American greasy hamburger and they were happy as hell."

Augie sold as many as four thousand greasy hamburgers a day on weekends, and almost as many orders of fries and malted milks. And he was making $100,000 a year when no one in baseball but Mickey Mantle was getting paid that much.

Augie claims he used to work sixteen, seventeen hours a day, seven days a week, and liked it that way. I think he worked so hard 'cause he was a bachelor and didn't like going home to an empty place. Least, that's what Gabby Smith says, and he took freshman psychology at USC before dropping out to sign a major-league contract.

Only thing Augie August cared about, aside from his business, was the Cincinnati Reds. "I loved that team as much as I loved my bank book," he told us. The Redlegs, as they were called back then, did have a pretty fair team. Fact is, they might have been a great team in today's league, with the talent spread so thin due to expansion. But the Dodgers had Snider, Robinson, Hodges, and Reese; the Braves had Aaron, Mathews, and Spahn; the Cards had Stan "The Man" Musial, and the Giants had Willie Mays. So the Redlegs had to struggle to finish even in the top half of the eight-team National League.

Now, back in the mid-1950's, the fans voted for the all-star team, just like you folks do today. Except instead of some company running voting, ballots were printed in the local newspapers each day. At the start of the 1957 season, Augie August decided that he was going to show the world how great his Redlegs really were. He was gonna do this by getting all eight regulars elected to the starting National League all-star team.

So he hired his neighbor's kid to be his all-star coordinator and borrowed a truck from the builder who constructed the Burger Bin. Each morning, the kid drove the truck downtown to the Cincinnati *Enquirer* printing plant and picked up five thousand papers. Then the kid drove back to the stand and spent a few hours pulling the ballots out of each paper. The leftover papers were piled out back of the stand and used to keep the grease grills burning. Augie August doesn't like waste.

People would drive up to the stand, order their greased hockey pucks, and while their orders were being filled, the counter girls would pull pencils from behind their ears, stick ballots under the customers' noses, and guide the customers' hands to the names of the Redlegs' players. Nobody got their food until they filled out a ballot.

When the stand closed each night at ten, Augie and his neighbor's kid sat up filling the day's leftover ballots. Well, seems the local radio announcers and newspapermen caught on to Augie's scheme and made his Burger Bin the official Redlegs all-star headquarters. The Redlegs invited Augie to visit their clubhouse and introduced him to the crowd before a home game with the Dodgers. And all the players started hanging out at the stand. One newspaper story, which Augie still has hanging in his office, called him, "the Redlegs' twenty-sixth man."

A local radio station asked Augie to be their weekend sportscaster, but he turned them down, since it would have meant taking time off from his work. But he did agree to do tape-recorded commentaries on the Redlegs, so the station sent an engineer to the Burger Bin each day to record Augie's opinions.

Well, Augie August became a local celebrity and his little white shack became a gold mine. 'Course, he claims he was only doing this for the team he loved. But we all know Augie better than that. He must have known that if his scheme worked, everybody in town would be stopping by his stand more frequently and buying a few more Augie Burgers long as they were there.

Sure enough, seven Redlegs got voted to the National League starting team. That's right. Ed Bailey was the starting catcher, Johnny Temple was the second baseman, Roy McMillan was the shortstop, Don Hoak the third baseman, and Frank Robinson, Gus Bell, and Wally Post were the outfielders. Stan Musial was the only "foreigner" to make the team, and even Augie couldn't argue much with that one. ('Course, he did insist on his radio show, and still insists, that George Crowe was a better all-around player than Musial.)

Commissioner Ford C. Frick was not real happy with

these voting results. So he removed Bell and Post from
the starting lineup and replaced them with Hank Aaron
and Willie Mays. This caused the first of Augie August's
many feuds with the commissioners of baseball. He used
his radio spot to call Mr. Frick every name that the station would let him get away with on the air. The next
year, the voting was taken away from the fans and given
to the players. Augie considered himself personally responsible.

On the day of the 1957 all-star game, which was
played at Sportsman's Park in St. Louis, Augie held a
day-long celebration at his stand and gave away free burgers. Cars lined up bumper-to-bumper on Reading Road
as far as you could see in either direction. The city had to
send out a dozen cops to direct the traffic in Augie's little
parking lot.

As it happened, that was also the day on which a salesman named Phil Kraft, from the Magic Mixer Company
in Chicago, came to Cincinnati to deliver two Magic Mix-
ers to Augie's Burger Bin. The guy was caught in traffic
on Reading Road for two hours and must have thought
that this August fella was a better salesman than Mr.
Fuller Brush, which he was.

Kraft went back to his bosses in Chicago and told them
what he had seen. A week later, those bosses came to
Cincinnati and asked Augie to go into business with them.
Their plan was to open Augie's Burger Bins all over the
country. Thousands of them. They would provide the
money and Augie would provide the knowledge. They
gave Augie a salary that was double what he was making
a year at his own stand, plus 50 percent of the overall
profits.

Well, the record speaks for itself. Augie August was a
multimillionaire before he was forty. And all because of
his love for the Cincinnati Redlegs. And they say nobody
ever got rich from baseball except Reggie Jackson!

Augie spent the next fifteen years traveling all over the
United States, opening up new Augie's Burger Bins, and

in 1972 he came to Washington, D.C., to open one on M Street. But in a taxicab on the way back to National Airport, he suffered a heart attack. He was rushed to D.C. General Hospital and spent a few weeks recovering there. As he tells it, while he was lying in the hospital ward with nothing to do, he reevaluated his whole life. It was the first time since he was in the Army that he had slowed down enough to think seriously about anything. Here he was fifty-two years old and killing himself from hard work. He had enough money to support himself for the rest of his lifetime and a dozen more lifetimes. He could afford to do anything he wanted to in the world. And the one thing, the only thing he ever dreamed of doing, was running his own major-league baseball team. He had no real background in the game, though he was sure that Freddie Hutchinson, the Redlegs' manager, used to listen to his radio commentaries and do everything Augie suggested. But Augie August knew that the only way he would get to run a baseball team was if he bought one.

As usual, Augie had a little luck working for him. The Washington Senators, the second franchise to have that name, had just left town and moved to Texas. And the men in Congress were furious. They wanted baseball games in town to go to. And since major-league baseball's right to ignore the antitrust laws is based on congressional cooperation, the people on Capitol Hill were in a position to demand that a new team be put in Robert F. Kennedy Stadium.

So when Augie got out of the hospital, he sold his stock in Augie's Burger Bins. He spent a few more weeks in Washington making friends with influential congressmen and then approached the commissioner of baseball with a proposal and congressional backing for a new franchise. He paid his ten-million-dollar franchise fee in cash and in 1973 organized the Washington National League Baseball Club, Inc.

Two teams had already gone broke trying to make it in Washington, but that didn't bother Augie. Like I keep saying, the man's a promotional genius. He did a study to find out why those teams had failed, and concluded that they had tried to appeal to the wrong audience. Washington is two separate cities in one, Augie discovered. One city is made up of the people, mostly out-of-towners, who come there to work for the government. They're the most visible part of the population, since they go to the restaurants and bars and get their pictures in the Style section of the Washington *Post*. They're mostly white folk and come from middle-class backgrounds and come to Washington 'cause they want to be close to power. But those folks only make up about 25 percent of the city. And even though they spend most of their time in Washington, their loyalties and interests remain in their hometowns, and if they're gonna root for a baseball team, it's gonna be the hometown team. Augie felt that the two previous owners had stupidly tried to cater to these people, which is like trying to sell No-Doz to insomniacs.

But there's another Washington, D.C. Though you'd never know it by reading the *Post,* almost three-quarters of the city is made up of black folk. And these were the people Augie knew he had to attract if he was gonna be a success. So he decided to do something that no owner of a team in any professional sport had ever done—create a team that black folk would feel belonged to them. The first major-league soul team.

First thing Augie did was to run a contest to name the club. Ballots were distributed only at unemployment offices. The name that appeared on the most ballots was Motherfuckers, but Commissioner Bowie Kuhn wouldn't approve it. So Augie went with the second choice and named his team the Dudes.

To go along with the nickname, Augie threw out the traditional baseball cap and replaced it with those short-brimmed floppy caps the dudes hanging out on Thirteenth Street always wear. The caps were made of denim that was dyed August auburn.

The man filled the stadium with soul music (Aretha

Franklin's "Respect" was the team's fight song) and put new signs all over the place. He renamed the dugouts the "cribs," the bullpens the "crow's nest," and the bleachers "downtown." He convinced the concessionaire to supplement the usual stadium menu of hot dogs, french fries, and beer with ham hocks, grits, and Ripple wine. And he tried to get the name of Robert F. Kennedy Stadium officially changed to Martin Luther King Stadium. That idea had already been proposed and rejected by Congress, who controls those things.

A lot of people in town said that Augie was nothing but a racist. 'Course, it was only white folk who said that. Black folk dug the old man. They figured anyone who was crazy enough to do these things was an all-right dude. And they started hanging out at the stadium like it was a street corner. Soon as the black folk started going there, the white folk knew it was the cool thing to do, so they went too.

Augie's only problem was that he couldn't find himself a black superstar. Chatsworth Chung was half black, but he was so bad that the black folk insisted he was 100 percent chink. The best starters on the team were Chi Chi Blanco and Aurelio Smith, and there's nothing black folk like to see less than successful Latinos. I heard the old man offered a million dollars for Reggie Jackson and the entire twenty-five-man roster for Joe Morgan, but got neither. And whenever I negotiated contract with him, he would say, "You'd be worth a lot more to me if only you were a nigger."

The funny thing is, Augie didn't like black folk no more than I like ladies with mustaches. But he always said, "Never let your personal preference get in the way of your business sense."

In 1973, when Augie started the Dudes, I was in the middle of my fifth and best minor-league season with the Charleston Comanches, one of the minor-league teams Augie acquired from the Washington Senators. I wasn't real happy when I heard about that. The only thing worse than pitching for the Senators was pitching for an expansion club.

Augie was his own general manager, even though he knew nothing about personnel. Near the end of his first season, when teams are allowed to expand their rosters, Augie combed his minor-league press guides looking for some people to bring up. He brought me up, he told me, not because of my statistics, but because of my name. He said anyone named Gather Morse could be a big star in the major leagues. He offered me one thousand dollars extra to change my middle name from Wesley to No. I said I'd be Gather No Morse if he'd change his name to August No August. He never mentioned it again after that.

I gotta admit, that at that point in my career I didn't care if he was bringing me up because I had a nice ass. I had had my fill of the minor leagues. I was sick of the bus rides and sick of the low salaries, like everyone else who's ever played bush-league ball. I think they have bush leagues so that when you come up to the majors you're so happy to be there that the owners can pay you a helluva lot less than you deserve.

Money's never been all that important to me, despite what you may have read about me in the papers. Fact is, the biggest reason I was desperate to get out of the minors was that I was ready for some good women. Bush-league towns have bush-league ladies, and you could quote me on that one.

We'd ride the bus from Mobile to Savannah to Charleston, we'd get to each town late at night, and if I was pitching, I just had to find myself my tranquilizer, which is something you already know about. I always ended up with a dog. One of the guys on our club whose name I'm not gonna tell you, 'cause it could get him arrested, got so disgusted that he took to shacking up with real dogs. I mean honest-to-goodness barking canines. I never got that low.

But it was so bad I often thought about doing without women altogether. Probably would have if I wasn't afraid it would screw up my career. So I took whatever I could find. One night in Pine Bush, South Carolina, I found myself with this lady who pumped gas at an all-night gas station. She was really into the smells of gas and oil and stuff. So she came to my room with a can of motor oil and insisted on using it to lubricate Fellini. Like I said, bush-league.

You can see why I was really grateful to Augie when he finally gave me the opportunity to put on the Dudes' August-auburn double-knits, even if they did make me look like a tomato with a five-o'clock shadow. But out on the mound, I didn't show how grateful I was. In my first few outings I was so nervous I had this bad twitch and the team doctor checked my medical history for signs of epilepsy. The worst hitters attacked my best stuff like Jimmy Connors attacks a tennis ball. Coming up to the majors is a bigger adjustment than you may think.

Minor-league teams usually have a few major-league prospects. But the rest of the players are burned out old-timers and no-talent young crackers who are just there to fill empty positions in the lineup. You go around the league once and you find out who the prospects are. Then you bear down and save your best stuff for when they come up. You can usually take a breather through the bottom half of any lineup.

But in the big leagues, you can't let up on a single hitter. Even the guys who hit in the low twos are capable of jumping on a weak pitch and knocking a line drive at your skull. You gotta think on every pitch. Some major-league pitchers may not seem like the brightest guys in the world, or even in a phone booth, but if they know nothing else, they know how to work hitters.

In my first major-league appearances I didn't know much about the hitters. Bubba tried to go over them with me before each turn, telling me what spots to avoid throwing to. But I only half-listened to him, 'cause I was thinking about my bedroom matinees to calm my nerves. I didn't know the hitters, I was awed by the beauty of the ball parks and the size of the crowds, and I was distracted by the noise. Most major-league parks have roofs over the stands, and more than one deck, and so the noise is much louder and deeper than in the open minor-league parks. Fart in a minor-league ball park and everyone in the place hears you. Fart in a major-league ball park and you can't hear it yourself. Now, that's disorienting.

After I got knocked around on the West Coast by the Dodgers and the Giants, we returned to Washington and Augie summoned me to his office. The phone call from his secretary shook me up. Based on my performance, I figured he was going to give me a one-way ticket back to bushtown. I thought seriously about going back home to Ohio and planting corn instead of to Charleston and making beans.

It was my first meeting with my boss, and so I dressed up in my only jacket and tie. It was a madras jacket and a red-and-blue-striped tie, and I wore them on top of a checked shirt. What did I know about fancy duds back then?

I walked into Augie's office and he got up from behind his desk and came around to shake my hand. He looked older than a man in his young fifties. I guess his heart attack had worried him gray. But he smiled and his gray eyes glistened and he gave me a real warm feeling.

"How you taking to living in Washington, son?" he asked me as we sat down on a pair of red leather chairs.

"I haven't really lived here yet, sir," I said. "We've been on the road since I came up."

"Well, I think you're going to like it here. It's got a little Northern sophistication and a little Southern hominess. It's exciting, but not too exciting for Midwestern people like you and me."

Later I realized from being around Augie that he always tried to establish common ground with people he spoke to. It was part of his charm and part of his con game. But at that first meeting, I sure appreciated it, whatever it was.

"I want you to be comfortable here," he said. "We'll get together on an off-night and I'll show you around town, and then if there's anything else I can do for you, like help you find a place to live or introduce you to some people, don't you be afraid to ask."

"Thank you, sir," I said, surprised by the tone of the conversation. "I'll sure take you up on that."

"Now, son," he said, putting his hand on my shoulder like Dad did when he lectured me. "I've been watching this game for almost fifty years and I've never seen a pitcher who can make the ball dance like you can. You got a real unique skill there. Major-league stuff. And I just wanted you to know that you're going to spend the rest of your career up here with the big guys where you belong. So I want you to go out there and forget about your worries. You hear me? Just make that ball dance."

I tell you, that little chat made me feel so good. I could've kissed him. 'Course, I didn't do that. But you know what I mean. Every player who gets a shot at the majors at the end of a season knows he's only gonna get a few chances to show his stuff. And if he blows it, come spring, he's gonna be back riding buses and meeting ladies who pump gas. Augie was saying that that wasn't gonna happen to me. And that sure made walking out to the mound a lot easier. Made me feel liked and wanted, which are the two best things to feel, I guess.

That night, I celebrated by picking up this Hill secretary at Clyde's in Georgetown. She had a great back porch and liked it occupied, which I gotta admit was a new experience for me. Sure gave me something to fill my mind till I walked to the mound the next afternoon to make my first appearance in RFK Stadium. I pitched against the Mets, who were involved in a tight divisional race with three other clubs that season. Every game counted for them. We were in the cellar, and no game really mattered for us. We were just playing for next year's salaries.

My ball danced so well that day that it coulda gone on *The Gong Show*. And won. I got through the first inning without even showing my greaser, and struck out Felix Millan, Bud Harrelson, and Cleon Jones. After that, I was one cocky sumbitch. Our guys made four errors behind me, but fortunately they were in four different innings. And we managed to score one run when Chi Chi got hit by a pitch, took second on a balk, went to third on an error, and scored on a sacrifice fly. That was all I needed. 'Cause, for my first major-league victory, I threw a no-hitter.

You had to be living in Washington to understand what that game meant to the town. I made the front page of the *Post* and the *Star*, right up there with the Watergate stories. I was invited to the White House and signed a baseball for the President. Mr. Nixon took me aside and told me, in a whisper, that if he was a major-leaguer, he would throw a spitter too. I denied throwing one myself, but said I was sure he would.

Augie bought me a yellow Stingray and gave me a gas credit card, since gas prices were too steep then for my minimum salary. He said I wouldn't look right behind the wheel of that car in my checked flannel shirts and overalls, so he took me over to this store in Georgetown called Britches and outfitted me to his liking.

He was treating me just like a son. I went all over town with him to the fancy places where people had gold American Express cards, and I met all these big shots whose pictures I always saw in the Style section of the *Post*. They all treated me like *I* was someone special. I was sure indebted to the old man. First he gave me an opportunity and then he made me a celebrity. I couldn't walk down the street without a crowd gathering around to tell me how terrific I was. I felt bigger than the Washington Monument, and it was all because of Augie August.

I finished that year three-and-one and was ready to

head South for spring training the day the season ended. Augie asked me to spend the winter in Washington, helping him to sell tickets for the new season, and I was more than happy to help him out. He said he'd pay me fifteen thousand dollars for the off-season, which was more than I'd made the whole previous season, then negotiate a new contract with me just before we went South.

Augie said that we had to spend the winter hitting up the white folk who could afford to buy season tickets.

"But you told me we gotta draw in the black folks to make it in this town," I said.

"I'll get them too," he said.

"How you gonna do that?" I asked.

"I got my ways," he said, and I assumed he knew what he was doing.

We were inseparable during the early part of the off-season. We were together day and night and weekends, visiting offices to sell season tickets and making appearances at stores and social events. We ate all our meals together, got a little drunk together, talked seriously with each other about things that meant a lot to us, like attendance figures and trading for better players. And I really thought that the man was my friend. My best friend.

At Christmas, I asked Augie if I could go home to Ohio for a few days to visit with Mom and Dad. But he said that people are more generous with their money at Christmas than at any other time of year and we had to do some serious pitchman work during those few holiday weeks. So I stayed in Washington, but being away from home for the holidays made me feel real lonely. I was seeing a few girls at the time, trying to sort them out and line up the best ones for the next season, but none of them meant a thing to me.

On New Year's Eve Augie threw a bash at his house. When he invited me, I asked if I should bring a lady along, and he said definitely not. There would be plenty of available young things, and I, being me, would have my pick of the crop. Now, back home, any lady who can't get herself a date New Year's Eve might as well hang up her spikes. I told Augie this, and he said, "Son, in this town, the women outnumber the men by ten to one. So there's a lot of choice meat out there waiting to be taken home for dinner."

And I gotta admit, he knew what he was saying. There were some prime cuts hanging around his living room waiting to be chosen. Since most of the men Augie knew had no excuses for ditching their wives on New Year's, the ratio of women to men in the room was the same as the ratio in the town. Like I said, Augie didn't seem like a ladies' man, and all the guys used to joke about it. But like he said, "I may not have played the game, but I got a good eye for talent."

From the minute I arrived, wearing an outfit of brown slacks, a tan turtleneck, and a tight-fitting waist-length leather jacket that Augie had picked out for me at Britches, I was the center of attraction. I just stood in a corner of the huge living room and, one by one, the foxes stopped by to offer me compliments, drinks, and phone numbers. There were blonds and brunettes, short girls and tall girls, Americans and foreigners. Augie was obviously a collector with a variety of tastes. The only things the ladies all shared were sweet smells and *Cosmo*-cover cleavage. It was as if the invitations had instructed them all to wear dresses that showed off their speakers. It was the kind of atmosphere I imagined Hugh Hefner lived in, but I never imagined it for Gather Morse.

As the night went on, Frank Sinatra sang melancholy songs in the background and my mind grew soft from the taste of wine and the smell of good perfume. Some folks were pairing up and leaving when I realized there was only one woman in the room who had not paid any attention to me. All the high-cheekboned faces were beginning to look the same, but I noticed her because she was the only black lady in the room.

She had shoulder-length hair pinned at the neck, and

soft features that showed there was some white blood in her somewhere. She wore a silver blouse and black velvet pants. She wore no makeup, no jewelry, no bra. She needed no adornments.

I had noticed her occasionally throughout the party talking quietly with other people, laughing at other people's jokes, touching other people's arms and legs, something that always indicated interest to me. But I don't think she even looked at me the entire evening. That bothered me. It also attracted me. Everyone else there was too easy. She presented the one challenge.

Finally she was alone, sitting on a love seat sipping from a brandy snifter. I left the corner I had stood in all night and wove through the crowd toward her. Before I was close enough to say anything without shouting, she got up and headed out of the living room. I wanted to follow her, but I knew that would be too obvious. I watched her go down the hallway and into the bathroom. She had a tight little ass that swayed from wall to wall as she walked.

When the bathroom door was closed, I walked down the hall and waited for her to come out. She had provided me with a convenient way to meet her. I was just standing there, I could say, because I had to take a leak. Of course, I wouldn't have put it that way. Not to that classy lady.

If I really had had to take a leak, I would have ended up doing it down my leg. She didn't come out for what must have been half an hour. What the hell is she doing in there? I wondered. I thought something might be wrong, so I knocked. No answer.

I grabbed the doorknob and turned it slowly. She had not locked the door. I opened the door slightly and stuck my head in. The sunken bathtub was filled with white bubbles, and only her head was above the foam.

She turned her head and saw me, but said nothing. I was embarrassed that I had intruded, but I had to act

cool. "Do you always take baths at parties?" I said, which
I thought was a good opening line.

"I've been waiting here for you for half an hour," she
said without looking at me. "Come on in. The water's
fine."

I blinked my eyes and shook my head to make sure, in
my drunken state, I wasn't just imagining this scene.
wasn't. I didn't say anything, because if I did, it surely
would have come out in a high, squeaky voice. I just
walked in, locked the door behind me, and began to peel
off my clothes. I undressed slowly to try to hide my excitement, but that was foolish. As soon as I took off my
Jockey shorts, she could see how excited I really was.
That's one thing that has always troubled me about being
a man. When you're excited, there's no way to be subtle
about it.

I climbed into the bubbles with my head at the opposite end of the tub from hers. The water was very
warm, but even so, a chill ran through my body. I sat
there looking into her brown, almond-shaped eyes. Her
pencil-line smile showed me she was amused by what was
happening.

"I'm Bernadine Green," she said in a whisper. "What
took you so long to get here, Gather?"

I was surprised she even know who I was. "You didn't
look at me all night," I said. "How was I supposed to
know?"

"I didn't want to share you with all those other
women," she said. "I only wanted you if I could have you
by myself."

I felt her foot rubbing softly against my inner thigh and
then against Fellini. The warm soapy water formed a silky
film over both our skins, making her touch smoother than
any touch I had ever felt. I moved close and she took Fellini in her long smooth fingers and rubbed him between
her palms. I touched her lips with mine and she guided
Fellini into her. It slid in easily, and I felt another chill

run down my back. My body shivered for an instant in the warm water.

I put my hands under her silky, soapy ass and our bodies rotated together. The water moved with us like a whirlpool, massaging all the parts of our skins that we were not massaging. I closed my eyes and continued to move with her.

We moved slowly and the whole world seemed to be moving slowly with us. It was a feeling I had never had before, but wanted to have for every minute of the rest of my life. Every inch of my skin and of her skin was at its most sensitive. Every touch, every movement forced both of us to moan with pleasure. And when I came, it was not in an explosion, or even short spurts, but in a slow, steady, endless flow.

We lay there in the bubbles for what seemed like hours, touching each other softly. We finally got out of the tub and rubbed each other with soft, fluffy towels. We pulled our clothes on, still in slow motion, then walked out of the steamy room.

The house was dark and silent. We didn't know how long it had been since everyone else had disappeared, and we didn't care.

We drove in my car to my apartment, stopping along the way to touch our lips and our tongues, always slowly, always softly. The breeze and the trees and the lights all seemed to be moving at our rhythms, as if we had re-created the world at our own tempo. And we climbed into my bed together and made love again. And again. And again.

Something happened to me with her that night. I felt something that I had never felt before. I wanted Bernadine to be with me forever. She kept her own apartment, but spent every night at mine. It wasn't easy for me to part with her each morning, and I couldn't wait to get back to her at night. When we went out together, I always held her close to me, as if, if I let go, I was afraid she'd disappear. Before I met her, I was always shy in public, embarrassed by public displays of affection. But I could not keep my hands off her rosewood-colored skin.

We spent the rest of that winter together. We went everyplace together, and there always seemed to be a photographer around to snap our pictures, which seemed to appear in the papers nearly every day. I thought Augie might object to the relationship, feel as if it might hurt business, me going out with a black lady and all. But he approved and encouraged me.

Bernadine worked for the Urban Redevelopment Corporation and was very dedicated to building up the broken-down ghetto neighborhoods in Northwest Washington. She had grown up in those neighborhoods, still lived there, even though it was beneath her means, and she loved them. And because she loved them, I loved them. At night, we often walked through those dark littered streets, streets I wouldn't go near by myself. We stopped and chatted with people whose idea of a good time was hanging out on the streets and talking. I had always thought that black folk object to their women going out with white men. But those folks accepted me. I guess it was because Bernadine was so well-liked in the neighborhood. And because I played for the Dudes.

I had heard about poverty, but I never knew what it was before that winter. I never imagined families of seven sleeping on mattresses on the floors of one-room apartments, with exposed leaky pipes and no heat, living with rats and vermin as if they were neighbors. It sickened me to see this at first, but Bernadine was strong, so I couldn't be a pussy. That lady taught me that all I had ever been concerned about was getting laid and making big money, but there was much more to life. So I spent all the time I was not working with Augie, playing with the kids in those streets, teaching them the only thing I really knew, how to play baseball.

As the winter thaw began to set in, I realized it would soon be time for me to go off to spring training. That made me melancholy. I didn't want to leave Bernadine. I knew she couldn't leave her work and come South with me. It would only be for six weeks, and then I would come back to her, but even that seemed like too long to go without her. And when I did come home, I would be traveling half the time and she could not travel with me. I suggested quitting baseball and finding something else to do—that was how much I wanted her—but she laughed and said she would never let me do that.

So in February I went to Orlando with the Dudes. It was a lonely spring. I called her every day, sometimes twice a day, and usually found her at home at night. The tone of her voice often sounded farther away than the thousand miles between us, but I told myself she was struggling with herself to get along without me. I just knew that when we broke camp and I returned to Washington, it would be just as it was before I left her. At least I wanted it to be.

Fellini remained inactive that spring. The usual array of bikini-clad bimbos hung out at our training base, many of whom I had spent some pretty wild nights with the spring before. But I couldn't imagine letting them near my bed anymore. With those other girls, screwing was just calisthenics, an exercise I had to perform and get through as quickly as possible, with little interest. But making love to Bernadine was the peak experience of my life. Everything else I did seemed boring and insignificant by comparison.

I spent each night in the Holiday Inn in Orlando holding my pillow close to me, imagining it was Bernadine, pretending my hands were her hands. It's a good thing Bubba, who was my roomie, slept facing the other direction so he didn't see me.

We broke camp on April Fool's Day and flew back to Washington to begin the new season. As soon as I got off the plane, I called her apartment. There was no answer. I stopped by my apartment briefly to drop off my luggage, then drove to her place. I was anxious to see her, and also a bit nervous. My heart was pounding so fast as I drove there that I felt as if Nolan Ryan was in my chest throwing his fastball against my bones.

I parked on the street in front of her building and ran up the four flights of stairs. I knocked on her door. There was no answer. I stood leaning against the door, waiting for her to come home. Ryan was throwing even faster.

Each time I heard the door to the building open and footsteps on the stairs, I held my breath waiting to see if it was Bernadine. I must have been waiting there for two hours when finally I heard her throaty voice.

"Man, am I exhausted," I heard her say.

I wondered who she was talking to. Then I heard a man's voice. "You ain't going to sleep on me yet, bitch," it said.

When I heard that, I was embarrassed to be waiting there. If there was another flight of stairs, I would have climbed it and hid. But there was nowhere to go without them seeing me.

She arrived at the top of the stairs and saw me standing by her door. Her face suddenly grew long and troubled. The man whose voice I had heard came up behind her. He was big and strong like Willie Stargell. His flowered shirt was open down the front and he looked as solid as the brick wall at Wrigley Field.

Before she said a word to me, she told him, "Bill, please go inside. Give me a few minutes to talk to Gather."

A few minutes! After six weeks of waiting for this moment, she was going to give me a few minutes. I was angry. Sad. I felt my airplane meal tumbling around in my stomach. If I closed my eyes, I'm sure I would have seen the medicine ball heading at my skull. As Bill walked by me, he stuck out his hand. "Hey, you Gather Morse?" he said. "I seen you pitch. You all right, brother. Make that ball wiggle like Tina Turner." I just left his hand hanging there in the air. He got the message and walked into the apartment.

Bernadine and I were left in the hall, staring at each

other, trying to come up with the right thing to say. She sure did look pretty standing there, and I could've just swept her off her feet and carried her on home with me. 'Course, that's not what she had on her mind.

"I'm sorry, Gather," she said. "The gig's up."

"What gig?" I said. "What are you talking about?"

"You don't know yet?" she said. "Hey, man, I ain't gonna be the one to tell you. You better ask your boss."

I didn't know what in tarnation she was saying to me. What'd Augie August have to do with me and her?

"I done bad, Gather," she said. "I done real bad. But I needed the bread, man. You gotta know I needed that bread. Without it, my man would've up and left. I'm not what you think I am, Gather. I'm nothing more than a junkie's bitch."

"What bread? What man? What junkie?" I said. "What the hell are you talking about?"

She fumbled around in her purse for a cigarette. Her hands were shaking. Her purse dropped to the floor. We both bent over to reach for it. She took advantage of the chance to skirt past me and into the apartment.

I pounded on the door with my fists. No answer. I pounded again.

The door opened and Bill blocked the door frame. He wasn't trying to look mean, but he didn't have to. He had this white ring of powder around one of his nostrils. I was gonna tell him, but he didn't give me a chance to speak.

"Gather Morse, you get your ass the fuck out of here, man," he said. "And don't you never come back. 'Less you want that pitching arm of yours broken in pieces."

He slammed the door in my face.

I couldn't believe this was happening to me. This wasn't the same lady I had left six weeks before. I'd been counting the days till I could see her again, and now she was in there with some coke-snorting sumbitch and I was by myself in the hall. What was going on? What could Augie possibly know about all this? I had to find out.

I got in my car and drove up to Augie's house. I pounded on the front door like a madman. There was no answer. I thought maybe he was still at the stadium, so I drove there.

I ran into the team offices. The whole staff was there, working late, getting ready for opening day.

I stopped at Cynthia's desk. She's Augie's secretary. I demanded to see the old man. She asked me to wait while she told him I was there. I paced the floor of the office. Bernice, the bookkeeper, got up from her desk and went to the john. I walked by her desk and pounded my fist down into her open accounts book. I looked down at the book. I was stunned by what I saw.

Sitting there on one of those green lines was an entry for two thousand dollars paid to one Bernadine Green. I turned the pages of the book and saw two more entries like that. They had all been paid to her since January 1, which was the day I met her.

I picked up the book and stormed into Augie's office. Bernice came out of the john and ran after me, but I pushed her aside. I was a crazed maniac.

Augie was sitting calmly behind his desk, wearing his bifocals. He smiled when he saw me.

I threw the ledger down in front of him. "What the fuck is this?" I said.

"Take it easy, son. Calm down," he said. "What is what?"

"This," I said, pointing to the entry of the payment to Bernadine. "And this. And this," I said, pointing to the previous entries.

"Cynthia, will you please excuse us," Augie said. "And close the door behind you."

Cynthia left the office.

"Son, sit down for a minute," Augie said. "I want to explain something to you."

"I'm not sitting down," I said. "Just explain."

"Gather, son," Augie said, "I never expected you to fall in love with a Negro woman. But I know how much you like women and I thought you'd get a kick out of a little black ass for a change. I also thought that, since we don't have a black superstar, it might help us to sell some tickets if you were seen with her. I was only thinking of the team, son. Our team."

I couldn't believe my ears. I couldn't believe any human being would stoop so low. "You mean you paid her off to go out with me?" I said.

"Well, I guess you can say that," Augie said, like it was nothing out of the ordinary. "It was a promotional expense. I didn't tell her to stop seeing you, though. I was willing to go on paying her. But she insisted I stop."

"You motherfucking cocksucking shitkicking asslicking sumbitch," I said. "I'm going to kill you."

I lunged at Augie, but missed him. Before I could catch him, his two bodyguards charged in and grabbed my arms.

I admit it, I was the dumbest sucker who ever lived. I should have known all along that Augie August didn't give a shit about me. I was just a piece of merchandise he was selling. I tell you, at that moment, as I stood there in that office, my arms pinned behind my back by the two thugs, my stomach soured on baseball forever. The game would never be the same to me again.

The next day, I announced my retirement and drove home to Mantua, Ohio. Augie told the press that we were having some contract problems. I didn't care what he said. I never intended to go back to Washington again.

My dad was disappointed when he heard I quit, but I couldn't tell him what really happened. He wouldn't have understood. Especially since the lady in question was black.

I spent the next two weeks lying in my bed, just like I did after Herb Score got hit in the skull. Only time I left the room was to throw up. Mom and Dad were really upset, but they didn't know how to deal with me. It was as if they had a little boy on their hands again.

I had no plans to leave that room. But while I was home, my dad had a heart attack behind the wheel of his

truck, crashed into a maple tree, and died. The day of his
funeral, Mom said to me that the only thing I ever did
that really gave Dad pleasure was play baseball. I knew
she was right. So I went on back to Washington and re-
joined the Dudes.

I ignored Augie, bad-mouthed him in the papers every
chance I got, did anything I could think of to make him
want to trade me. But like the man said, I was his only
annuity.

Then, last year, the Messersmith-McNally court decision threw out the option clause and gave us the opportunity to become free agents. We could make our own
deal with the team of our choice after our contract expired and we played one additional option year. When
that decision was made, I had one year remaining on a
two-year contract I had signed before the 1975 season.

I like to say that they replaced the option clause with
the Santa Clause. The new agreement was the best Christmas present I ever got. It finally gave me the chance to
get away from the only person I could honestly say I ever
hated.

So now you got it. First time this story's ever been told
anyplace, far as I know. And you can see the position I
was in. Like I said, I'm not just another one of those
money-loving jocks who has no loyalty to anything but his
bank account. I had good, solid personal reasons for
wanting to leave Augie August and the Washington
Dudes.

4

Well, I sure am glad I finally got all that off my chest. And while I'm on chests, I wanna go back to that night when I met Melinda Towers and her quadraphonics in the shower room.

I was feeling lower than an ant's asshole when I left the ball park that night after blowing my no-hitter in the bottom of the ninth. Watching Mark Fidrych having a conversation with a baseball wouldn't have made me smile that particular evening.

I was in a real quiet-type mood. You know, the kind of mood when you just want to sit in the corner and feel sorry for yourself even though you're making $100,000 a year and still have your whole life ahead of you. I guess everybody feels that way sometimes.

Bubba Bassoon knew just how I was feeling and he dragged me over to Clyde's in Georgetown for a few libations. On Wednesday nights, which that was, there's enough foxes prowling around the bar there to stock every zoo in the USA. And the place smells like the inside of a bottle of French perfume.

We walked in and waded through the sawdust on the floor and the smiles from the foxes who recognized us, then found an open space at the bar. Benjy the bartender, who was working there while he tried to find a real job as a social worker, served us up two light beers on the house. He always gave us free brews, which was his way of letting the ladies know that he was buddies with the ballplayers.

Bubba met this squeaky little thing who said she always wanted to meet him 'cause she played the bassoon in her high-school band. After talking with her for no more than ten minutes, Bubba went home with her so she could try out his instrument. I wasn't in the mood for that kind of music, so I drove home alone and got into bed with my own crazies instead of somebody else's.

I didn't sleep much that night. I was plagued by regrets at having dished up that home-run ball to Griffey. They say you're supposed to leave the game behind at the ball park, but I never met an athlete yet who could do that. I never can. And I especially couldn't that night. I shouldn't have choked just because my Scrubble Bubbles had dissolved. Pitcher good as me's not supposed to panic like a junkie without a fix just 'cause one pitch don't wanna cooperate. Shoot, I've seen pitchers throw shutouts on nights when only one pitch is working for them. 'Course, fastball pitchers and knuckleballers have an easier time getting by on nights like that than breaking ball artists like myself. Still, I felt plumb dumb foolish letting that game get away from me. I feel bad anytime I get knocked around, but I feel worse when I let one lousy pitch ruin an otherwise perfect evening. I sure wished I had that last pitch back to throw again.

I gotta admit, I also wasn't real happy with my performance in the shower room after the game. I wish I had that one back to do over again also. Augie had some nerve interrupting my moment of privacy in the clubhouse, and I should have let him know it. Shoot, an owner should know better than to bother a player after he just blew a game like that. Guy's gotta have some time by himself to clear out his head.

And besides, what kind of dumb bitch broad walks into a locker room full of naked men and shows no more reaction than a schoolgirl walking into her classroom? I'll tell you what kind. A no-class, two-bit floozy. That's what kind. I mean, I certainly don't pretend to be one of those moralist types, but when sex doesn't mean nothing more than going to school, well, then, I'm gonna hang Fellini in my locker right up there next to my spikes and retire. Yes sir. And won't that be a sight for sore eyes.

I guess I shouldn't be saying these things so loud with Melinda sitting right in the next room watching the soaps. I don't want her to think I'm calling her names or nothing. But she knows, though I love her now, I ain't real crazy about the way we met. A good lover is, after all, like a good pitcher. He saves some of his best stuff for late in the game when the opponent thinks he's got nothing left. But Melinda, she got to see some of my best stuff before we got out of the first inning.

When I finally did fall asleep that night, I had this real embarrassing dream. I dreamt that I was standing out there on the pitcher's mound, in front of fifty thousand fans and the Cincinnati Reds, and I wasn't wearing a thing besides my spikes and cap. It was just like that story you hear as a kid about the emperor's new clothes. I was standing there naked as the day I was born, and no one said a thing. No one, that is, until Pete Rose came up to bat. He couldn't keep his mouth shut about something as obvious as this. He stepped into the batter's box, the place got real quiet, and he shouted, "Hey, Gather. You forgot your belt." Well, all of a sudden fifty thousand people started laughing together. And I didn't know what to do. I put my glove over Fellini, and my whole body turned August auburn. I looked over at the old man's box and saw Melinda Towers sitting there. She wasn't laughing. She was running her tongue around her lips.

Now, you can imagine how humiliated I felt at that particular moment. Fortunately, the phone rang just in time to rescue me from that situation. I picked up the receiver and grunted into it.

"Am I speaking to the owner of the million-dollar arm?" asked a peppy voice on the other end.

"Yeah," I grunted.

"Well, then," the voice said. "This is the hundred-thousand-dollar agent."

It was just like my agent, Payton Forrest, to have his 10 percent of the take figured out before he even made a deal for me. You probably remember Payton from his days as a United States Senator from Alabama, especially from his appearances on the national tube as a member of the committee investigating that Watergate break-in. Payton was the gray-haired old buzzard with the deep drawl who appeared to be trying to make those folks who testified before the committee look cleaner than Steve Garvey. 'Stead of investigating a crime, man seemed to be whitewashing a picket fence. Lot of friends of mine who watched those hearings told me Payton was losing his mind. But that just shows they don't know the man. When I heard what happened, I knew that Payton knew precisely what he was doing.

You see, Payton's term was about to expire and he wasn't going to run for the Senate again. He had himself a plan where he could make more money than he ever made in government. Payton once told me that the only group of people in this country who were writing more books than the athletes were the politicians. And he figured, with all those government types becoming celebrities by appearing on television for five minutes, there was going to be a whole store full of books on Watergate. So Payton was determined to get in on this action.

His plan was to nuzzle up next to the crooks at those hearings, become a literary agent when his Senate term expired, and corral all these politician-celebrities as clients. Clever, huh? Only trouble was, by the time Payton was out of office, some little Jew wiseacre agent had beat him to the punch. "All that public ass-kissing for nothing," Payton said to me.

Since he was cut out of the book field, Payton did what every lawyer who wants to make himself a quick buck does these days—he became a sports agent. I signed with him on the advice of Gabby Smith, who said Payton was real crafty when it came to money. After all, Gabby did take freshman accounting at USC before dropping out to sign a major-league contract. Besides, I figured a smooth-talking Southern senator was the only person I could find who would lie as good as Augie August, which made him the perfect man to negotiate for me.

"And how is the preeminent professional pitcher?" Payton said into the phone.

"I feel like warmed-over shit," I said. "Didn't sleep much last night."

"A pity, my son," he said. "But you can supplement your sleep during our meeting this morning. Your future is in my able hands.

"Now, before we embark on this great meeting of the minds, allow me to recapitulate our position. If, and only if, the honorable owner makes an offer worthy of your unique talents, then, and only then, will we award our consent to a new contract."

"No way in hell, Payton," I said. "I don't give a fuck what he offers. I ain't signing again with that sumbitch."

"Aha! Excellent," Payton said. "Then we are in complete, utter, total, and unanimous agreement. We will, therefore, overlook the fact that Mr. August allowed you to enter the major leagues sooner than any other owner might have, that he escorted you around this city and introduced you to a mélange of distinguished people, and that he honored you with a six-figure contract before such numbers were *de rigueur*. Despite all these considerations, we are not going to be reasonable and bargain in good faith."

"Fucking right, Payton," I said. "And don't you forget it for a minute. I don't care if that sumbitch offers to suck me off in front of a standing-room-only crowd at RFK Stadium. There's no way I'm signing a new contract with him."

"Superb, my son," Payton said. "I gather then, Gather, from the gist of your overly emotional remarks, that there is no further need for discussion between us. We are approaching this confrontation with complete, utter, total, and unanimous unity. Our heads are joined like Siamese twins. You, after all, are my constituent and it is my duty to represent your interests and opinions, no matter how irrational they may be. I will look forward then to seeing you at noon. Until then . . ."

He hung up. I moved the receiver away from my ear and stared at it. Sure sounded to me like Payton was trying to con me into signing with the Dudes. But that couldn't be. He had to be on my side, didn't he? I didn't want to be so loony that I thought my agent was working against me too. I never understood anything Payton said to me anyway.

I sure need an agent. Fact is, agents and hair dryers are the two things every athlete's gotta have these days. I need an agent 'cause I don't know any more about money than Bowie Kuhn knows about raising hogs. Money's just something I never worried much about as a kid. Never even learned how to use a checkbook. I kept all the money I had in my shoe when I was growing up, and there was still room for me to wiggle my toe.

Now I find myself in this here business where people make in a year what most people back home must have made in a lifetime. Back home, people used to worry about paying the mortgage and affording new wire for the chicken coop. Today the people around me are worrying about these tax shelters. I still pick up the paper every day and turn right to the batting averages, but a lot of the guys in the clubhouse turn right to the stock quotations. I tell you, as good as I pitch, which is damn good, I still sometimes think that I'm in over my head in this game.

My worst moments in baseball are sitting across from

Augie negotiating a contract. I mean, here's a guy who's spent more time playing with money than I've spent playing with a baseball. So of course he's better at his thing than I am. What would really be fair would be if Augie had to get up there and hit against me, and my contract would be based on how well he did. He wouldn't stand a chance. 'Course, Augie would probably send up a designated hitter. And I guess that's what I do too. My agent is my designated hitter at the negotiating table.

He's also what I like to call my "no man." And I guess that makes the negotiating table no-man's-land. You see, if I was negotiating for myself, the owner might make me an offer and I might even turn it down. But then, all the owner would have to do is start calling me an ungrateful sumbitch—which they always do—and I'd immediately accept what he offered. I couldn't bear sitting there in a room with the man I was working for listening to him call me names like he didn't like me or something. So I go in with my agent, let him say "No," and listen to the owner call him names. Let him be the bad guy. He doesn't have to come back and face the owner every day.

This all reminds me of when Dad used to tell me, "Son, when you get yourself married up, don't go to bed angry. If you do, the rest of the night won't be no fun." Well, I always figured that advice also applied to negotiating a contract. Let your agent fight with your wife for you, and then you jump in bed and still have one helluva time.

So, after hanging up with Payton, I got dressed and drove through a pretty spring rain over to my meeting with my agent and the old man. I had only agreed to this meeting to let Augie know once and for all that he had less than two weeks left to make a deal for me or I was going, going, gone.

I walked into the team's offices and saw Augie's bodyguards standing at attention outside his door, which indicated that the old man was ready for me. The two heavies were there to discourage me from threatening to kill the old man like I did that day when I discovered that Bernadine was on the Dudes' payroll.

"Hey, fellas. Good to see you," I said with a smile, and I went to open the door. I felt a heavy hand land on my shoulder and spin me around. This thug with a shaved head was sniffing at me like a watchdog or something.

"Stick 'em up," he said. "The boss wants me to make certain you're not carrying a piece or nothing."

I looked at the ugly mother like he was loony. He stuck a finger in my gut, which made me throw my hands up above my head. He frisked me, which kind of annoyed me at first. But thinking about it, I was glad that Augie was so intimidated by me that he took such precautions.

Baldie opened the door for me to walk into Augie's office. "Thanks," I said to him. "Felt good." I winked at him and walked in.

Augie and Payton were already in the room, which is decorated with August-auburn drapes and carpeting and resembles a whorehouse in a Hollywood western. They each sat in a high-backed leather chair, puffing away on cigars that made the whorehouse smell like a glue factory. I didn't know how long Payton had been there, but the office was already filled with more smoke than my bathroom after I take a hot shower.

Augie and Payton seemed real chummy and had smiles on their faces like they shared some secret that I wasn't in on. Soon as I saw those grins, I got worried. It was as if they were working together against me.

Augie got up from his chair, asked me to sit there, then walked behind his desk and sat down. He offered me a cigar even though he knew I didn't smoke. He was just postponing getting to the business at hand. I looked to Payton for some support, but he wouldn't even risk making eye contact with me.

"Pitched a helluva game last night, son," Augie said. He always called me "son."

"Thank you," I said.

"Game had all the tension of one of those Alfred

Hitchcock movies," Augie said. "Couldn't leave your seat for a minute 'cause you might miss something. Exciting baseball. Of course, when the game's that exciting, it hurts me at the concession stands. But I can live with that . . . I guess."

Augie puffed away on his cigar, and I just kind of shook my head in disbelief. I figured he was now going to use the fact that I pitched so well against me. Try to knock down my price by claiming I didn't sell enough hot dogs. "Don't worry," I said. "Next time out, I won't make it so exciting."

Payton tapped on my forearm, advising me to calm down and refrain from making such biting remarks. I raised my arm and brushed his hand away.

"Dammit, we should be able to get you enough runs to win a game like that, son," Augie said. "And I'm going to promise you one thing right here and now. You be my witness, Senator. You stay here with me, son, and I'm going to do everything within my powers to get you a long ball hitter. Maybe even two. Get someone who can hit it out of the park, give you some breathing room . . . and draw some more fans."

"Superb," Payton chipped in.

"You're a guaranteed twenty-game winner with this lineup," Augie said to me. "Now, just imagine how many games you're going to win next year when I fulfill my promise to you. You'll win more games than any pitcher has ever won. You'll be the biggest star in baseball today. Maybe in baseball history. That's what we have to look forward to. Right, Senator?"

"Right," Payton shouted. Then he looked at me and could tell he had said the wrong thing. He cleared his throat, then said, "Uh, Augie. Who have you considered acquiring?"

I wasn't there to sit and listen to the pep talk. "Cut the shit, Augie," I said. "The only way you can get a slugger for this team is if you trade me. So why don't you just go ahead and do it already."

"Gather, Gather, Gather," Augie said as he walked around in front of his desk. He sat on the edge and looked me in the eye. It was the look of a desperate man pretending he was in control. "Look at it from my viewpoint, son. If you owned this team, would you trade away the best pitcher in the major leagues? The very best, and I mean that. And that includes Seaver and Sutton and Tanana and everyone else. What kind of baseball man would I be if I traded you away? Huh?"

I waited for Payton to pick up our end of the discussion and tell Augie that it was too late for such flattery. But my loyal agent just sat there chewing on his cigar like it was a pacifier. I was forced into being the "no man." "In the past, Augie," I said, "you would have been out of your mind to trade me. I used to think owners were assholes when they traded away people like Frank Robinson or Nolan Ryan when they didn't have to. But the free-agent system's changed all that. Game's changed, and a good baseball man's gotta change with it. I've got the upper hand now. Trade me in the next two weeks and get what you can, or I'm leaving at the end of the season and you'll end up with nothing. You know that. You're no idiot."

"Thank you, son," Augie said. "I appreciate that."

"I didn't mean it," I said. "You are an idiot. But you're a smart idiot."

Payton reached for my arm again, but I pulled it away.

"Okay, then," Augie said. "Here's what I'm gonna do for you." He reached behind him and took a pad and pen off his desk. "I'm going to write a figure down here on a piece of paper, and I want you to take a look at it."

I was familiar with this routine by now. Augie never mentioned dollars. He always wrote a figure down and showed it to you. He had written down so many figures for me in the last few months that I could have wallpapered my apartment with them. "Forget it, Augie," I said. "You're wasting paper."

"No, no, no, son," he said. "Don't be impetuous. I

want to do this. And I think you're going to be very happy with this figure."

"Tell him to forget it, Payton," I said to my alleged agent.

"Don't be impetuous," Payton said. I wanted to punch him.

"Just take a peek at this," Augie said. He folded a slip of paper and handed it to Payton.

"That's nice. Very nice," Payton said, bobbing his head approvingly. Then he handed the slip of paper to me. Without even glancing at it, I crumpled it up and dropped it on the floor. I felt like picking it up and taking a quick look, but I resisted. "It's not enough," I said. "Whatever it is, it's not enough."

Augie looked to Payton for help, but my agent just shrugged his shoulders. Augie started pacing back and forth in front of me with his hands in his pockets. He was trying desperately to look like a man who has been wronged. "I've lived a good life . . ." he began in a melancholy tone that he must have rehearsed for the occasion. "A damn good life. I had a great success in business and made more money than I ever dreamed of and at a very young age. And I've had the opportunity to fulfill my childhood dream and own my own baseball team. I've been a very fortunate man. I've worked hard. Damn hard. But still, I've been a very fortunate man.

"Oh, it hasn't been a cakewalk. No, don't ever think that. I had some serious illness, but I fought my way through it. And some people along the way let me down, but I fought my way through that too.

"Regrets? Yeah, I've had a few. But then again, too few to mention. I did what I had to do, and did it all without . . . without . . ."

"Dissension," I said.

"Why, yes, that's it. Oh, there's been some dissension. There always is. I can live with that. But there is something that's hard to live with . . . and that's the feeling that you've let down those who are important to you. It happens all the time, of course. When you're in business like I am, you sometimes find yourself in a position where some of your business decisions might not be the best thing for some of the people who work for you. Making those decisions is the toughest thing in your life. You make them—you have to make them—and you hope that in the long run it all works out all right. But sometimes it doesn't, and then you have to find a way to live with that . . ."

Listening to this, I was squirming around in my leather chair. I was sorry I had agreed to attend the meeting. I had never seen the old man humble himself before, and I wish that I had never had to see it.

He stopped pacing in front of me, put his hand on my shoulder, and looked into my eyes. I turned my head away, but he grabbed my chin and turned it toward him. "Son," he said. "I have wronged you. On occasion, I have put the interests of my business ahead of your best interests, and you know when those occasions were."

Thoughts of Bernadine flashed through my mind like slides projected on a screen, and I felt my stomach tighten.

"Believe me, son," Augie went on, "I don't like myself for having done that to you. I want to repay you for the injustices I have committed. I want to repay you in the only way I know how." He took the pad off his desk again. He scribbled down a figure, thought for a second, threw that slip of paper away, and wrote down another figure. He folded the slip of paper and handed it to Payton. Payton looked at it, bobbed his head up and down, and handed it to me.

It was a tense moment. If they ever made a movie of my life, there would be violins trilling in the background as I sat there deciding whether or not to take a peek. I know how much money means to August A. August, and one brief glance would have told me just how much I meant to him. But it also would have indicated that I was folding under his outpouring of regret and humiliation.

All I had to do was crumple it in my fist, as I had done with the previous offer, in a dramatic demand to end our relationship once and for all. I honestly can't tell you what I would have done right then. I might very well have looked at the slip, signed with Augie, and stayed with the Dudes. But I didn't get the chance to make a decision.

Before I thought the situation through, the door to the office flew open and who came bursting in but Melinda Towers.

"Hi, guys," she said. And she walked on into the office, real slinky-like, wearing this yellow dress that looked like it was affixed to her body with Duco cement, shaking her booty like there was something between her legs that she was trying to shake out. It's amazing, isn't it, how a lady like that can take grown men's minds off whatever they're doing and make herself the focus of attention? When they saw her, Augie and Payton jumped to their feet, flashed these little-boy grins on their pusses, and started competing with each other to tell Melinda how beautiful she looked. It was as if the strong smell of her perfume had made them instantly drunk with desire. They were at her mercy. If she suggested that they fuck themselves, I'm sure they would have found a way to do it.

Well, you gotta know how pissed-off this whole scene made me. Lady had interrupted *my* meeting. I sat there, stunned by the behavior of these supposedly dignified old men, hoping that I never acted so plumb foolish in front of any woman.

Melinda just kind of ignored Augie and Payton, which is something beautiful ladies tend to do when they know they got men drooling down their shirts. She could tell that she hadn't stolen my attention, so she came over to do her act and try to win me over.

"Gather, sweetheart," she said to me. "Now, you just can't go off and play for those Cincinnati Reds. A boy like you just isn't gonna have any fun living in a town like Cincinnati."

"Cincinnati? What are you talking about?" I said.

"Didn't you boys tell him yet?" Melinda asked. There was an uncomfortable silence. Augie and Payton exchanged the embarrassed look of co-conspirators who have just been caught in the act.

"What the hell is going on here?" I demanded.

"Oh, did I say something I shouldn't have?" Melinda whined.

"No, of course not, sweetheart," Augie said, since that was just what Melinda wanted to hear. He walked over to her, kissed her on the cheek, then guided her to the door. "I was just about to tell Gather myself," he said. "But why don't you go outside and have yourself a Fresca while the men finish talking. Then I can devote all my attention to you."

"Well, gee," she said. "I hope I didn't say the wrong thing. I was just trying to help the Dudes."

"Of course you were, sweetheart," Augie said. He opened the door and let Melinda out like she was a cat. He stood facing the door for a few seconds, composing himself. I jumped to my feet and demanded to know what was going on. I stuck the slip of paper that Augie had handed me in the pocket of my slacks and started banging my fists on his desk.

"Okay, Gather," Augie said, "if you're going to insist on being an ungrateful sumbitch, then I'm going to have to do something that I really don't want to do." He walked back to his desk, offered me a cigar. I refused again. He lit another one up for himself. "As you might know," he said, "Dick Wagner was in town with the Reds the last few days, and he expressed serious interest in you."

"No shit?" I said, leaning forward in my chair. I don't have to tell you that this was just about the best news I had heard in my whole life. "What does 'serious interest' mean?" I asked.

"Well, we discussed a lot of possibilities," Augie said. "I think we're going to be able to make a deal in the next few days."

"Oh, my God. I can't believe this," I said. "Playing for the Cincinnati Reds. This is terrific. Isn't it, Payton?"

"Nice," Payton said. "Very nice."

"Let me have one of those cigars, Augie," I said behind a wide grin.

"Just calm down a minute, young man," Augie said sternly. "There is one catch."

"Catch?" I shrieked. "What kind of catch?"

"You better explain it, Senator," Augie said. "It will sound better coming from the agent."

Payton flicked his ashes into an ashtray and stared at his cigar stub. "Gather, I assume that you are cognizant of the fact that the Cincinnati organization, which has the unpatriotic gall of referring to themselves as the Reds, is nevertheless the most conservative and tradition-oriented organization in this great American game."

"That's cool," I said. "I'll cut my hair. Throw out my leisure suits. Buy some ties. Wear wing tips. Name it. I'll do anything."

"That's nice. Very nice." Payton said. "But the organization's concern is not so much with your countenance as with your contract. Cincinnati, you may recall, refrained from indulging in the free-agent auction this winter past. Indeed, they recently dealt away the talented Rawley Eastwick rather than risk the possibility of losing him at the end of the year without compensation. They lost Don Gullett when he played out his option last year and do not intend to have that distasteful experience again."

"Don't worry about a thing, Payton," I said. "As soon as the deal's made, I'll sign a contract with the Reds. We'll have no problem over money."

"I'm afraid that that is not the sequence of events that they would agree to," Payton said. "They will only trade for a signed player."

Augie pulled out the middle drawer of his desk, removed a pile of papers, and held them in the air. "Here's your new contract, son," he said. "If you want to play for the Reds, you gotta sign this." He tossed the contracts across the desk to me. I caught them and glanced at them.

"But this isn't right," I said. "This is a three-year contract with the Dudes!"

"Precisely," Payton said. "The terms outlined in that contract were specified by the Cincinnati organization. The procedure for the deal is that, first, you sign that contract, and then, Mr. August trades that contract to Cincinnati. In that way, they know that you are bound to them for what they consider a reasonable amount of time."

I smelled a rat. After being screwed a few times by the old man, I knew that he was as good at lying with a straight face as most guys are at telling girls they love them if that's what it takes to get laid. I had to do some checking of my own before I signed three years of my life away. "Why don't you let me sleep on this overnight?" I said.

Augie and Payton exchanged another one of those skeptical glances. "That seems to be a valid request," Payton said.

"Well, all right," Augie said. "I'll go along with that. But I want you to come in here tomorrow at eleven o'clock and tell me your decision. When there's trade rumors around, it makes a lot of players feel insecure. If this takes too long, it can screw up my ball club."

"Screw them up?" I said. "You can't drop any further than last place."

"Eleven tomorrow," Augie said. "Now, give me back those contracts."

I started to hand the pile of papers back to Augie. I realized I hadn't even looked at the salary figure that the Reds were proposing. My eyes went right down to that dotted line, the only part of the standard player's contract that I ever read. The only part that I can understand. Well, sitting right there on those tiny little dots was the number $750,000 and a little ways across the line there were some more dots with the words, "for three years" sitting on top of them. 'Course, I could've gotten myself least twice that much if I played out my option and sold my pitching arm on the open market in the winter. But no sense being greedy. As it was, I couldn't really imagine just how much $750,000 was. But anything was enough if it got me away from Augie August as soon as possible and gave me the opportunity to pitch for the world champions. I handed the contracts back to Augie.

"How 'bout that cigar now, son?" he said.

"Tomorrow," I said, and I got up and walked out of the office.

Melinda was sitting outside on a secretary's desk, sipping a Fresca and looking through an issue of *Cosmopolitan*. I walked over to her and said, "Thanks for coming to our meeting, ma'am. Wasn't for you, I might've never found out about the Reds."

"I hope I didn't do anything wrong," she said.

I smiled at her. "Wrong?" I said. "Honey, you've never been so right-on."

She didn't understand what I was saying, but she was thankful for anything that sounded like a compliment and smiled back at me. As I left the offices, I remember thinking that she wasn't that bad of a lady, like I first suspected. She just wanted to be liked and admired, which was something I could understand, since I wanted the same things.

In the parking lot, I asked Payton to get me some kind of verification from the Reds.

"Easier said than done," he said to me. "It's contrary to baseball protocol for a team to admit to an impending trade before it is official. As soon as word gets out, those players who are about to be traded will surely get upset, and if the deal falls through, then the team is left with disgruntled men who feel unappreciated."

"All ballplayers feel unappreciated," I said.

"Correct," Payton said. "But those who are about to be traded have a right to."

Well, I didn't care what the complications were. Far as

I can tell, there's a way to find out anything if you're clever enough. And I was paying Payton 10 percent to be clever. He said he'd see what he could find out. And I intended to do some snooping of my own.

I drove back to my apartment and tracked down Pete Rose at the Sheraton in Philadelphia, where the Reds were holed up for a weekend series with the Phillies. I told Pete that I had been informed that the Reds were about to deal for me. Imagining me pitching for the Reds excited him as much as it excited me.

"But, Gather," he said on the phone, "they don't tell me nothing around here. I ain't sure just how to check it out."

I knew one way to make sure he'd do some snooping. It was mean, but I had to do it. "Do your best, Pete," I said. "You know Augie didn't tell me who he was getting in return. I sure hope it isn't you. It wouldn't be as much fun pitching for the Reds without Pete Rose."

"Me? You think they'd trade me?" he said.

"Never can tell," I said. "You are getting up there in years."

"Yeah, but they can't trade me, can they? Bastards. They never appreciate a thing. I'm gonna check this thing out right now. Get back to ya."

I sat there nervously waiting to hear back from Rose. I flipped on the tube and tried to watch the soaps like I always did when I wanted to get into someone else's problems instead of my own. You're not gonna believe this one, but that day, Dan Prendergast—you know, the stockbroker on *Heart Full of Tears*—well, old Dan was sitting there in his apartment nervously awaiting a call about a new job with a rival company. Damn if it wasn't like I was sitting in my living room watching my own story happening right there on the national tube. I imagine I was feeling right then just like Lou Gehrig would have felt watching Gary Cooper playing him in *Pride of the Yankees*. Bet old Lou would have shut it off before it got to the end part where he dies. He wouldn't want to watch that on television. And I shut off old Dan Prender-gast. I couldn't bear to find out what happened to him—especially if he didn't get the job.

I picked up the sports section from the Sunday *Post,* which I kept all week so I could look at the ERA's over and over. My name was right up there near the top of the list, behind Rich Gossage of the Pirates and Bruce Sutter of the Cubs. We were the only three pitchers under 2.00. Most of the Reds' pitchers were close to or above 4.00. 'Course, I gotta admit my ERA was a bit deceiving. You see, our guys made so many errors that almost all the runs we gave up had to be unearned. On our team, a pitcher could give up ten runs a game, lose twenty games, and still lead the league in ERA. They say statistics are for losers, and when you play for the Dudes you spend a lot of time looking at the stats.

After reading through the sports again, I turned to the stock-market quotations, figuring I better start thinking about that kind of thing with my new salary and all. Those stock fellas sure got a lot more statistics then we do in baseball.

Anyway, around three o'clock, Payton called me with some news. A top Red official had told Payton that they were looking to deal for an all-star pitcher. Now, that's not real strong evidence, but I seemed to be the only all-star pitcher available, so that had to mean they were try-ing to get me. Payton had also checked it out with a baseball writer for the Cincinnati *Post,* who said his column that day reported the deal for me was about to be made. I wasn't totally convinced, but I figured if I got a positive report from Rose it was bye bye Dudes.

Little while after I hung up with my agent, Rose called. "Hey, Gather, you asshole," he said. "They ain't gonna trade me."

"Good, Pete," I said. "What'd you find out about me?"

"They can't trade me if I don't wanna go," Rose said. "I'm a ten-and-five man. Ten in the league and five with the same club. They need my approval, and I'd be a horse's ass to go to a team like the Dudes."

"You're right, Pete," I said. "What about me?"

"And besides. After all I've done for this town. Shoot. If they wanted to get rid of me, they would have done it before I signed my new contract this year. It was real nasty negotiatin' this time around. Always is. But they came through. They want me here."

"Great, Pete. But what about me?"

"But shoot, if they want to give up one of the most consistent players in the game for some pitcher who plays every five days, well, they can go right ahead and do it. 'Course, they ain't gonna do it. You don't win championships doing things like that."

"Terrific, Pete. Great. I'm glad to hear it. . . ."

"The fans would never let them get away with it either, Gather. Fans appreciate me. 'Course, management does too. If you saw my new two-year pact, you'd know what I'm saying. Now, as far as you go . . ."

"Yeah, what about me?"

"Well, I checked with the trainer. He's got ways of finding out everything that's happening around here. And he says we're gonna get ourselves an all-star pitcher in two or three days. He tells me we're gonna give up Dougie Flynn, this kid Henderson we got in the minors, and probably a pitcher or two. 'Course, if I was your boss man, I wouldn't give up an all-star pitcher for guys who don't play every day. But I'm not your boss man. And trainer says we're gonna pull this one off."

"What all-star pitcher are you going to get?" I asked.

"Seems to me you're the only one available," Rose said. "Shoot, you don't think we're gonna get ourselves Seaver or Sutton without giving up some of our starting eight, do you?"

That was all I wanted to hear. I was going to run into Augie's office the next morning, put my name on that contract, and end my days as a cotton-picking slave for the hamburger king. Yes sir, freedom was but a few days away. I figured I'd be gone by the time my next pitching turn came up. Come Sunday, I'd be standing on the mound wearing the double-knits of the Cincinnati Reds. 'Course, signing that contract would just make me their cotton-picking slave for the next three years. But if you gotta be a slave, it might as well be a world-champion slave.

"Thanks for everything, Pete," I said. "See you in a few days."

"Sure, Gather," he said, as if he wasn't listening to me. "Hey, Gather, you just don't trade away a Pete Rose, a Joe Morgan, a John Bench. No sir. Those guys do a lot more for you than shows up in the papers. Nah, Pete Rose is staying in Cincinnati. You bet your ass he is. See ya, Gather."

I hung up the phone, jumped to my feet, and gave myself a standing ovation right there in my bedroom. What a cool motherfucking dude I was. Getting myself traded to the Cincinnati Reds. Going from the shithouse to the promised land. Stopping at Go to pick up my 250 G's a year. I can't imagine anyone's ever been more excited than I was at that moment.

I lay back on my round-as-a-pitcher's-mound bed trying to picture myself in a Reds' uniform. Had to lose just a few pounds round the waist so I killed the ladies in my clinging double-knits, I figured. I got out of bed, pulled a Fruit of the Loom T-shirt out of my drawer, and drew the Reds' logo over the left breast. I put it on and walked into the bathroom to admire myself in the mirror. Looked real fine, I'll tell you that. I turned around to see what I looked like from another angle. I was missing a number on my back. I realized right then that I had a minor problem. I had worn number 13, my lucky number, throughout my career. But Davey Concepcion already wore that number for the Reds. At first I thought of asking Davey if he wouldn't mind changing his number, but you know the Latinos are real superstitious and I didn't want to risk causing any problems right off with my new team. And

besides, the way that lanky Latino covers the infield, I
had to be glad to give him the shirt off my back. I had to
try out a different number.

A number might not seem like such an important consideration, but it's part of your on-the-field personality,
just like how much white you let show under your wool
socks and the puka shells some players wear around their
necks these days. Even though everyone on the team
wears the same uniform, today's players want to have a
little bit of their own style—which is one of the major
contributions those flashy-dressing black folk have made
to the game.

Some players like to wear the great historical numbers
like 14 or 32. Number 32 is real class since 1963, when
the MVP's in both leagues—Sandy Koufax and Elston
Howard—each wore it. Other players, the individualists
you might say, like to wear numbers that no great players
have ever worn, thinking that they can make it famous.
That's why you see Seaver wearing 41 and Dick Allen
wearing 99 with Oakland. Can you dig it? 99! Then some
of the teams have their own numbering system, like the
Dodgers, where almost every one of their starting eight
wears a single digit on his back.

It seems to be kind of a rule of thumb that pitchers
wear high-digit numbers up in the 30's or 40's or even the
50's. But to me that always had a bad connotation, like
the pitchers weren't athletes or something. Ever since I
played shortstop in high school, I've felt qualified to wear
an athlete's low number.

Figuring I had to let Concepcion keep his 13, I went
over the Reds' roster trying to pick out an available number that would look right on my back. I came up with a
fitting solution to my problem. Morgan wears number 3
and Bench wears number 5, but no one on the team
wears number 4. And I figured if I went in and signed in
the morning and the deal went through tomorrow like it
was supposed to, then I would have been traded on June
4. So it was only fitting that I commemorate the day I got

my freedom by wearing number 4 on my back. I wrote number 4 on the back of my T-shirt and stood staring at it in the mirror. It was gonna take some getting used to, but I liked the whole idea.

If there was ever a time in my life for some real celebrating, that was it. So I called some of the guys to try to find someone to go down a few brews in my honor.

I tried Bubba's line, but there was no answer. He must've been out playing some golf like he does every off-day. I called Gabby and told him the news, but he didn't seem real happy for me.

"Well, I hope you're happy with yourself now Gather," he said.

"Happy, man?" I said. "I'm more than happy. I'm super happy. I wanna go out and celebrate. Why don't you meet me over Clyde's."

"Hey, I got nothing to celebrate," Gabby said. "I'm still stuck in the shithouse. And besides, I gotta spend the off-day with my kids. My wife wouldn't let me out of the house on an off-day to go to your funeral."

I called Pinky Potts and Tony Smith, but got pretty much the same riff I got from Gabby. They couldn't leave their families and they weren't real thrilled for me. They all made it sound as if I was deserting them, which I guess in a way I was. Still, I was kind of hurt. I had spent lots of lonely nights on the road with these guys, sharing all kinds of personal bitches. I knew things about them that they wouldn't tell their wives. 'Course, if they did, they wouldn't have wives for very long. But we weren't just teammates. We were friends. Least, that's how I looked at it. I could understand they were envious of me going from a cellar-dweller to a front-runner. Who wouldn't be? But that's the breaks of the game, just like a ground ball that hits a rock, takes a bad hop, and costs you a ball game. If you're gonna play baseball, you gotta learn to live with those things.

As I went down the team list of phone numbers, looking for someone, anyone, to share my happiness with, I heard more excuses and more resentment. It was as if my teammates didn't give a shit about me. When we were on the road sharing planes and hotel rooms and losses and groupies, we were friends because we had to be. But now, just because a piece of paper I was going to sign was to be sold, I was no longer one of them.

All this rejection made me think back to the minors and high school and even my Little League days. I hadn't thought about it before, but my friends had always been my teammates. I began to wonder if, were it not for the teams, any of them would have been my friends at all. Thinking about this made me sad. It was the happiest day of my life and I was feeling sad. I had to change that fast.

I decided that if my teammates didn't see fit to carouse with this traitor, then I could always dig me up one of my lady friends. I called Suzy Quentin, the cute little blond who worked as a waitress at Paddy O'Brien's, but she said she was working dinner and then meeting "a friend." I tried Mary Zachary, a stew for United, but her roomie told me she was flying. I had a lot of other ladies' numbers lying around the apartment on cocktail napkins and matchbook covers. But most of those chicks had just been one-nighters and it wouldn't have been appropriate to spend the happiest day of my life with them.

It was all getting real frustrating and depressing. I had to know someone who would enjoy celebrating with me. I jumped in my Stingray and drove over to Clyde's by myself. I knew Benjy would be behind the bar and he was always more than happy to shoot the shit with me.

When I arrived, it was in between lunch hour and cocktail hour and the place was quiet as the clubhouse of the losing team in the World Series. There were two men in business suits sitting at a table too drunk to make it back to the office for the afternoon. I was the only soul at the bar.

Benjy put a brew down in front of me. "I don't ever remember seeing you here in the afternoon," he said.

"Well, it's kind of a special day for me, Benjy," I said. "And I came over here for a celebration."

"You getting married or something?"

"Nah, it's better than that. I'm getting traded."

"Traded?" he blurted out.

"Shhhh," I said. "You can't tell a soul till it's made public. I'm going to the Cincinnati Reds."

Benjy just kind of stared at me for a minute. Then he walked away, mixed a couple of martinis, and brought them over to the leftover lunchers. He came back to the bar, rang up a check on the register, and put it facedown in front of me.

"Hey, this is the first one you charged me for all season," I said with a giggle that echoed in the empty room.

"Go find yourself a bar in Cincinnati if you want drinks on the house," he said, and he walked to the sink and started washing some dishes.

Well, I didn't need to take any shit from that little twirp. I threw a buck on the bar and started walking through the sawdust to the door. I heard a drunken voice behind me yell, "Hey, Morse, ya bum. We love Augie August. He brought baseball back to Washington. If you don't like him, why don't you go cry someplace else? Who needs you, Morse, you bum?"

I turned my head and saw the two red-faced businessmen yukking it up and banging their glasses on the table. I walked out of the bar and to my car.

Only a handful of people knew about the deal, but already I felt as if the whole damn town was turning on me. I'd pitched my heart out for the team and the fans for over three years, but that didn't seem to matter. It never matters, I guess. The fans love you while you're playing for their team and hate you as soon as you leave. And even when they love you, if you have a dispute with the owner, you always find out they love him more.

My mood had rolled rapidly downhill since Rose called back and verified the deal in my mind. It was as if someone up there wasn't gonna let me enjoy my good fortune.

What I needed was something to lift my spirits. As I drove up M Street out of Georgetown, it occurred to me that I could use a good strong shot of Laura's medicine. Damn right. Just thinking about her as my Stingray bumpity-bumped over the cobblestone street made my body feel good all over. That soft shiny brown hair. Those big-as-a-half-dollar eyes. And the flittingest little tongue I ever did feel. I wiggled in my bucket seat thinking about that tongue.

Laura and I didn't have another appointment scheduled until Sunday, when my next pitching turn came up, but I needed to feel her smooth skin right next to me right then. I knew she spent her afternoons sculpting at her apartment, and I figured I had a few hours before her Panamanian art-dealer friend came home from his gallery. If I called her, she would have had the opportunity to discourage my visit, but if I just showed up there in the flesh, my body would be hard for her to resist.

So I drove on over to P Street, parked in front of her building, and sneaked over to the stairwell when the doorman's back was turned. I didn't want him to ring up and warn her I was on my way. I was a little nervous as I ran up the five flights of stairs, since I had never disregarded our schedule like this before.

I ran to her door and knocked. There was no response for a few seconds. Then I heard her little feet shuffling to the door. She opened the door just a bit and stuck her head out. Her cheeks were all rosy, and soon as I saw that face, I was glad I came over.

"Gather?" she shrieked. "You don't pitch for three days. What are you doing here?"

"This is an important day for me, sweet thing," I said. "And I wanted to share it with someone important to me."

"I'd like to, Gather," she said. "But I just can't now."

I started getting angry. She was the one person I didn't expect to reject me. "Come on, Laura," I said sternly. "This is important to me. Let me in."

"Gather, if you ever want to see me again, you'll leave," she said.

"What kind of shit is that?" I said. And I pushed my way past the door and into the apartment. Man, did I live to regret that move. For, lying there on her convertible couch, in the buff no less, was none other than Sticky Thomas, our starting pitcher for the next night's game against the Mets.

It was no small surprise to me. Laura had insisted she knew nothing about baseball, and whenever I mentioned one of the guys on our club, she pretended she never heard of them before. Well, she knew them, all right. And in the biblical sense. For all I knew, she might have been going down on our whole starting rotation. Wonder what she did when we played doubleheaders?

Without saying a word to Laura or Sticky, I walked out of that apartment, down the stairs, and into my car. I drove south on Twenty-first Street, heading for the reflecting pool across the way from the Lincoln Memorial. It's a real pretty spot and good for doing your reflecting, which is where the name came from, I suppose. Maybe it was good that I had had such a disappointing day, I thought to myself as I followed the flow of traffic around Washington Circle. Now, at least, I wouldn't feel like there was anything worth staying in Washington for. Fact is, at that moment I was ready to take the next plane out. I figured I had blown it in that town. But I was determined to make things different in Cincinnati. I like people, and I want people to like me, and I was gonna go out there to the Midwest and make myself some real genuine-type friends.

I left my car beside the ballfield across the street and walked over to the reflecting pool. The circle around the Lincoln Memorial was lined with scenic-cruiser buses. The lawn around the pool was filled with schoolkids snapping away with their Instamatics. I wasn't up for mingling with a crowd, so I walked among the oak trees that line the pool, looking for a peaceful spot.

This little blond kid in his blue school uniform jumped out from behind a tree, which startled me a bit. "Hold it," he said, and he snapped my picture. I started to walk on.

"Hey, mister," he shouted after me. "You're Gather Morse of the Washington Dudes, aren't you?"

"Who?" I said. "No, I'm not him."

"Yeah, you are. You are," the kid said. "I got your baseball card at home. You're Gather Morse."

"Wrong guy," I said, and I kept on walking. Just when I thought I was far enough away from the crowd to be by myself, I heard hundreds of little feet rustling through the leaves. I turned around and saw this swarm of little buggers in their school uniforms running toward me. They surrounded me so that I couldn't move without stomping on them. They stuck papers and pencils in my face and begged for autographs. Some of them snapped away with their Instamatics.

"Who is he?" a girl's tiny voice said.

"Dummy, that's Gather Morse," a boy insisted. "He's the best pitcher in the major leagues."

I looked out at all those little round faces pushing to get close to me, and I smiled for what must have been the first time in hours. Kids are terrific, I thought to myself. Sure is great being a major-league ballplayer.

5

I did, by the way, end up with some female company that evening after all. Those little buggers, who turned out to be a sixth-grade class from a Catholic school near Montreal, may have been excited meeting a major leaguer. But they were not nearly as excited as their teacher, this giggly, freckled little carrot-top who introduced herself as Miss McNamara, with the emphasis on the *Miss*. Miss McNamara insisted that I accompany her admiring class back to the Howard Johnson's Motor Inn, across the street from the Watergate, where they were staying. She claimed it would please the children, but it wasn't just their pleasure she was concerned with.

When we got to that hotel, she left her kids running wild and screaming in the lobby, as if she had dispossessed them, and escorted me up to Room 412. She excused herself for a minute and then returned with two other giggling young teachers, whom she introduced as Miss McIntire and Miss McGillicuddy. Seems all these teachers were chaperoning the annual sixth-grade trip to Washington and had chosen me to be their souvenir. I started giggling too. We were all giggling, naughty-type giggles. Before I had time to figure out the various configurations, Fellini was hustling from hole to hole faster than a scratch golfer. I never figured out what parts belonged to whom, but it didn't seem to matter much. A good time was had by all. Must have been near sunrise when I left Misses McNamara, McIntire, and McGillicuddy strewn out on the bed motionless as an Irish stew and headed back to my apartment. It wasn't exactly the kind of celebration I had planned for myself, but you know what they say about the best-laid plans.

I'd only had a thimbleful of shut-eye when my Selectricon digital clock radio (which I and all the other participants in the 1975 all-star game had received as a memento) went off at ten. I only had an hour to get to Augie's office to sign my contract. I jumped out of bed and shaved with the Techmagic razor I had received from the folks who run the all-star balloting. I pulled on my green Tartan slacks (a memento of the 1974 Tartan Celebrity Frisbee Tournament), my Barzini tennis shirt (a memento of the 1975 Barzini Celebrity Tennis Tournament), and my Adonis sneakers (a memento of a visit to our clubhouse by the local Adonis salesman). Then I made myself a nice tall glass of Instant Pro Breakfast, a case of which was given to each member of our team before the season. I don't mean to sound like a talking billboard, but all these folks are nice enough to give me their products, so I figure the least I can do is mention them when I get the chance.

I guess jocks are fortunate in that we don't have to go out and buy ourselves a lot of the everyday necessities that the average Joe has to worry about. Fact is, just about everything a gentleman needs to look good, eat well, and smell fine is handed to us free of charge. 'Course, sometimes we end up with things that we wouldn't think of using if we were just the average Joe. Like this Insta-Tan shit that Payton talked me into endorsing last year. *Just rub a little on and look like you just got off the plane from Florida* it says right there on the box. Actually, you look like you just moved here from Puerto Rico.

Since I was endorsing the stuff, I felt obligated to put it on in the clubhouse when the reporters were around. So after one home game against the Braves, this young reporter from some Georgia hick paper comes over and asks me, "Why do you play so shallow in center field?" Sumbitch mistook me for Chi Chi Blanco! Now, I don't have nothing against the Latinos, but I wouldn't want to be one. That was the end of that endorsement.

When I arrived at the stadium, Augie was not in his office. His secretary said he had a brunch meeting, but I assumed he was home with Melinda, which is where I would have been if I had her speaker system filling my house with music. He had left my contracts with Nat Horowitz, the Dudes' vice-president in charge of operations, which I always thought made him sound like he worked in a hospital instead of for a baseball team. Nat Horowitz's main responsibility, far as I can tell, was to find the cheapest way of doing anything, whether it was buying uniforms, making hotel arrangements on the road, or ordering the turkey for the team's annual Thanksgiving party. Nat was in the construction business before he came to work for Augie. He was forced out of that business when an entire development he had built collapsed. He was hit with millions of dollars in lawsuits because the cheap materials he had used did not meet the legal standards. When Augie heard about this, he knew he had to have Nat Horowitz as his vice-president of operations. "He's the cheapest sumbitch I've ever met," Augie always said. "And I love him for it."

As I signed my contracts, Nat, a pudgy, balding little fella with a nose as big as his belly, said, "Well, I'm glad you've changed your mind and decided to stay with Augie's ball club."

I assumed that Augie had simply not informed Nat

about the upcoming deal with the Reds. I wasn't going to let the cat out of the bag. "Yeah," was all I said.

Nat rubbed his hand over his bald head, which was always sprinkled with beads of sweat and looked like the hood of a car when it was raining. "I just knew Augie would find some way to convince you to stay with his club," he said. "It would have broken his heart to lose you. After all, we get twice our normal crowd every time you pitch. You gotta love a player who does that for you."

"Sure do," I said, and I handed the contracts to Nat. "That should do it."

Nat looked them over. "Lot of money for a young man to be making," he said. "I've been thinking of suggesting to Augie that we take out the water fountains. That way people will have to go to the concession stands when they're thirsty and give us more money to help pay your salary. What do you think of that idea?"

"Why don't you just put in pay fountains?" I said sarcastically.

Nat rubbed his hand on his head and then wiped the sweat off on the leg of his pants. "Helluvan idea, Gather," he said. "Wonder if we can get a quarter for water?"

I treated myself to a steak at Duke Ziebert's for lunch, but I didn't dare tell Duke about the deal. Tell him something like that, and everybody in town'll know before nightfall. And besides, I wasn't in the mood for more of the kind of reaction I had gotten the previous day.

I spent the afternoon at home watching the soaps and listening to the Carly Simon albums the nice people at Radio House had given me for just letting them use my name in an ad. Now, Carly Simon's one lady I'd really like to get acquainted with. I may be vain, but I'd give her something to sing about.

Fact is, being an athlete you do get to meet a lot of show-biz folk. Especially at the all-star game and at those celebrity-type tournaments we all participate in during the off-season. I once got paired up with Don Rickles in a golf tournament in Las Vegas. He had me laughing so hard I thought I was gonna croak. "What kind of a name is Gather?" he said to me.

I told him that Dad wanted to name me Gary, after his dad, and Mom wanted to name me Luther, after hers, which is the truth. So they compromised. "Very clever," he says. "Too bad their names weren't Sherm and Muckie. Then they could have named you Schmuckie. Which would have been as good as Gather. Gather Morse. What kind of name is that? Sounds like something to kill fungus."

I laughed so much that day that my whole golf game fell apart. I should have known that that was Rickle's intention. He beat my ass.

Funny thing about those tournaments is, the show-biz folk always want to be good athletes and the athletes all want to be in the movies. No one's ever happy with what they are.

Anyway, I went back to the stadium around five for our game with the Mets. I walked into the clubhouse and discovered I was no more welcome than a lady with clap at an orgy.

"Hey, Gasser, Gasser," Chi Chi said as he danced in his spikes and cap. "This no you clubhouse. You go to visitors. No? And, Gasser. You get me World Series tickets for me mother? Maybe? No?"

"Maybe no!" I said.

Skip Thomas saw me and ducked into the trainer's room to hide. No one else said a word to me. I sat down on the stool in front of my locker, turned to Bubba, sitting next to me, and said, "How was your golf game yesterday, bro'?"

"Whaddaya care?" he barked at me, and he spit a wad of tobacco on the floor.

"Hey, Bubba," Gabby said, looking up from his game of dominoes. "Better be nice to Gather. Otherwise he may throw at you when he pitches against us. 'Course, his pitch won't hurt no more than a wad of cotton."

"Throws at me, I'll break his fuckin' arm," Bubba growled, and he got up and walked away.

"Well, Morse is going to the right team," Tony Smith said. "You know what they say—if you can't beat 'em, then join 'em."

"But just think, Tony," Gabby said. "Now maybe Gather will groove a pitch to you like he grooved that one to Griffey the other night."

"Hey, bro'," Tony said. "Morse did the right thing. He won one for *his* team."

Everyone in the clubhouse started laughing at that crack. Not good-time laughing, but real mean laughing. That was a little bit more joshing than I was willing to shake off. I'd done everything I could to beat those Reds Wednesday night, and I wasn't gonna stand for these wiseacres accusing me of dumping. I couldn't in my rightful mind just sit by and accept that kind of donkey shit.

I jumped right up off my stool like it was a gas burner and slammed my fist down in the middle of the bridge table. The dominoes went flying up into the air. All the Smiths could tell I wasn't messing around. Three of them went scampering faster than Joe Morgan gets down to second base.

But Gabby was slower getting away, just like on a steal. I grabbed him by the neck of his T-shirt. I looked into his eyes and called him a motherfucking, cocksucking sumbitch. And I threw him into his cubicle. As he fell backward, he grabbed onto his clothes hanging on hangers. They ripped off and fell onto his face. Before he could pull them away and see me, I was flailing away at his midsection with right-left combinations. I was a crazed man and I was pounding him as a symbol for the whole fucking team.

Next thing I knew, I felt a ton of lead, that happened to be Bubba, landing on my back and wrestling me to the August-auburn carpet. Bubba pinned me to the ground and slapped my face a little. Gabby jumped on and pounded away at my midsection.

Then I heard Skip's high-pitched voice yelling, "Break it up, fellas," as if anyone was gonna listen to his say-so. Bubba and Gabby would have surely put me on the injured reserved list if Benny the Nip didn't come right over and start splashing wintergreen all over us. Bubba fell off me and covered his eyes. I felt the stuff splashing on my face, and my whole body started burning. I jumped up, ran into the shower room, and turned on the water cold as it would go. Damn, that stuff makes you feel like you're burning at the stake.

The shower got rid of the stinging. But it didn't do much for the bruises Bubba and Gabby had inflicted on my face and stomach. I tell you, I felt like crying right then. Not so much because of the hurting, but because everyone in that there clubhouse, guys I'd worked with and traveled with for three years, had all turned against me. I can't stand being in the same room with even one person who doesn't like me, so you could imagine how I must have felt surrounded by twenty-four of them.

Craziest thing was, when you think about it, every one of those guys used to bitch and yell that they were slaves to the owners. When the Messersmith-McNally court decision came down, we said, to a man, that it was the greatest day of our lives and even held a beer blast to celebrate. 'Course, all of them went right out and signed new multi-year contracts, opting for the security rather than taking the risk of putting themselves up on the open market. They didn't think enough of themselves to take the chance. But I did. And I had my own reasons for getting away from Augie August. So here I was, taking advantage of a new bargaining system that they all approved of, and they treated me like I was doing something wrong. Now, when they hear what I'm saying here and find out what went down between the old man and me, they might feel bad about the way they treated me back then. But at the time, I was flaming mad.

I took my uniform into the trainer's room, closed the door, and suited up away from the other guys. Then I went out to the field to run some sprints and calm myself down.

There's no more exciting place than a filled stadium, and there's no lonelier place than an empty stadium. The tall grandstand walls hold all the sounds of the street outside. The seats are all folded up waiting for bodies to fill them and give them life. And what's left is a vast, quiet meadow, like the farms back in Mantua. I sat down in our dugout and stared out at the meadow, thinking about how much fun it was playing baseball on the farms when there were no owners and contracts and money and jealousies. My eyes roamed the field, not focusing on anything until they reached the visitor's dugout. Sitting there, by himself, staring out at the empty peaceful field like I was, was Tom Seaver. I always like talking with Tom. He's one of those real deep-thinking-type individuals, and as much of an expert on pitching as you can find anyplace. I walked across the field to talk with him.

"Gather Morse from the great town of Mantua, Ohio," he said behind a pretty-boy smile as he saw me approaching.

"Mr. Tom Terrific, the man who made the New York Mets famous," I said as our huge hands grasped.

"Well, we're just about to close the covers on that book," he said.

That was the kind of line I expected from him. Any other player would talk about things in terms of either baseball or sex. But Tom Seaver talks about books. "Whaddaya mean?" I asked him.

The smile that always seemed to decorate his face disappeared. It was replaced by one of those real sad and serious-type expressions. The kind you see on managers about to be fired, but not on Tom Terrific. "Well, Gather, my man," he said, putting his arm around my shoulders. "It appears that my days as a New York Met have just about come to an end."

"You're not gonna retire, are you?" I asked. I figured retiring was the only way the Mets would let the man they called "the franchise" get away.

"Retire? Not me," he said. "I got four or five good years left in this body. No, old buddy, I'm afraid Mr. M. Donald Grant has decided that it would be best for his team if he traded me away."

He had to be putting me on. I knew he had had some disagreements with Grant. But far as I'm concerned, you just don't trade away a Tom Seaver. You do anything you have to to keep that man happy. "You gotta be shitting me," I said.

"I wish I was, but I'm not," he said, staring out into the wide-open spaces of the field.

"But why?" I asked.

"Oh, it's a long, involved story," he said. "Personality conflict, I guess. Has to do with loyalty and conduct unbecoming a New York Met, whatever that means. And a little bit about money, though that's not really the issue with me."

"Hey, that's just bulltwang," I said. "None of those things matter. You made this team a success, and if they gave you some help, you could make it a bigger success. That's all that matters."

He laughed a little. But I could tell it was a sad laugh. "I'll tell you one thing, buddy," he said. "If all you had to do in baseball was walk from your house to the field, this game would be as easy as pitching pennies. But you gotta stop in the clubhouse along the way. And that's not so easy. Ah, well. It doesn't matter anymore. Mr. Grant asked me today for a list of four teams that I'd agree to go to, and I gave it to him. Now I just wait."

Suddenly a gong went off in my head. It dawned on me that if what Seaver was telling me was true, as it had to be, I was no longer the only all-star pitcher available. My own situation could be affected by this. "What four teams are on your list?" I asked him with detectable worry in my voice.

"Well, the Dodgers and the Padres, of course," he said. "I'm from that area, after all, and I like the weather out there. And Atlanta, because I like what Ted Turner's trying to do with that club. The man's not afraid to spend some money. And, of course, the organization that no one in his right mind wouldn't want to play for . . ."

"Cincinnati?" I shrieked.

"You bet," he said.

"Holy fucking shit!" I said.

"What's wrong?" he asked. "Wouldn't you want to play for the Reds? From what I hear, they're the ones who are ready to deal for me."

"I gotta run, Tom," I said. "See you later."

I ran across the field toward our dugout. This was like a bad dream come true. My teammates were coming out to hit, and Skip yelled, "Come on, Gather. Let's get some hits in here." I ignored him. I ran down the runway, through our clubhouse, into the hallway, and up the three flights of stairs to Augie's office. I couldn't let this situation get out of my control. My deal was too close to happening to let it evaporate now. I had to see if Augie knew about Seaver, and if so, what that meant to me.

I walked through the glass doors and into the team's offices. Just as I reached Augie's office door, E. J. Acton of the *Post* and Bobby Ward of the *Star* came out.

"Just the man we were looking for," Acton said. "Augie just told us about your new three-year contract with the Dudes. Tell us, Gather, in your own words, what made you change your mind about playing out your option?"

Now I knew I was in serious trouble. Augie had conned me once again. "I haven't changed my mind at all," I said. I pushed Acton aside and burst through the door into Augie's office. He was sitting behind his desk in the August-auburn blazer he wore to every home game. He looked up and saw me, his eyes opened wide, he pushed down on his intercom. "Send my bodyguards in here," he yelled. "Hurry up. Get them in here."

"You no-good fucking liar," I said, walking toward him with my fists clenched in front of me. "You fucked me again. I can't believe you fucked me again. I'm gonna beat the living shit out of you this time, old man."

He jumped up and scooted around the desk to try to stay away from me. I chased him around it. He ran for the door. I ran after him. He pulled the door open. The two reporters were standing there with their ears to the door. Augie pushed past them, and I ran after him. As I was about to go through the door, the two bodyguards pulled the reporters away and stood blocking the door frame. But I was an animal. Even they weren't going to stop me from beating the old man.

I let out a war whoop, ran at the thugs, and tried to dive between them. They caught me in the air as easy as you catch a pop fly. They put me on my feet and pinned my arms behind me. I jumped around, trying to free myself, but it was no use.

They dragged me down the hallway toward the double glass doors. "I'm gonna get you yet, old man," I yelled. "Goddammit, I'm gonna ruin you."

The thugs deposited me outside the glass doors and stood in front of me with their arms crossed and their muscles bulging. I was breathing heavily and my chest was pumping up and down. Every muscle in my body tightened. I never thought I had it in me, but at that particular moment, for the first time in my life, I felt as if I was capable of killing a man. But to do so, I had to get by the two goons, and I could not have accomplished that.

I was helpless. I turned away and walked back down to the clubhouse. I wasn't staying for the game. I didn't care how much the old man fined me. I wasn't ever going to show up for one of his games again.

I walked into the clubhouse and grabbed my clothes out of my locker. I wasn't even going to stop to get dressed. I reached into the pocket of my jeans to pull out my car keys. I found the keys. And I also found that slip

of paper on which Augie had written down his last offer
at our meeting the previous day. I had stuffed the slip into
my pocket without looking at it when Melinda came into
the room.

Now I unfolded it to look. There was no figure written
on it. Augie knew I wasn't going to look at it, which is
why he had dreamed up his whole lying, deceiving scheme
to get me to sign. Instead of a dollar figure, the slip of paper said *"Sucker!"*

I could hear the crowd in the stadium cheering as I
pulled out of the player's parking lot. There were only
about ten thousand fans at RFK that night to watch Tom
Seaver pitch against the Dudes. But their voices ricocheted off the concrete walls and formed echoes so loud it
sounded like a full house.

That screechy sound, which had usually thrilled me,
sounded different to me that evening. It repulsed me. I
didn't want to hear the idiots screaming for their heroes. I
didn't want to be one of those heroes. I just wanted to be
as far away from the team and the game as possible, and
I was relieved when the noise faded in the distance behind
me.

As I drove up Massachusetts Avenue toward downtown, I was just reeking with hate. I hated Augie August
and knew that if I ever saw him again, I would immediately burst into a rage and attack him like a mad
dog. I hated my teammates for turning on me as soon as
they found out I wasn't going to be one of them anymore.
I hated the fickle fans who rooted for a uniform that said
"Dudes" and didn't care who was in that uniform. Fact is,
I hated the whole idea of major-league baseball.

Now, I'm a person, and that's how I like to be treated.
But people don't count in baseball. It's a game of teams.
Put nine jackasses out there on the field, call them the
Dudes or the Mets or the Dodgers, and the owners would
pay them, the fans would root for them, and the chip-
munks would interview them. Athletes ain't nothing but

jackasses with numbers on their backs. And when they get old, they bring in younger jackasses to replace them.

I wondered if the average Joe felt this way about his job. Dad never told me much about his work, but one thing he did always say was that his success was based on his personal relationships with folks whose loads he hauled. I liked hearing that. It made me real proud of Dad. Made me think people liked him. I wanted my life to be just that way. But it wasn't, and so I felt pitiful sorry for myself. Here I was, bound for three years to a team I didn't want to play for, surrounded by people I didn't want to be with, living in a city I no longer could live in. How'd I get myself into this mess? I wondered as I drove by the Capitol and into the Northwest section of town. And now, how do I get out of it?

What I needed was someone to help me out. When you're an athlete, there's always someone around to help you. You're guided through your young life by coaches and agents and traveling secretaries and accountants and owners. There's always someone else around to do your thinking for you. Only decision you have to make is what to order for dinner—and since we all live on meat and potatoes, that don't take too much smarts. But now I didn't have anyone to help me. For the first time in my life, I was all by myself. I was pitching without a team covering the field behind me.

I drove up Constitution Avenue past the back of the White House, which was real fitting at the moment. I'd seen some of our Presidents get on the national tube and say what a lonely place the White House was, and I could never understand what they meant. After all, they have all those servants and advisers nipping at their butts, and they're always having big parties. But that night I understood why it was so lonely. I pictured myself sitting there alone in that oval office having to make big decisions by myself. Making decisions is an underrated chore, tell you that. But I had to do it. I just couldn't accept what Augie had done to me and fulfill my new contract with the Dudes.

I turned up Twenty-first Street and left my car across from the Lincoln Memorial again. I crossed the street and walked up the steps. It was a muggy night and I felt a good sweat accumulating under my uniform just from walking. I was in no mood to change into my civvies, but that didn't matter 'cause there was no one at the Memorial that late to recognize me. The reflecting pool across the street, which was always noisy and crowded during the day, was empty and quiet now. Looking up the Mall, I could see the Washington Monument and the dome of the Capitol illuminated in the distance. It was a real serene-type setting, which was just what I wanted.

I sat down on a concrete step, leaned back against a stone wall, and looked up at Abe sitting there watching over the city. It was kind of appropriate, his being there with me, since he's the man they say freed the slaves, and I was there to think about my own freedom. I wished he could just say the word and set me free, just like he did for the black folk. 'Course that wasn't gonna happen, his being made of stone and all. I had to free myself.

My first thought was that I should get out of baseball completely. Just up and quit. So I thought good and hard about retiring and all the things it meant giving up. Some of the things—like ladies and teammates—didn't mean as much as they used to after my experiences of the last few days. And money was never that important, since I didn't take real advantage of it anyway. I could even live without the freebies.

But the thing I really regretted giving up was the competition. I just loved standing out there on the mound matching my wits against the best hitters in the world. It was in those moments, when I was trying to beat the batter with my pitches, that my mind and body seemed to be working at their fullest capacity. The intensity of that struggle is something no one can imagine unless they've been through it. But I'll tell you, it gave me the greatest high I ever had. When I was in control, deceiving one hitter after another, it was as if I was in another zone. I couldn't imagine anything else that could duplicate that sensation. Maybe playing tennis or boxing, but I was too old to take up those games. I was just going to have to live without that high. There didn't seem to be any other choice. It was get out of the game I played every five days for half the year or feel miserable every single day of my life. So, for a while there I thought I had my mind made up. I was gonna quit baseball and find a new life for myself. I didn't know how or where, but it didn't really matter. I'd have the burden of baseball off my shoulders and that would make everything else in my life easier.

I was enjoying imagining my life without Augie and Payton and the fans and all the other goodies that come with baseball, when this skid-row-bum type appeared on the step above me.

"You're sitting in my space, man," he said to me.

I was lost in my daydream, and the sound of his voice startled me at first. I looked at him and stared without saying a word. He was this scrawny black man wearing a dirty black raincoat, black shoes without laces, and black pants that were cut off at the bottom 'cause they must have been too long when he found them. He wore no shirt under the raincoat and no socks. His chest bones and ankle bones looked like they were about to pop out of his dirty skin.

"I said you sitting in my space, man," he said.

"Your space?" I said. "There's a hundred steps here and I'm only sitting on one."

"Yeah," he said. "But that one's mine. Been mine for a year now. Since I moved here from Paris."

The sight of the man saddened me, but his feistiness was amusing. "You're from Paris?" I said from behind a smile.

"Get off my space and I'll tell you," he said.

I got up, climbed two steps, sat down again. He opened his coat and took out some newspapers that he must have picked out of a trashcan. He spread them out carefully on the concrete, like he was making a bed, then sat down on them. "Fine space," he said to me. "Wall blocks the north-northwesterly wind currents that blow in from Canada. And you get a good view of the lights. Lot of lights in this city. Oughta go into the light-bulb business."

I'd often seen his type sleeping on a bench downtown, and I was curious about how they lived. "So you came here from Paris," I said.

"Paris. London. Timbuktu. Name it. I've been there."

"I see," I said. "And why'd you come to Washington?"

He thought for a second. "Gonna work for the U.S. government," he said.

"Did you take the test?" I asked.

"What test?"

"To work for the government, I think you gotta take this civil-service test. Least, that's what some lady told me."

"Yeah, well, that's why I ain't working yet, man," he said. "Didn't take the test."

"Maybe you could do something else, then," I said.

"Yeah, man. Maybe I can. What else?"

"I don't know," I said. "There must be something else you wanna do."

He shook his head. "Lotta things I wanna do. Not much I can do. You think I'd be living in this space if I could do something? Nah, can't do nothing else." He thought for a while. "What do you do?"

He didn't recognize me by my uniform, and I was glad. "Nothing much," I said to him.

"Dressed pretty fancy to do nothing," he said. "Where'd you find those fancy duds?"

"Found them in a trashcan," I said.

"Shit, man, why don't I find pretty things like that?" he said. "So why don't you do nothing?"

"I'm planning on doing something," I said.

"Yeah, what can you do?"

"Well, I'm not sure yet."

He laughed at me. "You see, man," he said proudly, "you and me, we's in the same boat. Can't do nothing but keep on pretending we can. But let me tell you something, brother. Don't fight it. Now, me, I've been all over this world. Michigan, Russia, Timbuktu. All them places. And one thing I know, some people just can't do nothing. Simple as spelling 'cat.' People who can, do, and people who can't, don't, if you know what I'm saying."

"You like it this way?" I asked.

"Gotta like it," he said. "Anyway, people who are doing something don't like what they're doing. So why should I mind doing nothing?"

Well, I couldn't much argue with that one. Man didn't even know me, but he knew about me.

He pulled the ends of the newspapers up around him and lay back. "Now, if you don't mind," he said. "It's been a long day. And I gotta get some shut-eye so I can do nothing again tomorrow." He closed his eyes, then opened them and looked at me. "Hey, man," he said. "When I'm not here, you use my space. Be my guest."

I left him and walked back to my car. I drove around the Memorial one time to get a last look at him before I went on. Sure was a sight for sad eyes—which mine were—lying there wrapped in those newspapers. Poor bastard, I thought to myself. And I tried to picture myself in his situation. Funny thing was, just a few minutes earlier I was identifying with the President of the United States, and here I was identifying with this skid-row-bum-type. I didn't know who I was like.

But I did know one thing. There was something I could do, and do well. And as I drove back up Constitution Avenue, past all the museums and government buildings, I realized it was foolish to think I could give up baseball. Took that man to make me find that out. I was being emotional 'stead of rational, which is something Mom always said about me. I shouldn't be forced to give up baseball just because I couldn't get along with a few people.

I felt a little better by the time I reached my apartment.

I took off my uniform and fell onto my bed. Lying there, I thought back on the time Dad said to me, "No son of mine is a quitter." Guess a lot of dads have said that. But my dad forced me out into the yard to play catch with him. He knew I was no quitter and he proved it to me.

Well, I still wasn't a quitter. I could go on playing. All I had to do was find some way to get myself traded. I didn't know how, but there had to be some way.

I looked at my Trinitron digital watch, a memento of the 1976 Superstars competition, and pushed the little button down until the date appeared.

June 3.

I had twelve days left until the trade deadline. Not much time. I had to work fast.

But I made up my mind that night that I was going to do anything within my powers to get myself traded. Anything. I didn't care what kind of a conniving sumbitch I had to be. I didn't care what Augie August would think of me. Or anyone else, for that matter. I was going to find a way.

It was hot in my room, so I got up and turned on the air conditioner. Then I got back in bed, closed my eyes, and all I could see was that scrawny little man sleeping on the steps of the Lincoln Memorial, covered with newspapers. The thought made me shiver. I pulled my blanket up over my body, and the shivering went away real fast.

I liked my blanket. I liked all my things. I liked my home. I was lucky to be able to do something and get paid for it. You just don't turn your back on things like that.

Part II

Why Get Angry
When You Can Get Even?

6

We had some weather on Saturday, June 4, the day I was *supposed* to be traded. The sky was a dull gray like the old flannel road uniforms teams used to wear before Charlie Finley made Technicolor uniforms fashionable. Most of the buildings in Washington are also gray, and when there's a sky like that overhead, the whole town feels like a jail cell. Setting seemed only fitting, though, since I was like a jailbird planning his escape.

About two hours before the start of our game against the Mets that afternoon, I walked out into the light drizzle falling on the field to take a little batting practice. Soon as the reporters spotted me standing behind the batting cage, they rushed over like a swarm of bees and surrounded me, just as I expected they would. Right off they started shooting questions about my new contract. The chipmunks' questions are always predictable, and I was anticipating this opportunity to put my first plan of escape into action.

"Tell us, Gather, in your own words," E. J. Acton from the *Post* said, trying to look at me through the raindrops on his glasses, "why did you decide to sign a new contract with the Dudes?"

Twenty chipmunks stood there with their pens poised at their little spiral notebooks, anxiously awaiting the word from this here big famous baseball star. And the word was, "I signed to keep the black folk off this team."

Not a pen moved. Twenty pairs of beady eyes stared at me in disbelief. It was as if they couldn't dirty their white pieces of paper with my colored remarks.

"To keep the blacks off the team?" Acton repeated as if he thought he heard me wrong.

"Yeah, E. J. You got it right," I said.

"Would you mind elaborating on that statement, Mr. Morse?" asked this reporter who must have been from out of town, 'cause I didn't recognize him.

"What did I say that you didn't understand?" I asked. The little guy was intimidated, which is just how I want reporters to be when they're interviewing me.

"Th-th-th-the blacks," he said with difficulty. "Are you saying you want to keep the b-b-b-blacks off your t-t-t-team?"

"Don't you guys listen? Yeah, that's just what I said. I found out that Augie August was planning on trading me for just one white folk and three black folk. Can you imagine him trying to pull a stunt like that? Best thing about this here team is that there ain't one black face in the whole starting lineup. Now, you don't expect me to be responsible for changing that, do you?"

There was an uncomfortable silence. You could almost hear the reporters sweating. No one knew how to respond, and I was enjoying their discomfort. Finally one guy said, "Do you have something against the blacks, Gather?"

"Why do you guys insist on calling those folk blacks?" I said. "They ain't blacks. They're niggers. That's what they are. Nigger coon bugger jigaboos. Let me see all of you write that down, or I ain't saying no more."

They all started scribbling in their notebooks. So I gave them some more to scribble. "There's too many coons in this great American game. It ain't good for baseball. Let 'em go play basketball. That's their sport. Or let 'em go dance someplace. They're good at that. Like the Earl Butz fella said, all they want is loose shoes, a warm place to shit, and some tight pussy. Well, we ain't got none of those things here on this team."

"Come on, Gather," Bobby Ward of the *Star* said. "Stop putting us on."

"Hey, Bobby baby," I said. "When have I ever put you on? It's time someone took a stand on this."

"I'm not sure you understand what you're saying," a reporter said. "Washington's primarily a black town, and the best thing Augie August has done is make the blacks feel welcome at his ball park. We can't write this stuff. If we do, no one will come out to see this team."

"I didn't know you guys were in the business of selling tickets," I said. "If you don't want to write my true feelings, that's fine with me. But you're gonna get scooped, 'cause the television guys are gonna have it. And you know they'll show anything on the air.

"Hey, Joe. Joe Henderson," I yelled to the sportscaster for WWBC television news. "Stop talking to Seaver and get that camera over here on me. I got a statement to make to the television audience. I'm gonna give you a scoop."

Soon as Henderson heard the word "scoop," he hustled his crew over, stuck his microphone in my face, and started the camera whirring away. "I've got Gather Morse, the Dudes' all-star pitcher, here with me," Henderson said in his artificial television voice. "Now, Gather, tell the viewers out there why, after demanding to be traded for months, you have changed your mind and decided to stay with our team?"

" 'Cause Augie was gonna trade me for niggers, that's why," I said.

"Hold it. Hold it. Stop the camera," Henderson said, and the camera went silent. "Come on, Gather. Don't bullshit me, man. This film costs money."

"Ain't no bullshit, Joe," I said. "You guys always say

we're holding back on you to preserve our image. Well, this time I'm giving it to you straight."

Henderson just kind of looked at me like I was loony. "Well, all right," he said. "But don't use the word 'niggers'. They'll bleep it."

"What's the acceptable television word for 'niggers'?" I asked. "How 'bout 'buggers'. Is 'buggers' all right? Gotta call 'em what they are."

"Well, blacks can call themselves anything they want," Henderson said. "But whites should call them blacks."

"Okay, let's roll it," I said.

The camera started whirring and Henderson went back into his television voice. "I've got Gather Morse, the Dudes' all-star pitcher, here with me," he said. "Now Gather, tell the viewers out there why, after demanding to be traded for months, you have changed your mind and decided to stay with the team."

"Well, Joe," I said in my television voice, "I was privy to some inside information and I know that Augie August was planning to trade me for one American white folk and three black folk. I refuse to let that happen. To be honest with you, Joe, I like looking behind me when I'm out on the mound and seeing only white faces backing me up. There's no other team like ours in that regard. 'Course, there's a lot of black faces in the stands, too, many in fact, but ain't nothing I can do about that. But there is something I can do about this. So I signed my contract instead of letting Augie bring those fellas here. The way I see it, Joe, there just ain't no place in baseball for buggers."

The interview went on just like that for a few minutes. Henderson winced every time I called those folks anything but blacks. But when I was finished dishing out my little pearls of wisdom, the sportscaster said excitedly, "Great stuff. Great stuff. We got a real, genuine scandal here. Bet I can get the lead story on tonight's show."

"That would be terrific, Joe," I said.

As I walked into the batting cage, I saw all the little

chipmunks whispering to each other. I knew my plan was working as effectively as a drop pitch on a humid August afternoon. Augie was gonna have to get rid of me fast or his team would find themselves playing in front of an empty house. By the time the next morning's papers hit the stands, I figured I'd have my locker cleaned out and be on my way to the promised land. The promised land, far as I was concerned, was any city other than Washington, D.C.

Later that afternoon, Kong Kingman dropped a routine fly ball in the ninth inning, enabling us to score a run for our second straight win over the Mets. Thanks to two errors by Kong in two nights, the Dudes were only a game under .500. If I didn't know better, I'd suspect that Augie had the Mets' left fielder on the Dudes' payroll.

I missed the game's dramatic ending myself. I had sneaked out of the bullpen before the ninth inning began, dressed, and left the clubhouse before my teammates and the chipmunks arrived.

I was home in my living room in time to catch the six-o'clock news. I pulled two tiny portable televisions, mementos of some event or another, out of my closet and set them up right next to the big color console I received from the VFW to honor me after I pitched that no-hitter in my rookie year. I turned on all three local news shows at the same time and sat back, with a can of light beer, to watch myself get interviewed. I felt like a genuine genius when all three stations put my story right up there at the top of the show.

"This afternoon, Gather Morse gave the most stunning performance of his career," Joe Henderson said. "And it wasn't on the pitcher's mound. . . ."

"Sports and particularly baseball is one facet of our American society where racial harmony seems to exist on the surface," said Wally Winters of WPIT. "But all that may have changed this afternoon at RFK. . . ."

"So often, athletes tell reporters what they think they want to hear," said Judy Rauchman of WCPA. "Well, this afternoon Gather Morse of the Washington Dudes told me something I didn't want to hear. . . ."

And then there I was on all three screens at the same time saying some of the craziest things I ever heard myself say. I probably would've been pissed off if I ever saw any other player saying those things. I actually like having the black folk around. Only thing that bothers me about them is I never know how I'm supposed to shake their hands. Soon as I learn the fashionable handshake, they've invented a new one. But I can live with that.

But up there on the screen, I managed to sound like a sincere racist. It was an act of complete, utter, total, and unanimous desperation. I knew I'd have a lot of explaining to do once I got myself traded. I hoped people would understand my situation and not hold those remarks against me forever.

After the sportscasters editorialized about what a disgrace I was to the great game of baseball, the news shows switched their attention from the Gather Morse scandal to the Bert Lance scandal. I shut off the tubes and headed to the fridge for another beer. The phone rang and I answered it.

"Gather Morse?" said a deep rough voice.

"Yes," I said.

"You a dead man, honky," the voice growled, and the caller hung up.

I wasn't sure if it was an outraged viewer or one of my teammates playing a joke on me. Since my number wasn't listed, I assumed it was a joker, but I wasn't gonna take any chances. I pushed my brown leather living room couch against the door of my apartment and made sure to stay away from the windows all evening. I carried a Louisville Slugger around with me just to feel a little safer.

I was scheduled to pitch in the first game of the doubleheader against the Mets the next day. I knew if I was forced to take the mound, I'd be an easy target for any gun-toting fan who wanted to be an instant hero. But I was counting on the outrage being so great that I'd never be able to pitch for the Dudes again.

I spent that night in bed with my Louisville Slugger. Not my idea of a perfect evening. I will say that that piece of oak was as exciting and responsive as one or two pieces of tail I've ended up with. And at least I didn't hate it or myself when it was still lying there in the morning, which is how I feel with ladies lots of times.

My doorbell started ringing round about ten o'clock Sunday morning. Afraid it might be some angry black folks who didn't take kindly to my television appearance, I stood in bed hoping the visitor would go back where he came from. But the bell kept right on ringing. So I wrapped my blanket around my naked body, grabbed my bat, and walked to the door.

"Who's there?" I said without opening it.

"It's me, Gather. Laura."

I'd damn near forgot that me and Laura had ourselves scheduled for a little tumble that morning. Fact is, I didn't know if she'd ever show her pretty face at my place again after I'd caught her in the altogether with Sticky Thomas. Didn't know if I wanted her at my place either, even though she always did make Fellini gush like a broken fire plug. 'Course, today's man's gotta live with the fact that a juicy piece of meat like Laura's gonna end up on other fella's plates too. But, at the same time, he don't wanna think that every man he knows is eating off the same bone. For one thing, it ain't healthy.

I wasn't sure how I was supposed to act toward her. But I moved the couch aside, opened the door, and let her in.

"What are you doing here?" I said real unfriendly like.

"Aren't you pitching today?" she said.

She was wearing those tight-type French jeans, and her tiny nipples—I love nickel nipples 'stead of the half-dollar size—were pushing their way out of her white sweater. Tough to be mean to a lady who looks like that, but I

forced myself. "Yeah, I'm pitching the first game," I said.
"But Monty Sturgis is pitching the second. And I bet he's
sitting at his place right now just waiting for you to come
over and get him up for the game."

"Don't be a prick, Gather," Laura said. "If you don't
want me, I'll leave."

"Go ahead," I said. "Be easy enough to find myself another groupie."

Now, that made her furious. Her hazel eyes got fiery.
Her lips started to quiver. She sure did look pretty when
she was mad. "I don't need to take that crap from you,"
she said. "You've got no reins on me. You're nothing to
me but a good fuck."

She turned and headed for the door. But I couldn't let
her leave without being hospitable.

I dropped the blanket I had wrapped around me to the
floor. I grabbed Laura by the arm and pulled her back
toward me. I lifted her up in the air, held her above my
head, and spun her around a few times.

"Put me down, prick," she shouted.

So I obliged. I slammed her down on the rug. She
screamed when she hit the floor. I put my hand over her
mouth and sat over her belly. Then I pinned her arms to
the floor and started barking at her, real angry like,
through gritted teeth.

"You whory little bitch," I said.

"You dumb shit animal," she said, wiggling to get free.

"You're nothing but a dumb, hungry cunt," I said.

"Fuck you, you pig," she said.

We continued exchanging pleasantries. It was as if we
were punching each other with words. Strange thing is,
looking at her lying there cussing me really turned me on.
She could see Fellini growing like corn in spring. Bigger
he got, more she cussed.

I felt angry and violent. I tore off her sweater and
jeans. She had nothing else on but sweet-smelling perfume. I went to force myself into her. I expected to have

to struggle to find my way. But cussing had excited her too.

I was used to soft, gentle-type lovemaking. But this time it was rough and mean. I was hating her by loving her. Punishing her by pleasing her. I pumped up and down like a piston on a Formula One car. We set a beat for our movements, like a marching cadence, by cussing.

"Bitch!"

"Prick!"

"Cunt!"

"Bastard!"

"Cocksucker!"

"Motherfucker!"

"Animal!"

"Pig!"

"Dog!"

"Horse!"

"Oh . . ."

"Oh . . ."

"Oh, God . . ."

"Oh, God . . ."

"Laura . . ."

"Gather . . ."

"Baby . . ."

"Honey . . ."

It was over quicker than a TV commercial. And then it was real quiet in the room, except for the sounds of us breathing. Kind of peaceful, like a storm had blown over.

I went to kiss Laura gently, the first gentle move either of us had made. But before I touched her lips, the doorbell rang.

"Who the fuck . . ." I said.

It rang again.

"Who's there?" I shouted.

"Police," yelled a husky voice.

Laura's eyes asked the same questions I was asking myself. My first thought was that a neighbor had heard us grappling and groping and had reported a rape. Would've been great publicity coming on the heels of my performance the day before. *Gather Morse, the Racist, Is Also a Rapist!*

Laura scampered into the john while I wrapped the blanket around me and opened the door. There were two Smokeys standing there, big guy and little guy, looked like Toody and Muldoon from the old *Car 54* show.

"Gather Morse?" the little guy said; then he puffed his cheeks like he was trying to hold down garlic.

"Yeah. What can I do for you'?" I said.

"Sorry to bother you," the little one said. "We're from D.C. Security Corp. Mr. August sent us here to pick you up."

"Augie?" I said. "Is he sicing the cops on me now?"

"For your own protection, sir," the big fella said in a froggy voice and very apologetically.

"My protection?" I said. "Shoot, what do I need protection for?"

"Well, Mr. Morse," Toody said, then he excused himself and puffed his cheeks again. "Sorry. Italian food . . .

"Anyway, as I started to say, there are now twenty-five thousand blacks demonstrating outside RFK Stadium. We figure they're waiting for you to arrive, and they aren't planning on singing 'Happy Birthday.' "

"Biggest black demonstration we've had in this town since Martin Luther King's days," said Muldoon. "It was peaceful in those days, but you get too many of them in one place, never know what can happen. I know you agree with that, Mr. Morse."

"Sure liked what you had to say on the news last night," the little Smokey said. "We were down at the office looking at the tube, and when you said what you did, every guy in the place stood and cheered. You're a great American, Mr. Morse. Ain't he, Al?"

"Got a real good drop pitch, too," Al said with a wink.

I sure was the Smokeys' hero that day, I guess. And these fellas were bringing me both good news and bad.

The good news was that twenty-five thousand people

were angry enough to picket, which gave Augie twenty-five thousand good reasons to trade me. My plan seemed to be working.

The bad news was that those same twenty-five thousand folks were a threat to my welfare. I might not live long enough to put on the uniform of another team, which wasn't part of my plan at all. Back in grammar school in Mantua, teachers had told us about Americans who had died for their cause and made them sound real brave. But I never saw no premium in being brave, 'less of course it was an Atlanta Brave. I wanted to get traded, but I wasn't willing to die for it. Wouldn't be much of a deal for my new team if that happened.

"I don't know if I should show up at the stadium today," I said to the Smokeys.

"Hey, don't worry about a thing, Mr. Morse," the little fella said. "You come with us in our car. We got it all worked out. We'll wait outside for you."

I started to close the door. "Hey, Mr. Morse," the little cop yelled. "Forgot your paper."

With a smile he handed me the Sunday *Post* that was lying on my welcome mat.

As I pulled on some civvies, Laura sat on my bed reading the paper. I told her to pull out the sports section and check where I ranked in the ERA column, which was the first thing I did every Sunday morning.

"Hey, Gather, you gotta see this," she said. She came into the john, where I was shaving with my Techmagic, and showed me a page in the sports section. Sitting there above the baseball stats was another one of those advertisements Augie ran the day of every game.

"Today. Doubleheader. Dudes vs. Mets," it said. "Come out and see Gather Morse, the Baseball Bigot, on the mound."

Sounded like an invitation to a lynching to me, which might be humorous, provided you're not the one being lynched.

It was a pretty spring morning in the nation's capital. Washington's cold as up North in winter and humid as down South in summer. But early June sometimes brings the finest weather you're ever gonna see. As comfortable as it was outside, I was just that uncomfortable inside the rent-a-cops' rent-a-car.

Downtown was lazy and quiet, like it is every Sunday morning, and there wasn't a soul on the streets as we headed over Capitol Hill out toward the stadium. We were still half a mile from the entrance when some muffled noise interrupted the silence. It was a repetitive rhythm. Chanting of some kind. When we neared RFK, the chant became clear.

"Gather's Gotta Go! Gather's Gotta Go!"

It was a real catchy tune. I might have enjoyed it the day before. But now it worried me.

As we pulled into the stadium parking lot, I glanced out the back window and saw this mass of angry black faces. Fists and signs were bobbing in the air to the rhythm of the chant. Black folk sure looked like they were having a good time on my account, which didn't make me feel no better. Augie always said I was his drawing card, but I didn't think this was what he had in mind.

As the car neared the crowd, I saw this flatbed truck filled with people holding bullhorns and leading the rally. Standing right there in the center of the platform, yelling her considerable lungs out, was my old, old, old lady, Bernadine Green. I hadn't seen her in two years, since her coke-dealing boyfriend had advised me to stay away. She sure looked beautiful as ever. Chill started at Fellini and ran to my head when I spotted her.

Saddened me to think she was rooting against me now. Hate to admit it, but I had to hold back a tear or two. Here was this lady I was once insane for, and now she must have thought I was insane period. I told myself, "Don't you worry about all this, Gather. You're doing what's right for you. Come tomorrow, you'll be playing for a new team in a new town, and all this won't mean bulltwang."

The tall cop turned around and told me to duck down out of sight. We were about to drive through the crowd and he didn't want none of them black folks to get a look at me. They probably wouldn't have if twenty additional policemen didn't run over and surround the car. But as soon as the rent-a-cops arrived, the folks knew there was something in the car that they weren't supposed to see and they all rushed over to have a look. Next thing I knew, there were these angry black folk lying on the hood and banging on the roof. The cops took out their billy clubs and started applying some corporal punishment to those folks who refused to get off the car. The cops were swinging and the black folks started swinging back, and the thing turned into a rough street fight.

I lay there on the back seat with my eyes closed, hoping I wouldn't get hurt. But closing my eyes didn't relieve my fears. I saw this whole string of line drives heading at my skull. My stomach started tumbling. I was sure glad I hadn't had time to eat anything besides Laura for breakfast, otherwise I would have decorated the back seat for sure.

Somehow the Smokeys managed to drive through the riot and into a raised garage door next to the players' entrance. When I got out of the car, the door was closing behind me and I heard hundreds of fists pounding on the aluminum. Sounded like it was thundering in RFK on that pretty spring day.

I was sure relieved to be inside, protected from the mob. I didn't look forward to exposing myself to them again when I trotted out to the mound. As I walked down the concrete corridor to our clubhouse, I daydreamed that Augie would be waiting at my locker to tell me that he was left with no choice and had traded me away.

I walked into the locker room, and as soon as Gabby spotted me, he shouted, "There he is, guys. Man of the hour."

My teammates all rushed over and surrounded me. These were the same exact folks who had kept away from me Friday night like I had stepped in dogshit. Then I was a traitor. Now I was a hero.

"Gasser, Gasser," Chi Chi said, interrupting his bare-assed Latin hustle to greet me. "You tell eet like eet ees, Gasser."

"Right on, bro'," Tony Smith said, and everyone cracked up.

" 'Bout time someone here had the guts to say what should be said," Bubba cracked, wrapping his big hairy arm around my shoulders.

"Keep the dudes off the Dudes," Gabby shouted.

" 'Less of course the dude can hit .350 and steal sixty bases." Bubba added, and everyone agreed.

I sure was surprised by the reception, though I can't say pleasantly surprised. I never realized that all you gotta do is toss out a few racist remarks and you get treated like you tossed a no-hitter. Guess I should've realized it, though. All the guys had often said the very same things I had said, but they never said it to the press. Racist just ain't the thing to be these days, especially on the tube.

'Course, what the players think don't matter none to the owner. So I didn't expect this celebration of the Baseball Bigot would change my status with Augie. I was the hero in the clubhouse, but I'd be the goat at the gate. And we all know which one counts.

I walked through the swarm of happy ballplayers. And sure enough, Augie was standing at my locker waiting for me, smoking his big cigar, just like I'd daydreamed. I approached him with a smile, which was something he hadn't seen decorating my mug in quite some time. And he smiled right back at me.

"Son, allow me to congratulate you," he said, extending his hand. I assumed he was coming on like a wiseacre, congratulating me when he really wanted to damn me.

"Sorry, but I had to do it, Augie," I said, ignoring his

hand. "All's fair in love, war, and contract negotiations." I was proud of that little poetic remark.

"Sorry?" Augie said, flicking his ashes into the pocket of Bubba's trousers, which were hanging in his locker. "Don't be sorry, son. You're a promotional genius."

"What are you talking about?" I said.

"This is the greatest day of my baseball career," Augie said. "And I have you to thank for it. Today is the first time in my four years in baseball that we've completely sold out the stadium. There's gonna be more than fifty thousand people out there this afternoon and it's all because of you. They're all here to hate you, son, and I love you for it. That was a great bit you pulled yesterday. Wish I'd thought of it myself."

I was stunned. My mouth was open so wide you could drive an eighteen-wheeler through it. My surefire plan had backfired. The black folks were so outraged that they were actually paying their way into the ball park to harass me.

" 'Course, I had to hire two hundred extra cops just to protect you," Augie said. "But don't worry about that, son. We'll more than make up for it at the concession stands. Gonna sell a lot of grits today.

"Yes sir. Best thing I ever did was get your name on a new contract. You're not only a great pitcher, you're a promotional genius."

He patted me on the back and walked away. My jaw was still hanging to the August-auburn carpet. I thought I was having a bad dream. I always have this dream where I can't get to where I'm going or finish what I'm doing. I wake up just before the happy ending. But now I wasn't waking up, and the ending wasn't so happy. I was stuck with the Dudes. And, what's more, I had to go out and pitch in front of fifty thousand fans who wanted a piece of my hide for a souvenir.

It rained cans and bottles at RFK that pretty afternoon. People bought pop just so they'd have a can to throw at me. 'Stead of keeping the foul balls they caught, the fans chucked them back, aiming at the Dude on the mound. My teammates all wore their batting helmets when we took the field for protection. And Bubba said it was the first time in twenty years of wearing the catcher's gear that he felt he was in the most protected position instead of the most dangerous. They had to stop the first game of the doubleheader again and again to clear the debris off the field.

I don't have to tell you that I was scared shitless. I was perspiring so much in the very first inning that my uniform turned a deep purple.

Melinda was sitting pretty in Augie's box, but I didn't take but one glance at her. Well, not more than two or three. My eyes were too busy peering around the stands between pitches. I was sure there was someone sitting there waiting for the chance to play sniper and fill my uniform with lead.

I had no mind for the hitters. Fact is, I didn't even know who was standing in the batter's box most of the time. I just glanced quickly at Bubba's sign, threw whatever he called for, then started peering cautiously at the crowd again. My body was flooded with fear. I was pitching in a semiconscious daze.

Since we were only playing the Mets, I was able to get by with less-focused concentration. And I didn't have to worry much about a line drive putting my lights out, since they didn't even hit liners in fungo games. I just wanted to get on and off the mound as quickly as possible. I didn't dally with the hitters. I just threw strikes.

Kong Kingman parked two of those strikes in downtown D.C., which accounted for four runs, which should have been enough to beat us. But he also misplayed a single into a triple, which gave back three runs and kept us in the game.

We were all tied at 4–4 in the bottom of the eighth and I was our leadoff hitter. I can't hit much even when I'm concentrating, and that day I wasn't even looking at Jerry

Koosman's pitches. He threw at the plate and I kept my eyes on the stands. Standing up there, with my back exposed to one side of the stadium, I was an easy target.

That time up, just before Koosman threw his first pitch, I heard this loud noise. It sounded like the gun shot I'd been expecting. I hit the dirt.

The ump, Burt Sooty, walked out from behind the plate, stood over me, and said, "What the hell are you doing down there, Morse? Man didn't even throw a pitch yet."

"I heard this noise, ump," I said. "Sounded just like a gun shot."

"Shit, Morse, that was no gun shot," the ump said. "That was a popcorn fart. And I was the popper. Play ball!"

I stood back up, let three strikes go by, then trotted back to the dugout. At that moment, I was so scared that I really felt like I was losing my mind. I left my bat and helmet on the bench and walked down the runway toward the clubhouse. I stood under the stands trying to calm myself for the ninth inning. But I couldn't calm down.

I did feel a little better being away from the crowd. And that's where I wanted to stay. I heard a cheer go up when Pinky Potts hit one out, to give us a 5-4 lead. But I couldn't go back out to protect that lead. I had to get out of the ball park.

I ran up the runway toward the clubhouse. The door flew open and Chi Chi came out. He had spent our half of the inning in the john.

"Hey, Gasser," he said. "We back on field. Pitch now, shit later."

Chi Chi did the Latin hustle down the runway toward the field. As I watched him dance, pictures started flashing through my mind. Pictures of Chi Chi dancing nude in the locker room. And of me standing naked on the mound.

I don't know what came over me, but I pulled off my jersey, my T-shirt, my pants, and my jock and left them in a pile on the runway. Then I took a deep breath and trotted out onto the field wearing nothing but my cap and spikes.

"Lord have mercy. He's lost his mind," Skip shouted as I pranced through the dugout. Soon as the fans spotted me, the booing that had been the background music all afternoon started up again. But the booing changed quickly to laughter. Fifty thousand fans all came to their feet and laughed their asses off.

I picked up the ball like nothing unusual was happening. I was ready to start my warm-ups. But I had no target. Bubba was rolling around in the dirt at home plate, holding his stomach and laughing. Burt Sooty had his hands over his eyes.

I looked around the stadium, at the fans, the dugouts, my teammates in the field. Everyone in the place was having a good laugh on me. And I was so delirious that I was enjoying it. I pulled off my cap and started bowing in every direction.

When I was facing the outfield stands, I felt hands grabbing me from behind. Suddenly I was surrounded by a dozen rent-a-cops. They lifted me up in the air over their heads and carried me off the field like they were pallbearers. One cop held his cap over Fellini. I left the ball park to a standing ovation from the folks who had come out to hate me.

The cops carried me out the players' entrance and threw me into a paddy wagon.

"Hey, where are we going?" I shouted.

"The clink, buddy," a cop said. "You're under arrest."

"For what?" I asked.

"Indecent exposure," he said. And he slammed the paddy wagon door in my face.

7

I didn't get thrown into the ordinary clink along with your average everyday robbers, murderers, junkies, and child-molesting types. 'Stead, they locked me up with the criminally insane, disabled insane, and the just plain insane insane at St. Elizabeth's Hospital, the D.C. loony bin.

I spent the night in this tiny white room with nothing on the walls but roaches. Place was so cramped it made me long for the Holiday Inns we usually stayed at on the road. Least there I had my color tube and magic fingers. The loony bin is so uncomfortable, crazy people must get crazier there. And if they ever have any vacancies, they could lock the most normal people in the world in one of those rooms, and after one night they're sure to go crazy too.

Lying there, on a cot with broken springs that dug into my back. I wondered how anyone knows when they are losing their mind. I mean, if I saw a ballplayer making those racist remarks on the tube or walking out to the mound in his birthday suit, I'd sure think that he was either tripped out or flipped out. Since I didn't go in for drugs—except, of course, for some occasional social tok-

ing—I knew I couldn't be tripped out. But maybe I was
crazy. Maybe my situation in Washington was not so desperate and only looked that way to me because my neu-
rons were burned out. I really didn't know anymore.

But I did know that my resistance was wearing down.
I've seen a lot of shows on the tube where they put
uncooperative prisoners in solitary so that when they get
back to their group cells life there doesn't seem so bad.
The men are broken like wild horses. They're tortured
into acting sedate. I guess that's what was happening to
me. That night in that room at St. E.'s, I wondered if I
should just accept my life the way it was and stop trying
to change things. I wondered if anything was worth the
humiliation I was suffering. I'm sure that's just what
Augie August wanted me to think, but I thought it nonetheless.

It was somewhat of a relief to find out the next morning that Dr. Fine didn't think I was crazy. Never was a
person so aptly named as Dr. Fine. Her thin face, though
still attractive, showed her forty years. But her body
looked like it was taken off a girl half her age and attached to her head. She sat in a chair across from me in
her office with her legs crossed as if to taunt me.

"Do you do things like this often?" she asked, rubbing
her hand through her long dark hair, a gesture I always
find sexy.

"Like what?" I said.

"Well, walk into an open arena undraped?"

I was embarrassed to have such a pretty lady asking
me questions like that. "No, this was the first time I can
remember," I said.

"I see," she said. "And did you enjoy it?"

"Enjoy it? Well, yes. Uh, no." I didn't know what to
say to impress her. "Look, Dr. Fine, I'm not one of those
flasher types."

"I'm glad to hear that," she said. She smiled at me and
I smiled at her, and I figured I was on the right track.
Then she said, "So why did you do this?"

" 'Cause I wanna get traded," I said.

I knew that sounded weird, and she gave me a look that verified that knowledge. "I'm not a great baseball fan, Mr. Morse," she said. "But other players have been traded, and none of them have ever had to walk naked in front of fifty thousand people to do so."

"Yeah, that's true," I said.

"Have you had thoughts of doing this before?"

I wasn't sure if I should tell her about my dream, but I did. "I was standing there naked and everyone was laughing at me," I said.

"I see. Everyone was laughing at you. Tell me, Mr. Morse. When you were out there like that, did you have an erection?"

"In my dream or in the flesh?"

"Both."

"Neither time."

"I see," she said, and she scribbled down some notes. "Are you generally shy about your body?"

"Shy?"

"Do you walk around freely undressed when you have a woman in the room?"

Now she was getting too personal. So I got personal myself. "Do you?" I said.

"That's not our problem," she said.

"Yeah," I said. "But I'm interested."

She scratched her right knee. I was dying to scratch it for her. And I wouldn't have stopped there. "What you are asking me is totally irrelevant," she said. "But if it will comfort you, yes, I do walk around freely. I'm not ashamed of my body."

I was sure glad to hear that. "We got something in common, then," I said. " 'Cause I'm not embarrassed about my body either. And if you saw it, you'd know why."

"Well, perhaps you'd like to show it to me," she said.

I didn't know what the right answer to that question

was. "Yeah, I would," I said. I eagerly waited for her to call, "Play ball!"

"I see," she said in a businesslike tone, and she wrote down some more notes.

"Wanna see it?" I asked.

She looked up at me. "Of course not," she said.

"Well, why'd you ask, then?"

"I didn't ask to see it. I asked if you'd like to show it to me."

"Don't sound much different to me," I said.

"Look, Mr. Morse. I'm afraid we're talking about two different things here."

"No we're not," I insisted. "You're interested in my body and I'm interested in yours."

She noticed me staring at her legs, and she got uncomfortable. She walked behind her desk and sat down there where I could not see her pins. "It's not your body that I'm interested in, Mr. Morse," she said. "It's your mind."

"That's too bad," I said.

"Why is that?"

"Most ladies like my body better."

She laughed at me and I was real embarrassed. "I'm sorry," she said, and she stopped laughing. "Look, Mr. Morse. I like your body. I also like your mind. But we're not concerned with like or dislike here."

"What are we concerned with?"

"This is a hospital," she said. "I'm a doctor. My job is to find out if you are a healthy person who is capable of living within society. Yesterday you did something that is not considered normal, rational behavior. I'm trying to find out if you have some problems you cannot cope with by yourself."

It was all getting a bit too confusing for me. When I'm with pretty ladies like Dr. Fine and they ask me personal-type questions like she did, I always suspect they're asking for something other than what they're asking. Record proves I'm usually right. "Look, Dr. Fine," I said, "I didn't mean to offend you."

"I don't get offended," she said.

"The only problem I have is that I want to get traded, and Augie August, he owns the Dudes, won't trade me. He conned me into signing a new contract, which was a real dumb-ass thing to do on my part, and now he's got me by the cubes, so to speak. Only way I can get free, I figure is by doing something to humiliate him. But I keep humiliating myself instead. Now, if that's crazy, well . . . what can I say?"

She sat there with her hands crossed in front of her face, blocking an amused grin. "Well, I'm afraid I can't help you get traded," she said. "And I don't think you need any other help. So you're free to leave here, Mr. Morse."

She stood up and extended her hand across the desk. I took it and shook it gently.

"So you don't think I'm loony, Dr. Fine?" I said.

"Loony? No, I don't think you're loony. You suffer from the same problems that plague every other American athlete."

I waited for her to elaborate on that, but she didn't. I didn't know if I had been complimented or insulted, but I thanked her anyway.

As I was leaving the office, she called to me, "Mr. Morse. Can you please give me your autograph for my nephew?"

I walked back to her desk with a big smile on my face. Sure, it's for your nephew, I thought to myself. I'd heard that one before. So I wrote down my name. And my phone number.

"Why'd you give my nephew your number?" she asked, which took me by surprise.

"Case he ever wants to call me," I said. "You can call me too if you'd like."

Well, I never heard from that Dr. Fine again, which was too bad. But, looking back, I'm glad I got fixed up with a lady doctor. It's much easier for me to talk to ladies than to men.

I walked out of the hospital wearing some baggy clothes they provided for me, since I had none of my own. I was waiting for a cab in the parking lot when who should drive up but Augie August.

"What are you doing here?" I said.

"I was coming to visit you," he said.

"I'm waiting for a cab to go home."

"Jump in. I'll take you."

I got into the Mercedes, looked at Augie, and had to struggle to hold back my laughter. I'd known the old man for four years, but that was the first time I ever saw him wearing a rug. The thing sat up there on his sunburned head like gray astroturf on a basketball.

"Like it?" he asked.

"What, the hospital?" I said.

"No, my hairpiece."

"Oh, I didn't even notice," I said.

He smiled slyly. Augie loved secrets of any kind. "Melinda's idea." he said, which I should have guessed. "It was also her idea for me to come here and have a little heart-to-heart talk with you."

We headed out of the parking lot and on through the city toward my place. Augie was trying hard to be kind. "Let's just forget completely about what happened yesterday," he said, which I appreciated. "We'll just sweep it under the astroturf and go on like nothing happened."

"Did we win?" I asked.

"Sure did," he said. "Won your game five to four, which raises your record to nine and one, best in the majors. Won the second game too."

"Holy shit," I said. "That's four in a row. A miracle."

"Not only that," he said. "We're twenty and twenty, first time a team of mine has ever been at .500."

Both of us sat there thinking about what this meant for a while. To me it meant that Augie was less likely to trade me, since our team looked like it might even be a contender. But like I told you, my resistance was so low

at that point that I didn't have it in me to keep pushing
for a deal.

"Let's forget about the team for a minute," Augie said.
"I want to talk about you."

"What about me?"

"You're a troubled young man, Gather," he said. "And
I can sympathize with that. I was a troubled young man
myself once."

"I find that hard to believe, Augie," I said.

"What, that I was troubled?"

"No, that you were young."

He flashed a disapproving glance. "I'm trying to be
serious with you now, son. Trying to share some of my
experience with you and help you, if you'll let me."

The old man was so good at sounding sincere that
sometimes I even forgot what a conniving sumbitch he
really was. 'Course, he had me in a conciliatory mood after I'd spent a night in the loony bin, which I'm sure he
suspected before he decided to come see me.

"The problem with today's athletes, and that includes
you, son," he said, "is that none of you fellas have any
passion in your lives."

I laughed at that one. "You kidding me?" I said. "I
could have passion in my life every night of the week if I
want it."

"Aha," he said. "Precisely what I'm talking about.
What you're saying is that you can have sexual relations
every night of the week, with a different woman each
time—"

"Sometimes different ladies the same night," I said.

"But that's not passion," he said.

"Well, it ain't chopped liver."

"Look, son, let me try to explain this so you'll understand, which won't be easy. When I talk of passion, I
mean something that's so important to you, you can't live
without it. Something that you feel in your heart and your
loins. Sometimes it makes you feel good and sometimes it
makes you feel bad, but it's always there. Now, you don't

have anything like that. Those girls you spend a night with, that's not passion. You might as well be masturbating. And you don't have any passion for baseball anymore. None of you guys do. The game's nothing but a good paycheck and plenty of free time.

"I forgot what passion was myself for a while. But Melinda has revived it for me. Yes, sir, can't live without that lady. And having her makes everything else in my life seem better. If you had some passion in your life, I think everything else would be better for you too."

He sat there staring out over the steering wheel like he didn't see anything beyond the windshield, which worried me a little, since my life was in his hands. But what he was saying made some sense to me. Fact is, it made a lot of sense. There was nothing in my life that meant that much to me. And since I was feeling so low, I was willing to try anything that might revive my spirits.

So that evening, as we were beating the Cubs 3–1 to extend our amazing winning streak to five games, I sat out in the bullpen considering what I could be passionate about. It had to be some new dish, since I had no real feelings for any of the delicacies I'd been nourishing lately. What I needed, I decided after some serious thought, was a new lady who was both classy and mysterious. 'Course, it wouldn't hurt if she was constructed like a Playmate of the Month. These qualifications came to mind since Bernadine had all of them and she was the last thing I had in my life that I didn't think I could live without. I did eventually have to learn to live without her, which wasn't easy and—this is being more honest than I have to be, but what the hell—still isn't easy.

So that night, after the game, I went out to try to find myself a little bit of passion. I knew I was never gonna find it at Clyde's. Record had already proven that. There's a lot of goodies packed into the tight jeans that hang out there, but no passion. Not for me anyway. Only a handful of the ladies there had any class, and none of them had much mystery. There's nothing mysterious 'bout a lady who uses the overcrowdedness as an excuse to stand so close she's brushing her thighs up against Fellini.

The kind of lady I now had my mind set on would be attracted to the important men in town, to the powerful-type folks, and so I figured they'd be hanging out at the after-work haunts on Capitol Hill. On the Hill, after-work drinking runs from noon till closing time. So the bar was still busy when I arrived at a place called the Monocle around eleven o'clock.

The Monocle's a sit-down-type bar as opposed to the stand-up setup at most singles places. At a sit-down joint, there's some kind of commitment to conversation beyond the standard three-question routine (What's your name? What do you do? Your place or mine?) that fills the stand-ups.

I figured the best way to get rolling at a place like that was to sit down alone, pick out a lady who was also alone, make eye contact, then invite her over to fill the empty seat at my table. So I sat down, ordered a light beer, and sized up the situation.

Across the room I spotted this pug-nosed blond sitting with two guys and two other girls at a table for six. The seat next to her was empty, so I figured the odds were pretty good that she was the available one—'less of course they were all into something other than your basic couples. I stared at her until she glanced at me. She noticed me staring, smiled, then went back to her conversation with her friends.

I just kept on staring at her. After exchanging a few more brief glances, she focused her eyes on mine. We looked at each other for about a minute and I said to myself, "Gather, she's giving you the hit sign." So I got up to walk over and fill the empty seat next to her. But just before I reached her table, a guy in a three-piece suit came out of the men's room and took the seat I was heading for. I was caught standing there, embarrassed, with no destination. So I ducked into the men's room, pretending that's where I was heading all along.

I stayed in there for as long as a leak would take, then returned alone to my table. Just as I sat down, the guy sitting at the table next to me got up and went where I had come from. No sooner had the bathroom door closed behind him than the lady he had been buying drinks for, this tough-looking brunette with a tight mouth and dark slits for eyes, turned to me and said, "Hey, good-looking. What's your name?"

"Gather Morse," I said.

"What's your real name?" she said.

"Gather Morse," I said.

"What do you do, Gather Morse?"

"Pitch."

"You're being difficult. What do you really do?"

"Pitch."

"Terrific," she said. "My place is being painted. The smell of paint really turns me off. Why don't we try yours?"

The lady had popped the three questions. She sat there staring at me with a *vacancy* sign on her face, begging me to occupy the available room. It wasn't exactly what I had gone looking for, but I was excited by her directness.

"What about the guy you're with?" I asked.

"Fuck him," she said. "He bores me. You excite me. Let's go."

Well, we were out of there in no time flat. We didn't say much to each other in the car on the way to my place. I don't even think I got her name. We were both thinking about what was gonna happen. Least I was.

"Can't you drive any faster?" she said at one point, and I liked hearing that. The lady was revved up like a motorcycle. I always like those minutes before it happens, when you both know it's going to happen.

I know that Augie would have said that this wasn't passion. I don't know what it was, but whatever it was, I wanted it. She did meet some of my qualifications. She was mysterious all right, leaving her date behind like that. And she seemed classy, dressed like she was, in a silky blouse open halfway down, and a suede skirt. Who knows, I thought to myself, maybe it would turn out to be passion after all.

We got to my apartment, walked into the bedroom with our arms wrapped around each other, and started some basic kissing. Her kiss was a tease-type. She brushed her tongue back and forth against mine, then withdrew it. I reached my tongue deep into her mouth to find hers. She stepped back, ran her tongue around her lips, and said, "Get ready. I'll be right back." Then she disappeared into my john. I assumed she had to prepare herself, which did eliminate some of the spontaneity. But I couldn't object. Least I knew what I was getting into. Or I thought I did.

I ripped off my clothes and dived under my blanket. I liked to keep Fellini hidden until I had my lady all worked up, then, when she was gasping for him, have the big unveiling. That always got a great response.

I couldn't wait for her to appear undressed and crawl into bed next to me. After a few minutes waiting for her alone, I was tempted to knock the bathroom door down and drag her out.

Finally the door opened and she emerged. But she was still dressed. What's more, she was carrying a gun, pointing it right at my head.

"Just stay right there and tell me where your money is," she said.

"Oh, shit," I said. "This isn't really happening."

"I'll use this thing," she said. "Where's your money?"

I told her my wallet was in the back pocket of the pants I had left on the floor. She took the two hundred dollars in cash that I was carrying.

"What about jewelry?" she said.

"There's a few watches in the box on the dresser," I said.

She kept the gun pointed at me and grabbed six or seven watches, all mementos of various events I'd participated in.

"Stay there until I'm out the door," she said. "or I'll blow your brains out. Hey, this was really fun, Gather Morse. See you around."

She ran out of my apartment, leaving me alone, helpless, frustrated, humiliated, and two hundred dollars poorer.

So much for passion.

I guess something like that was bound to happen sometime with all the strange ladies I'd been bringing to my apartment or hotel room. You never think about it when you're all hot and ready to go, but there's as much risk involved in the sport of muff diving as there is in sky diving or skin diving. Funny thing is, lot of folks who wouldn't let a hitchhiking stranger into their cars never hesitate to let bar-hopping strangers into their homes. I guess we all get a little careless when it comes to sex.

Despite that little incident, I truly enjoyed myself for the first few days after I got out of St. E.'s. I guess you can call it my second honeymoon with Augie August. Augie had told the reporters to forget about my racial remarks and my bare-ass appearance, and they obliged. They had to, since Augie picked up their bills on the road.

The team kept right on winning, which didn't hurt my attitude none. We beat the Cubs, 2–1, on Tuesday night and, what's more, we did it by scoring two legitimate earned runs rather than benefiting from their mistakes. Chi Chi singled in the first and walked in the seventh and scored on hits by Gabby Smith and Bubba Bassoon. And what's even more surprising is that we got through that game without an error, which is like the Fonz getting through a show without combing his hair.

We went back to our normal style of play Wednesday night. We made three errors that led to three runs. But in the bottom of the ninth, with us trailing by a run and no one out, Chatsworth Chung came up with Pinky Potts on second and Rod Smith on third and rolled a slow grounder toward second baseman Manny Trillo. Trillo had to charge full steam, and his throw to first arrived late. As it was, Rod scored to tie the game. But that wasn't the end of the play. Instead of settling for a single, which don't exactly come to Soul Chink in bushels, Chatsworth rounded first and kept right on running. He got himself in a run-down and appeared to be a dead duck, which was a dumb thing to be at that point in the game. But he kept the Cubbies playing catch long enough to let Pinky score and give us a 4–3 win.

So we had swept our second series in a row, won seven straight, and moved into third place with a 23-and-20 record. The streak changed the whole attitude of our ball club. Skip cut down from smoking four packs a day to two packs, which, according to him, was like a .200 hitter becoming a .300 hitter. And all the guys were real friendly toward each other in the clubhouse. I guess they figured I was stuck with them, so they were treating me like one of the gang again. I even caught Bubba smiling once, though he insisted he was just stretching his gums.

It wasn't that we were playing good so much as the other teams were playing bad. But that was okay. It was a ton of fun sitting on the bench watching other teams suffering from the diseases we usually had an epidemic of.

Our fans responded too. Payton called me each morning to get tickets for his old cronies up on the Hill. Yes sir, RFK became the place to be at night in Washington, and once that happens in the capital, anyone who's anyone drops what they're doing and comes out to be seen. Folks in that town love to be associated with a winner, and I can't blame them for that.

Only the Phils and the Pirates remained ahead of us in the standings, and they were the next two teams scheduled to visit the Dudes' den. Sounds hard to believe even as I talk about it now, but it was possible that we could've ended that home stand in first place in the National League East. 'Course, it wasn't even summer yet, but that didn't matter. We were all pretending that we were legitimate title contenders.

We had an off-day on Thursday, June 9, and I was scheduled to open the series against the Phils on Friday night. Steve Carlton was matched up against me, and I figured I'd have to throw at least a shutout to beat him. But I was feeling good about myself and my team, so it didn't seem like an impossible task.

I woke up Thursday morning, got the Washington *Post* at my door, and made myself a big glass of Instant Pro Breakfast, which . . . I guess I plugged those folks already. Anyway, I pulled out the sports section and read E. J. Acton's account of our thrilling victory the night before. The story started on the front page, then jumped over to page three. Well, when I turned to page three, all those good feelings I was starting to have vanished in an instant. For sitting there on the bottom of that page was another one of Augie's teaser ads. Not the usual little box, but a whole half page.

"Tomorrow night. Dudes vs. Phillies," it read. "Come out and see Gather Morse on the mound. First he was Baseball's Bigot. Then he was the Nudist on the Mound. What will he be this time?"

As if the words didn't sting enough, there was a full-length picture of me standing there on the mound naked. A backside view, of course.

Man, was I pissed off. Just when I was starting to calm down and cope with the fact that I was Augie's slave, he went out and agitated me into being an uppity nigger again. Damn, the old man always found some way to get my dander up sky high.

"Let's just make like this never happened," he said to me when we were driving home from St. E.'s. Remember? And I believed him. He had erased all references to the incident from the press, which led me to believe that he was sincere. I guess he was, till he saw an opportunity to sell some tickets.

Seeing that humiliating ad ended our second honeymoon. I grabbed the phone and dialed Payton's office.

"Linda," I said to his secretary. "This is Gather. I gotta speak to Payton."

"I'm sorry, Gather," Linda said. "But he's in the middle of an important meeting."

I was frantic. "I don't care if he's in the middle of open heart surgery," I said. "Get him on the phone or I'm bringing my ten percent someplace else."

That was enough to interrupt Payton's important meeting. He got right on the phone.

"Did you see the ad the lousy sumbitch's running today?" I said.

"Yes, I did," Payton said. "I consider it in poor taste."

"Poor taste?" I shrieked. "Tastes worse than a shit sandwich. Man's supposed to be selling tickets to baseball, not to skin flicks. You gotta get me out of that contract, Payton. I ain't playing another game for that lying bastard. I swear it."

"Now, just extinguish your flame, boy," Payton said. "We must conduct ourselves in a gentlemanlike manner."

"Gentlemanlike? You call this ad gentlemanlike? This is an ad for those queer types. They may be gentle, but they ain't men.

"You gotta find some loophole that will get me outta here, Payton. Or I'll find me an agent who will."

"Fine, Gather," he said calmly. "Why don't we do this, then? Meet me for lunch in an hour at the Four Georges Inn in Georgetown. Together we'll come up with a solution to this latest problem of yours."

I was still as hot as some of that Szechuan chink food when I pulled into a parking space on Wisconsin Avenue an hour later. The street was filled with those swanky-type ladies from the Northwest part of town as well as secretaries on their lunch hours. They were all there to grab up the latest in hip-cool-type fashion, which is what the shops in Georgetown always offer. I exchanged brief glances with a few foxes who were probably looking for something like me to occupy the rest of their afternoons until the man of the house arrived home. But I didn't have time to pop the three questions. I kept on walking briskly toward the restaurant. I knew there had to be some way for me to weasel my way out of my contract, some way for me to twist Augie's arm until he yelled uncle, aunt, niece, and nephew.

Well, let me tell you, friends. After all that had happened to me, after being conned, screwed, and humiliated ten times over, I was bound to run into a little lady luck sometime. And, sure enough I did, right there on the gold-paved streets of Georgetown.

Before I got to the Four Georges Inn, where I assume Payton was waiting, I spotted, sashaying along the street about twenty feet in front of me, one of the great architectural phenomena of our time. It was one beautifully constructed back porch packed tightly into a pair of white slacks through which flowered panties were visible. And it was attached to the person of none other than the love of Augie's life, the passion of his soul, you guessed it, Miss Melinda Towers.

I stopped in my tracks when I recognized her strut. And I'd like to construct a monument to myself—something like the Lincoln Memorial, but not that big—right there on that spot on Wisconsin Avenue Northwest. For it was there where I was hit by a stroke of absolute genius, by the kind of idea that turns down-and-out losers into outright American successes in no time at all.

"Gather, old boy," I said to myself, standing in that spot, "the answer to all your problems is hiding in that there pair of pants. Augie August told you he can't live without Melinda Towers, right? Well, boy, you go steal the lady's affections right out from under the old man's nose and he'll have you out of this town faster than you can say Cincinnati Reds."

Yes sir. It was all so obvious. I don't know why I hadn't thought of it sooner. 'Course, it wasn't a sure thing. I didn't know how committed the lady was to the old man and his wallet. But I had as much confidence in

my sales pitch as in my drop pitch. And it was sure worth
the effort. "Gather Morse," I said to myself, "you make
that lady love you. You hear me?"

As I look back, that was one of the meanest thoughts
that ever passed through my head, making a lady love me
whom I had no intention of loving back. But I was a desperate man. I'd been used more times than a mattress in a
cathouse. And it was time for me to do some using.

Just as I got this brainstorm, I saw Melinda walk into a
boutique called Ruby's. So I headed in after her. It was
one of these mod-type ladies' shops with mirrors all over
the walls and ceilings. Place was filled with disco music,
and the atmosphere seemed more right for boogying than
buying.

This middle-aged fox in a denim jumpsuit and more
makeup than a circus clown came up to me and said,
"Can I help you?"

"No, I'm just looking for someone," I said, and I wan-
dered among the racks of clothing searching for Melinda.
I walked around the store twice and couldn't find her. I
felt a little silly being by myself in a ladies' clothes shop.
But I knew she was in there somewhere.

She must be trying something on, I figured. So I walked
to the back of the store, where the dressing rooms were. I
saw some nice pins beneath the ends of the curtains in a
few of the rooms. And then I noticed Melinda's white
pants lying on the floor of the very last room. I had her
just where I wanted her.

I pulled the curtain of her dressing room aside. She
gasped with fright until she saw who I was. She was
standing there undressed except for those flowered panties. Her speakers were nearly wall-to-wall. It sure was a
funny moment, me standing there like that, looking at her
almost in the raw. It was just like the time she walked in
on me in the shower room, only in reverse. That's obviously what she was thinking too, 'cause she smiled and
said, "Well, now we're even."

It was a great opening line and the beginning of a
beautiful relationship.

8

So that afternoon, instead of lunching with Payton and pleading with him to do something for me, I ate with Melinda and started to do something for myself. We went to this cute little place called Maison Crepe and had a real personal-type conversation, getting to know each other by exchanging a few stories from our lives.

I told her a lot of the things I've been putting into this tape recorder. And she told me about some of the bumpy waters she traveled. I was flattered that she felt comfortable enough to share her past with me like that. That kind of talk is usually the first sign that I'm connecting with a lady. 'Course, you gotta be careful. Some ladies feel obligated to pour out their entire life histories, with all the dirty details, to anyone they meet. It's as if they got a record sitting on their tongues and you're the switch that turns them on. Those kinds of folks bore me to tears. But Melinda's not one of those self-pitying types, I assure you of that.

I'd like you to hear her story just like she told it to me that day. And there's no better person to tell it than Melinda herself, in person. So I'm gonna call her out here into the living room and have her take over the microphone. ('Course, this here's one of those tape recorders without a microphone. You just talk into the black box. I don't know how it works, but it does.) Just one short minute.

"Melinda. Melinda. Come out here. There's something I need from you."

"Not again, Gather. I'm still charley-horse from last night."

"No, that's not what I need. Come sit over here next to me. Right here. Come on.

"Now, honey pie, I want you to tell the whole story of your life just like you told it to me when we had lunch that day in Georgetown. Remember?"

"Tell it to who? There's no one here."

"No, silly. Into this Sony tape recorder."

"Oh, come on, Gather. Just because you got yourself a new toy, that doesn't mean I have to play with it. Get a Scrabble set and I'll play with you."

"Hey, this is serious stuff, Melinda. I want to put the whole story of my feud with Augie August on the record. Well, on tape anyway. It's important. You see all those bad things people are writing about me in the papers. I gotta have my say."

"That's fine. But I don't have to have mine. I'm used to being called names. It doesn't bother me anymore."

"That's 'cause no one ever called you a killer. Look, sweet thing. Just do this one thing for me. Please."

"What do you want me to say?"

"Anything that comes to mind."

"Anything?"

"Sure."

"Gather Morse has a great cock."

"No, not that. Come on. I'm gonna have to erase that."

"Okay. Okay. Where should I begin?"

"I don't know. Talk about your mom and dad and all that kind of shit."

"Give me the microphone."

"Is none. You just talk out in the open and the

machine does the rest. I'll tell you what. Let's make like Johnny Carson. I'll be Johnny and you be my guest. Okay. Here goes.

"My next guest is Melinda Towers, the beautiful wife of Gather Morse, the famous baseball star. Tell me, Melinda, did you have a happy childhood?"

"Actually, Johnny, it sucked. Oh, no, I can't say that on television."

"Don't worry. You're not really on television. Come on. Just talk. Let's start again. Tell me, Melinda, did you have a happy childhood?"

"Well, all right. You asked for it. Let's see, now.

"I grew up in this ugly fleabag apartment on East Third Street in Manhattan. In case you missed East Third on your sightseeing trips of New York, it's a dark alley full of dogshit between Gramercy Park and the Village. It's where all the bums hang out. My father was one of the bums.

"Oh, yeah, he had a job working in the Ballantine Beer bottling plant over in Jersey. He was a taster. That's a little joke. But he sure smelled like he was. And he was always bumping into things and falling over.

"I guess I loved him despite it all. And I felt sorry for him too. But Mother felt nothing for him."

"Is this the kind of stuff you want, Gather?"

"Yeah, Melinda. Terrific. Go on."

"Well, Father would come home every night, eat supper, then lock himself in the bathroom with a six-pack. Really. He spent every single night locked in the john. I have no idea what he did in there. But if I wanted to pee after dinner, I had to run down to Mr. Federico's grocery on the corner. Guess that taught me something about self-control.

"Actually, I spent a lot of time at Mr. Federico's. He provided me with the only enjoyment I had in New York. The fat, bald Italian used to give me all the new movie magazines for free. I always thought he was being nice to me because he liked me. Later I found out that he and

Mother spent the afternoons going at it in his meat locker. Fitting setting, I guess, a meat locker. Though they both must have come down with frostbite in some uncomfortable places.

"I spent a lot of time sitting out on the stoops on Third Street, reading the movie magazines, dreaming about being Marilyn Monroe. I know how boring that sounds. It's trite, but it's true.

"When I was eleven, it must have been 1957, I came home from school one day and my mother told me we were leaving that night for California. Father wasn't going with us, which made me sad.

"I remember there was this street bum who used to spend the nights sleeping on the stoop where I read during the day. He was still there sometimes when I left for school in the morning. Seeing him always made me feel incredibly lonely. When Mother said we were leaving Father, I imagined him sleeping out there on the stoop like that, and I wanted to cry. Mother wouldn't even let me stay home long enough to say good-bye to Father. 'The bus won't wait for us,' she said.

"That day we left, Mother was wearing this shiny, clinging green dress. It was the only nice dress she had, and I wondered why she was wearing it for a three-day bus trip.

"Mother—Dorothy was her name—always seemed very beautiful to me. She wore her neck-length blond hair in a fifties flip and had a body that belonged on a teenager. I remember telling her that she was as beautiful as the girls in my movie magazines. 'That's just why we have to go to California,' she said.

"Mr. Federico came over to drive us to the bus terminal, and I was surprised to see him at my apartment. At that point, I didn't even know that Mother knew him. We left without leaving a note for Father. I questioned Mother about that. 'When he gets here, he'll know what happened,' she said.

"I can't really tell you how I felt about any of this. Sad

and bewildered, I guess. I haven't thought much about it over the years. Intentionally. Why should I? None of this was much fun. I'm good at pushing things out of my mind.

"Anyway, Mr. Federico drove us to the Port Authority in his Nash Rambler. He carried our suitcases into the terminal, took money out of his pocket, and bought us two tickets. He gave the tickets to Mother, threw his arms around her, held his hands on her ass, and hugged her warmly, possessively, which my father had never done. The sight made me a little uncomfortable, maybe even jealous. Then Mr. Federico handed me a pile of movie magazines and bent down to kiss me. 'Please watch over my daddy,' I said to him.

"Mother and I got onto this silver bus and Mother told me to sit by the window where I would have a view and could sleep better. She sat down in the aisle seat, pulled her dress up, crossed her thin legs, and dangled one foot in the aisle.

"Soon, this tall blond man walked onto the bus. I remember his head almost touched the ceiling. And he was a real hunk. Maybe even a movie star, I thought. When he reached Mother's dangling foot, he stopped in the aisle. Mother did not move.

" 'Excuse me,' was all he said.

" 'Oh, I'm sorry,' Mother said, and I could tell she didn't mean it. She removed the foot from the aisle, turned to me, and said, 'This trip will be just fine.'

"Later that night, I woke up and it was darker outside my window than it had ever been in the city. I couldn't see anything beyond the edge of the road. I was frightened. I turned to Mother for comfort, but her seat was empty. Then I looked through the space between her seat and mine.

"The tall blond man was sitting there with this expression on his face that I had never seen before. It looked like pain to me. There was a blanket on his lap and someone underneath the blanket bobbing up and down. I wondered what was happening to the poor man. I turned my head away. But then I heard him moan. I thought he was hurt. So I jumped up on my knees to make sure he was all right. As I did, the blanket fell to the floor and Mother sat up in the seat next to him.

"For the rest of the bus trip, Mother sat beside me during the day and beside Mr. Young—I think that was his name—at night. And each time the bus stopped, Mr. Young bought us a meal.

"When we arrived in Los Angeles, Mr. Young shook Mother's hand and went his own way. 'Isn't Mr. Young going to live with us, Mommy?' I said.

" 'Of course not, Melinda,' Mother said. 'Mr. Young lives with his wife.'

" 'Are you sad about that, Mommy?' I said.

" 'Sad?' she said. 'Why should I be sad?'

" 'I don't know,' I said. 'I thought maybe you liked him.'

" 'Now, sweetheart,' Mother said to me in this very serious tone. 'We're in this new city and we don't have any money and we don't have anybody to take care of us. So your mommy has to find men who will. It may seem to you that I like them, but I don't. When you get older, you'll understand this better. Okay?'

"But I did understand that. And I understood when Mother went into the bathroom with the man at the real estate office. And I understood when I had to sleep on the hideaway bed because the man who made the movie with Jayne Mansfield was sleeping beside Mother where I was supposed to sleep. I understood, and never asked Mother any questions. She didn't like to answer questions. She always appeared to know what she was doing.

"Mother was pretty busy out there. She was always working as an extra in one movie or another. And she was always going out with one man or another. She seemed to have some money, and we lived better than we did in New York.

"But I never really took to L.A. Palm trees look anemic to me. The air burned the inside of my nose. Mother always promised she would take me to the beach, but never found the time. And I spent a lot of hours alone, studying myself in the mirror, which is one of the most popular forms of passing time out there.

"One night, I was sitting up late, waiting for Mother to get home, worrying about where she could be. I usually waited for her to arrive before I got undressed for bed. But it was so late that I got undressed and pulled out my Lone Ranger nightie. There was a knock at the door. I thought it was Mother, so I ran over with my nightie in my hands. I opened the door and stood behind it so no one outside would see me undressed. It wasn't Mother at the door. It was one of her friends, the man who made the movie with Jayne Mansfield. I knew him only as Fritzie. I was cold and held my arms across my chest.

"Fritzie's hair was ruffled, his shirt collar was unbuttoned, his tie hung loosely. He always looked like he had a five-o'clock shadow. He smelled from liquor.

" 'Where's your mommy?' he said.

" 'Not home yet,' I told him.

"I stood against the wall trying to warm my body with my hands. I was shivering.

" 'You look so cold,' he said. He stepped toward me. 'Don't be scared, Melinda,' he said. 'I won't hurt you.'

"And then he lifted me in his big hairy arms and carried me into the bedroom. He put me in bed and pulled the blanket over me.

" 'I need my nightie,' I said.

" 'I'll keep you warm till mommy gets home,' he said. He undressed and crawled into bed beside me.

"You know the rest. I don't have to give you the lurid details. It wasn't really rape, I guess. I understood what was happening. I remember liking the feeling of warmth and liking him holding me and liking the feel of him lying on top of me. Mom really did know what she was doing, and I wanted to be just like her.

"Between that adolescent experience and the fine example Mother had set for me, I grew up thinking that the best thing in life was to have a man next to you, keeping you warm, providing affection, also providing money. I developed nicely, to men's eyes anyway, and it was never difficult to find what I thought I wanted. I wasn't a prostitute or anything like that. But I guess I wasn't much different. From the day I graduated high school, men paid me, allegedly to be a receptionist or a typist, but really just to have me around the office. Some men I met made me promises of stardom, the kind you hear ten times a day in L.A. But I never wanted to be a star. I don't know why, with all my childhood fantasies about Marilyn Monroe, but I didn't. I just wanted to be beside a warm body with its arms wrapped around me. I just wanted to feel protected.

"Most of the warm bodies I spent time beside lost interest in me after a short while, but I always found another. None of them ever gave a shit about me. I know that now. But why should they have? I never demanded more than company. And that's what I got.

"This all sounds so trite, now that I'm reliving it. But that's me. Little Miss Trite. Everybody's favorite piece of ass. There's a lot of women I know, especially in California, who would give anything to be everybody's favorite piece of ass. It may not be chic to admit it today, but it's true. Every woman longs to be desired. I was, and that alone was enough to live on.

"I may have been able to live on that forever, but I made a classic mistake. A trite mistake. I fell in love.

"His name was Brent Caring, and you probably know of him. He's a congressman from California. I met him at an ad agency where I worked as a receptionist. He came in one day to plan some media advertising for his first campaign. It must have been 1972. He saw me sitting there, joked with me, and offered me a job on his campaign staff at a much higher salary than I was making. I had no emotional commitment to jobs—I must have gone through ten of them in five years—and he was cute, so I accepted his offer. I was his personal aide, which meant that after a long day of campaigning, I came to his aid. Or I came as his aide. Or whatever. You get the picture.

"He was married, but so were most of the other men who had taken care of me. I found that married men offered me a more stable relationship. That may sound foolish, but I believed it. The single men I met were all intent on bedding down as many women as time and energy would permit. Their pleasure came from the numbers. Dates or appointments meant nothing to them if something new came along. And when they did keep appointments, I always felt I was an audience for their show rather than a participant in a relationship.

"Married men always made me feel more important, desired, wanted, even needed. Just by the nature of the intrigue attached to adultery, I represented something exciting to them, an alternative to the routines that were their lives. And since it was safer and much less complicated for them to have one affair instead of dozens, I found them more devoted and dependable. Of course, as a full-time other woman, I had to accept the fact that I would always spend Saturday nights by myself. Saturday is Wives' Night all over America. But I managed to cope. When I was with a married man, I always felt that I was the focus of his attention and affection, and the intensity of those moments together was enough to get me through the moments alone.

"Why, with all the men that I dated, did I fall in love with Brent Caring? Oh, I don't know. I've thought about that, but how do you explain what draws you to someone? I liked the way he crunched up his nose and eyes like a little boy when he was embarrassed. I liked the way he touched me, with a sense of possession and confidence. I liked his asking my opinions and feelings about whatever he did. I enjoyed listening to him thinking out loud in my presence. I was happy that we laughed in bed instead of treating our lovemaking like a melodrama. I was comfortable with him and with myself when with him.

"I know I'm just rambling now, but I'm enjoying it. Talking like this is new to me and actually kind of fun.

"Anyway, Brent got elected to the House, moved me to Washington, and set me up with a job and an apartment. Leaving California was never a consideration. He left, so I left. But our relationship deteriorated as soon as we got to Washington. The pressure and competition on the Hill was too much for him. He grew cold, preoccupied, distant. He had less time for me, less interest in me. I had come clear across the country just to be with him, and I wasn't with him. I had been spoiled, and now I was offended. And I did a dumb thing for attention, revenge, spite. When the Wayne Hays-Elizabeth Ray romance became public, a story I should have understood, even appreciated, I foolishly jumped on the bandwagon and told a reporter from the *Post* that I too was a woman being kept at the taxpayers' expense.

"The day my name appeared in the paper, I went to Brent's Hill office and found someone else at my desk. His administrative aide threw me out of the room. I tried to call Brent and apologize, but he did not take my calls. He cut off all contact with me. I sustained myself for a while on anger, but that faded and was replaced by loneliness.

"I had plenty of dates. The publicity surrounding the scandal made me a very popular woman. I guess men thought I was easy—isn't everybody easy these days? My phone wouldn't stop ringing with offers. I went out a lot to fill my needs for company, attention, admiration, but remained emotionally connected to Brent.

"I didn't hear from him or see him for two years. Then, back in May, he called me. He was very businesslike on the phone and I assumed he was in his office and could not talk freely. He had rented a yacht to entertain some clients and invited me to a party there. I know all about those Washington parties and the services women guests are expected to perform. And I think more of myself than to whore to help anyone's career, even

Brent's. So my first reaction was to decline the invitation. But I was anxious to see Brent again, and this was my opportunity. I also know that I never have to do anything for a man that I don't want to do. The one thing Washington hotshots won't do to women is commit rape.

"I bought a new outfit for that party—white pants and a cute little sailor blouse with a scoop neck. I wanted Brent to desire me. But when I arrived at the dock down in Southwest Washington—not far from where Gather lived—I found my former lover and benefactor ogling some tight-ass Southern bitch he'd found in the hallowed halls of Congress.

" 'I'm glad you came,' Brent said when he saw me. 'Let me introduce you to some of the men.'

" 'I don't want to meet them,' I said. 'I haven't seen you in two years. I want to talk to you.'

" 'Hey, Melinda,' he said with a chuckle. 'There's nothing between us anymore.'

"And then he smiled at me. I felt like knocking out all his teeth. But I just ran off the boat, into the parking lot, and started beating my fists on the hood of my car. I was hurting my fists and I was miserable and I was crying and my eye makeup was running down my face. This big, tough, wisecracking, ballsy lady was in the midst of an infantile fit. And standing there watching me was this sunburned, bald man old enough to be my father.

"This stranger walked over to me, took me in his arms, and patted my head. That embrace felt so good, I just melted in it. He introduced himself as Augie August, said he had come for Brent's party, but insisted on skipping it, took me home to his Tudor mansion, and made me some chili.

"I didn't leave that house for months. Augie August took better care of me there than anyone ever had. And as tough as I may pretend to be, I enjoy being taken care of. Who doesn't?

"I went everyplace with Augie. He enjoyed showing me off, and I enjoyed being shown. From what Gather tells me, Augie once did the same thing for him. It's as if the man is not complete without a star or a beauty accompanying him. There was nothing Augie wouldn't do for me, and I felt cared for and protected with him. I was his princess and he was the staff of servants. At the time that he found me, he was just what I needed, which may sound selfish, but all relationships are selfish. Maybe I should have thought ahead and realized that I could not stay in our kind of relationship forever. But I'm as bad at thinking ahead as I am at looking back. It was comfortable at the time, and that was all I considered.

"Then this cute, crazy, funny guy with the ridiculous name of Gather Morse came along. Why did he appeal to me? Again, how to explain? He's kind of good-looking, I guess, though none of his features are striking. I do love his dimples. And his little buns. And his curly brown hair. And he looks very sexy on the pitcher's mound in his tight-fitting uniform. And also in the showers in no uniform. And the first two times we met, in the showers and at Ruby's, which I'm sure he's told you about, were amusing and hard to forget. But I think I started to fall for him that first day we had lunch together in Georgetown. He told me all about himself, and he was funny, insightful, more sensitive than I ever expected an athlete to be. It was one of those exciting conversations when you get turned on and never want to leave. He's such a good storyteller, I loved listening to him.

"Well, after that lunch, I went back to Augie's and I felt like a teenage girl who was trapped in her father's house and desperate to get out. But I was afraid to hurt my father. If I could have had my way, Augie would have continued to play my father and Gather would have played my lover. But that was unreasonable to expect, so I—"

"That's enough, Melinda."

"Ah, Gather. Let me tell more. I'm really into this."

"Yeah, but you're getting into my part of the story

now, honey pie. Folks know enough about you for now. It's my turn again."

"Well, all right. But I gotta say just one more thing."

"What's that."

"I gotta say that I'm really sorry about what happened to Augie. I have bad dreams about it every night. But I do love Gather Morse. He's a sweetie. . . ."

"All right, Melinda."

"And he didn't kill Augie or anything like that. The idiots who are writing that stuff should get their ties caught in their typewriters and choke to death. . . ."

"Okay, Melinda. That's enough."

"Gather wouldn't hurt a fly. He's a gentle man. Real gentle. In fact, why don't you come into the bedroom and show me how gentle you are?"

"Not now, Melinda. I have to finish my story."

"We can keep the tape running and let everyone hear just how gentle you are.'"

"Later, Melinda. Later. Please. Oh, stop that. Not now. Oh, God. Stop that. Oh, God. Oh, my. Excuse me a minute."

9

I'm back.

Sorry about that. But the lady is on her honeymoon, after all. So am I, for that matter. Guess I should erase that last exchange. But that wouldn't be honest, would it?

Now, where was I? Okay, lunch in Georgetown with Melinda.

I'm a sucker for a pretty lady with a sad story to tell. Fact is, I'm a sucker for a pretty lady if she tells me "Snow White and the Seven Dwarfs." But I wasn't going to let my natural masculine instincts get in the way of my latest plan. Least, that's what I kept telling myself. Speakers, back porch, and all, Melinda was nothing but a means to an end. And if we made a little sweet music along the way, well, it was nothing more than strategy.

She'd been around, as they say. So I figured that if she was gonna want me enough to give up all that Augie offered her, I was gonna have to treat her differently than all her other guys had. I had to act laid back. Pretend that I was in no great hurry to explore her peaks and valleys. I had to make her want to make me.

After lunch, we said good-bye to each other on the street in front of the restaurant with a handshake. Her eyes were sad and I could tell that she was sorry our little get-together was over, which was just how I wanted her to feel.

"When will I see you again?" she asked.

"Oh, I don't know," I said. "You planning on going to the game tomorrow night?"

"Wouldn't miss it," she said.

"Well, I guess I'll be there too," I said. "Especially since I'm pitching."

I didn't want her to think I was overanxious. 'Course, I only had six days left before the trade deadline, so I had to work fast. But I didn't want her to know how badly I needed her. I figured I'd see her at the game and arrange another get-together sometime over the weekend.

On Friday morning I had an appointment scheduled with Laura. I was throwing against the Phillies that evening, and they hit me hard, even when I'm as calm as a corpse. I needed a diversion so that I didn't spend the afternoon worrying about their hitters. By noon, when Laura still had not arrived, I started to get panicky. All I could think about was Mike Schmidt and Greg Luzinski standing up at the plate with grins on their pusses, waiting to put a dent in my pretty face with a line drive.

My patience ran out and I dialed Laura's number. Her Panamanian art-dealer friend answered the phone. Though I had never met him, I knew it was his voice 'cause he said, "Jello!"

I hung up without saying a word. I didn't know why he was at home on a Friday afternoon or for how long he was intending to stay home. But I couldn't wait around to see if Laura could lie her way out of her house. I needed a fix.

I didn't know what other lady might be available on such short notice. But the sad look on Melinda's face when we parted the day before kept popping into my mind. My better judgment said I should bluff for a while rather than fold my hand too early. But I was in a rut and she seemed the right person to help me out.

Before I pursued her, I had to make sure she was alone. So I did a little checking. I called the stadium, said I was Bowie Kuhn, and asked to speak with Augie August. When the secretary put me on hold, I knew the old man was in his office. I hung up. When Augie picked up his phone, he probably figured the commissioner was snubbing him again, but he was accustomed to such treatment.

The coast was clear, so I dialed Augie's home number. Melinda answered and sounded glad to hear from me.

"You free this afternoon?" I asked.

"What'd you have in mind?" she said.

"I'll pick you up in half an hour."

So me and the lady took a pleasant afternoon drive deep into the woods of Rock Creek Park. I pulled my Stingray up beside this weathered wood bridge that crosses the creek, one of the most peaceful spots I knew of in the bustling capital. And we got out and walked together, listening to the water rushing over the rocks.

"You're one of the last of the romantics, Gather Morse," Melinda said to me as we walked along.

"What makes you say that?" I asked.

"You brought me to a place like this," she said. "Most guys I've known start right off by offering me scotch and sofa and sometimes they forget about the scotch."

That made me feel a little guilty since I am really just like the guys she was talking about. And all I ever keep in the house is beer. But I didn't let on.

"Yeah, I guess I am one of those romantics," I said. "Nature really turns me on. Sometimes I wish I was a tree living among all the other beautiful trees. Or one of those rocks there in the creek."

She giggled at that bulltwang. "You do not," she said.

I looked at her and she had this amused grin on her pretty face. Her unusually light blue eyes demanded attention and honesty. "You're right, I don't," I said. We both laughed. Then we stood there silently amidst thousands of trees, both wondering what we were gonna do next. She was as fresh and lovely as the setting. And I was tempted to pull her to me and kiss her right then, which would have been easy. I forced myself to hold back. Unfortunately, she didn't, which made things hard for me. She threw her arms around my neck and pulled my lips to hers. She smelled as pretty as she looked and she rubbed her long fingers through my hair, which excited me. But I was a little suspicious. I wondered what was on her mind. She was, after all, shacking up full-time at Augie's place. So what made her kiss and hug me like I had just returned from the wars?

I pulled my head away from hers and said, "Why are you doing this?"

"It feels right," she said, and she kissed me again.

I pulled away again. "But you're someone else's lady," I said.

She stared into my eyes and said, "Kiss me." I couldn't resist. Then we held hands and continued walking along the creek.

"Augie's the nicest thing that ever happened to me in my life," she said without my inquiring. I waited for her to say more, but she didn't.

"Yeah. So . . ." I finally said.

"That's all. He's just the nicest thing that ever happened to me. And I love him for it."

"So why are you here with me?" I asked.

"Why'd you ask me to come?"

I shrugged my shoulders and tried to think of the right answer. " 'Cause it feels right," I said.

"Well, that's why I'm here with you," she said.

She didn't want to tell me any more, so I didn't ask. After walking for a while longer, we got back in my car, kissed some more, and headed back to Augie's mansion.

"Why don't you come in?" she said when I pulled my car onto the driveway.

It seemed like an appropriate thing for me to do, go into Augie's house and have his lady in his bed. And Fellini was ready to go, which I'm sure someone with Melinda's experience noticed. But it was all too easy. At that moment, she wanted me, which I wanted. But she couldn't have been ready to give up everything else in her life for me yet. Right then, even if the old man had walked in and caught us in the sack—which wasn't gonna happen, since he was at the stadium and would stay through the game that night—he would've been mad and they would've had a fight and she would've cried and the whole thing would've blown over without the desired result. It wouldn't have been threatening enough to force Augie to ship me out of town. Not yet. So I fought off my natural masculine instinct and resisted Melinda.

"I really can't come in now," I said. "I have to get to the clubhouse early for a rubdown."

I could tell she didn't believe me, but she didn't press. "When will I see you again?" she asked.

"Real soon," I said, and I kissed her good-bye.

She disappeared into the house and I was left with time to kill before I really had to be at the stadium. So I passed the afternoon watching *Casablanca* at the Circle Theater, the dollar movie-revival house on Pennsylvania Avenue, a few blocks west of the White House. Tits flick, I'll tell you that. Bogey sure knew how to handle ladies. Watching him, I thought to myself that I was handling my situation with Melinda just like he would have. Too bad he's not still around to play me in the movie version of my life. Only thing wrong with him was that he wasn't a southpaw.

That night, I was nervous in the clubhouse before I went out to face the Phils. It was the first time in my major-league career that I didn't have myself a lady before pitching a game. I guess I'm a little superstitious—all pitchers are—and I thought my abstinence was a bad omen. 'Course, I'm not as superstitious as some of the guys, like Sticky Thomas for example. Sticky's so crazy, he's worn the same pair of socks for every game he's pitched in the major leagues. Gabby says those socks now run out to the mound every fifth day even if Sticky doesn't put them on. I don't do anything that loony. But I do make sure not to step on the baseline when I walk out to the mound.

Anyway, even though I didn't have my usual pregame meal, I did have a rare delicacy watching me from a front-row box seat at game time. Melinda was sitting beside Augie but smiling at me like I just pumped her full of my own high-octane fuel. Every time I glanced over there, she was staring at me through bright, inviting eyes. Made me feel desired. And that made me feel potent as punch on the mound. I don't even think Augie noticed the little game going on between me and his lady throughout the big game.

In the first inning I got Garry Maddox, who hits line drives easy as I eat, Larry Bowa, a feisty little bugger, and Mike Schmidt, the most consistent long-ball hitter in the league, to slap routine grounders at our infielders. It was a humid night and my pitches were breaking like I had a string attached to the ball that I could pull at just the right moment. I felt so good out there, I bet I could've made the ball loop-de-loop if I wanted to. 'Course, that would've just been showing off.

I ran off the field at the end of that easy inning and didn't tip my hat to the lady, which would've been tipping my hand to her escort. As I sat in the dugout, my adrenalin was flowing like Rock Creek. I knew I had it that day. As my teammates plundered at the plate, I took a handful of sunflower seeds and shoved them in my mouth. Sunflower seeds have pretty much replaced chewing tobacco with most major-leaguers. I like them much better myself. I tried chewing tobacco one night during my rookie year when I was pitching in Candlestick Park against the San Francisco Giants. It's so windy out there that during one all-star game a pitcher named Stu Miller got blown off the mound. But I figured if I was gonna be a tough major-leaguer, I had to chew the stuff. So I stuffed this thick wad in my jaw, started munching on it, and went out to pitch. After a few pitches, I figured it was time to spit out a trail of tobacco juice, like you see all the fellas do. Well, I spit this juice out in front of me and the wind blew it right back into my face. My eyes started stinging and they had to stop the game so that Benny the Nip could run out to the mound with a towel and wipe the juice out of my eyes. I never tried that stuff again.

Sunflower seeds are much neater and your breath don't smell like dogshit to the ladies you meet up with after the game. I never could understand how the foxes put up with tobacco breath. Maybe that's why so many of the guys complain that the ladies they meet just give a little head, then scoot on home before the guys get to do some genuine loving of their own. I guess you could say sunflower seeds make for a well-rounded sex life, which is another strong argument in their favor.

Anyway, we went down in order and I spit out a mouthful of shells and strutted back to the mound for the second inning. Greg Luzinski started off the frame by poking a routine fly to left field, which Pinky Potts managed to play into a double. But I didn't let that rile me none. "That base is where you're staying, Polack," I said to myself. And I struck out Jay Johnstone and Tommy Hutton and got Bob Boone to chase an inside screwball that he bounced to Aurelio at first for an unassisted putout.

I don't know why I was so cocksure of myself that particular evening. But looking back, I can guess. That walk in the woods with Melinda made me feel like I was starting to get my situation under control. I wasn't a free man yet, but I was on the right track. And since I had control of my life, I had control of my pitches. That's the way it is with ballplayers, you know. 'Course, I'm the same pitcher with the same tools every time I walk out there, and so my confidence should not waver. And if I didn't have to live my everyday life in between pitching turns, it probably wouldn't. But things happen on those days between games that affect the way I feel about myself, and end up affecting the way I throw. It's like there's this little guy sitting on my shoulder, just like that Jiminy Cricket fellow in *Pinocchio,* and some days he says to me, "Gather, you're hot shit," and other days he says, "Gather, you're pure shit." I don't know what the guy looks like, he may be a black folk or a Latino for all I know, but I always seem to believe what he's telling me. They say that a ballplayer's supposed to leave his home life outside the ball park and leave the game at the ball park, but I never met one yet who could do that. I sure can't.

But that particular evening, I liked myself a whole lot and my performance showed it. While I continued to baffle the talented Phillies' hitters, my teammates managed to put three singles together and give me a run. I'd scattered three singles myself, but took a 1-0 lead into the ninth inning.

For some reason that I can't explain, when a pitcher has a one-run lead in the ninth, he always ends up facing the meaty part of the opponent's lineup. This game was no different. Schmidt, Luzinski, and Johnstone were coming up and each one of them was capable of poking the cowhide into the parking lot.

After taking my warm-ups, I stepped off the back of the mound to consider the task at hand. I was determined not to let this game get away like I had against the Reds the week before. Even if a break went against me, I had to stay composed and win the game. I reached down into my crotch to make sure my Scrubble Bubbles were ready for some serious action. As I felt them, I looked up and saw Melinda watching me with her eyes wide open. She must have thought I was shaking hands with Fellini, and she was amused by the gesture. She was probably wishing that I had called her out there to shake hands for me. I hoped she had enjoyed the show and climbed the mound to challenge Mike Schmidt.

Schmidt waited for the first strike, which came on my second pitch, a good curve. He's a heads-up player, and even with his power, he was willing to take a base-on-balls if I was offering. But after he saw that I was delivering strikes, he gritted his teeth and started looking for a fat pitch.

Bubba called for my drop pitch; I went through my fidgety routine and delivered. Schmidt's eyes lit up as the ball headed toward the center of the plate, waist-high. You could almost hear him thinking, "Don't drop, ball. Please don't drop." But the ball dropped. Schmidt swung anyway and topped it, sending an easy roller toward Gabby at short. Gabby charged hard, scooped it up, and went to throw. But the ball got stuck in the web of his glove. Schmidt was on first with a cheap hit. I should have been pissed off, but I wasn't.

Greg Luzinski, the ox they call the Bull, stepped into the right-hander's batter's box. Luzinski hits both with power and for average, and it's never pleasant to have to face him. Facing him when you're protecting a one-run lead and there's a good runner on first is downright nauseating. But I kept my cool, moved the ball around, and got him to hit a bouncer at Tony Smith, who was well-positioned in the hole just to the right of second base. It was an easy double-play ball. Easy for anyone but Tony. He fielded it all right, but flipped it way wide of the bag. Gabby was covering second and the ball flew over his head and into center field. By the time Chi Chi reached the ball, Schmidt was on third and Luzinski was on second. Two little sure-out nibblers and I was in trouble.

Skip came charging out to the mound to make sure I was still calm. "Now, don't panic, Gather," he said, wiping the sweat off his forehead. "Forget about the pressure. Forget that you blew a game just like this one last week. Just don't panic. You can get out of this, and if you don't, you really stink."

"Thanks for the encouragement, Skip," I said. We agreed that I had to walk Johnstone and set up a force at any base, which I did.

So now I had a one-run lead with no one out and the bases loaded. And I had no confidence in any of the fielders behind me. My options were limited—strike out Tommy Hutton, the left-handed-hitting first baseman, or lose.

I worked the scroogie on Hutton, high and tight, hoping that if he did hit it, he'd pop it up. My teammates had not been successful with grounders, and I thought a pop-up might be easier for them to handle. Sure enough, Hutton lifted a towering fly in foul territory just outside first base. Aurelio went after it, but he was circling around like a drunk, not sure where it was going to fall. I couldn't stand by and take a chance on him dropping it. So I ran into foul territory, threw my shoulder into Aurelio like a defensive back making a block tackle, knocked him to the ground, and caught the ball myself. I checked Schmidt back to third, then called for time. Aurelio was sitting on his ass, startled, and I helped him to his feet.

"You bastard," he said.

"Sorry," I said. "I didn't see you." And I walked back to the mound.

At least I had myself one out, as Bob Boone, their catcher, stepped into the left-hander's batter's box. In that situation, most pitchers would hope for a ground ball and a double play. But I was praying that Boone wouldn't hit the ball on the ground and give my infielders the chance to blow it.

On my first pitch, Boone squared around to bunt. The squeeze was on. Soon as I saw him level the bat, I charged off the mound. Schmidt was coming down the line. Boone bunted the ball right in front of the plate. On the run, I grabbed it with one hand. Schmidt went into a slide, and so did I. When his foot slid into mine, I knew I had beaten him home and he was out.

All the guys were whooping it up and congratulating me on my heads-up play. It was a super play, if I gotta say so myself, but it didn't leave the bases any less full. And I still had to get by second baseman Ted Sizemore,

who's a crafty little hitter himself. So I walked back to the
mound, tried to block out the noise of the crowd, and
planned my attack on Sizemore.

I was a bit too careful with him. I got him to swing at
and miss a pair of curves, but I missed with three drop-
sies. So there I was with the game riding on one pitch,
and my old reliable greaser wasn't working for me. Bubba
called for another curve, but I shook it off. Sizemore
would have been looking for it. Bubba called for a screwball, and I shook that off. Then he called for a fastball,
which I throw maybe ten times a season, and of course I
shook that off too. There was nothing left for him to request except the greaser, and he must've thought I was
one dumb sumbitch when I accepted the sign and went
into my routine. But, like I said, I was cocky that day and
I knew I couldn't miss with four greasers in a row.

Well, ol' Sizemore was craftier than I thought. He had
guessed with me. He saw the ball floating toward his letters, but swung the bat waist-high. He got under the ball
and lifted a Texas leaguer just beyond shortstop. Gabby
ran back and Pinky ran in. But I didn't trust either of
them. So I ran off the mound and out into the outfield. As
the ball dropped, I dived to the turf. The ball bounced in
and out of Pinky's glove, in and out of Gabby's glove, and
fell into my glove, which was resting on the grass.

My teammates quickly surrounded me. The fans were
damn near hysterical. The Dudes' winning streak was at
seven and I was 10 and 1.

I ran into the clubhouse and stripped down to my bare
essentials. But I didn't duck right into the showers. 'Stead,
I stood in front of my locker enjoying a beer and savoring
my superb performance. I expected Augie and Melinda to
come into the clubhouse to congratulate me. And I
wanted the lady to get another glimpse of what I was
keeping from her, make her want it all the more.

Skip opened the door for the chipmunks and they all
scampered over and started shooting questions my way. I
answered without much thought and all the while looked

over their shoulders at the door, awaiting Melinda's entrance.

After a few minutes, Augie walked in with his rug on his head and a smile on his chubby face. But, much to my dismay, he was by himself. He walked toward my locker, and the chipmunks spread apart to let him get to me.

"You were beautiful, son," he said, shaking my hand. "Miss Towers thought so too."

"Isn't she gonna come over and tell me herself?" I said.

"No," Augie said. "She didn't see the need to bother you."

Bother me? I thought to myself. This time I wanted to be bothered. I was counting on seeing her there so that I could arrange to see her over the weekend. Now she'd be tied up with Augie and I wouldn't even be able to get her on the phone without getting the old man's approval first.

I had to see her before she left the ball park. Without even showering a considerable sweat off my body, I pulled on my civvies. The reporters were still grilling me, but I pushed my way by them and ran out of the clubhouse. I ran down the corridor, out the players' entrance, pushed through the autograph seekers, and sprinted to the parking lot. But I was too late. Augie's Mercedes was already gone.

I stood there disgusted with myself for acting so standoffish with Melinda in the afternoon and not arranging another date right then.

"You're a fool, Gather Morse," I said to myself. "And you smell terrible."

As I hurried on home, anxious to get my butt in the shower, my mind was busy plotting and planning. There were only five days left until the trade deadline, and in that time I still had to convince Melinda that she wanted me, arrange for Augie to discover our affair, and leave the old man with enough time to deal me to another team. I knew I couldn't pretend to be a laid-back dude any longer. I had to start moving in for the kill.

I walked into my apartment and headed straight for the shower, peeling off my clothes along the way. Just as I reached in to turn on the water, my doorbell rang. I wasn't expecting anybody. And no one I knew would just drop by at eleven on a Friday night. I went to the door, making a pit stop along the way to pull on some jeans.

I opened the door and found myself eyeball to eyeball with this freckled, red-headed six foot or more foul-pole of a lady I had never seen before.

"Hi, Gather," she said. "I'm the Stick." Even though I didn't know her, I could've told her that she was the Stick. If she stood sideways I wouldn't have even seen her.

"Am I supposed to know you?" I said.

"I'm a friend of Johnny's," she said.

"Johnny?"

"Yeah, Johnny Bench. And Rusty Staub and the Bird and Reggie, too."

'Course, I understood what the young lady, who had to still be in her teens, was telling me. She was what Gabby called part of the office pool and what you would probably know as a baseball bimbo or groupie. Lot of the guys preferred messing around with bimbos, since they made things so easy—with them you didn't have to buy drinks or dinner or deliver your standard lines. And, what's more, you didn't have to worry about them calling your house after you made the plunge. Ladies like that just wanted to add you to their collection, like you're a stamp or something, and soon as they had you, they stopped thinking about you and let you sit in the drawer with your corners curling. Me, I usually avoided the office pool myself. I figured that anyone who just wanted to collect me could go out and buy my Topps trading card.

"Sorry, sweetie," I said. "I'm not interested." I started to close the door, but her long leg got in the way.

"Oh, please, Gather," she said in a very nasal voice. "I saw your picture in the paper and knew I just had to have your buns. I hitched in today all the way from Detroit just to see you, and followed you home from the ball park.

We gotta do it now, 'cause I gotta head home. I got school on Monday."

Lady sure had gone to a lot of trouble just to see me. I felt ungrateful turning her down. But I wasn't in the mood. What's a man supposed to do in a situation like that anyway? It was so much easier back in the days when the guy had to do the asking.

"Sorry, I can't help you," I said, and I closed the door and headed back for my shower. The Stick wouldn't give up. She started pounding away on my door. That made me angry. I walked back and flung the door open. And there she was standing with her blouse in her hand, and all my neighbors were hanging out of their doors looking at her freckled skin.

I took her hand and dragged her into my apartment. I knew the only way I was gonna get rid of her was if I gave her a souvenir. So I dragged her right on into the bedroom.

"You sure are a tall thing," I said as I lay on the bed watching her slip out of the rest of her clothes.

"Yeah," she said. "All throat."

Well, she sure was a lot of throat. Unfortunately, she was a lot of teeth too, which irritated Fellini, all right. She was so frail that I was worried I'd crush her, and so long that my lips couldn't reach hers when I was inside her. All in all, it was not one of your more memorable experiences.

But I managed to enjoy myself by pulling the old hidden-ball trick. While she concentrated on me, I kept my eyes closed and concentrated on another little experience I had hidden away in my mind.

As I rubbed my palms on the Stick's thimble-sized breasts and circled her penny nipples with my tongue, I imagined that I was working my best stuff on Melinda's ripe, tender melons. And as the Stick stroked me, I pictured Melinda's soft blond hair and her thin, gentle lips against my skin. Imagining Melinda was even better than I imagined.

It was as if the Stick wasn't there at all. Fact is, it wasn't much different from masturbating. The Stick was nothing more than a pinch hitter for my own hands. I don't think she knew or cared what I was thinking. Soon as we were through, she thanked me and started to pull her clothes back on. Before slipping into her white panties, she took out a magic marker and asked me to autograph them in the crotch. When I balked, she reached into her pocketbook and pulled out a half dozen similar pairs, all of which were autographed by some of the best-known major-leaguers. Lady did all right, despite her shortcomings. I guess with her you'd have to call them longcomings. She was like a .180 hitter who made a spot for herself on the all-star team. Anyway, she left quickly without my even having to ask her to, which I was thankful for.

I spent the rest of the night rolling around in my bed, looking for a comfortable position, but found none. I was anxious for the morning to arrive so that I could revive my pursuit of Melinda.

As soon as the first daylight sneaked in through my bedroom window on Saturday, I pulled on some civvies, drank some orange juice out of the container, and headed up to Augie's mansion in the Northwest corner of town. The sky over Washington was charcoal gray, which intensified my own dreary, frantic mood. I drove through the streets that are lined with fat trees and are without sidewalks in the wealthy section of town where Augie lived, and parked a block away from his property, where I had a view of his driveway. I sat there among the houses of all different architectural styles, houses that have nothing but great size and hefty mortgages in common, and waited for Augie and Melinda to appear.

My hope was that they would go out somewhere together that gray spring morning—shopping, for lunch, anywhere, I didn't care. I would then follow them at a distance, wait for Augie to leave Melinda's side for even a moment, then make my presence known to her and arrange a secret meeting between us.

At noon, I'd already been sitting and waiting for five hours and they had not appeared. I felt a little like Kojak staking out a house. My stomach was growling and I wished I had some flunky around to send out for sandwiches and coffee like Kojak always has. I even started hoping that the Good Humor man would come ringing his bell up the street, a thought I hadn't had since I was a little bugger.

I was about ready to start chewing on my leather-covered steering wheel when Augie's Mercedes rolled out of his driveway and headed away from me up the block. I could see Melinda's shiny blond hair hanging over the passenger's seat, so I trailed the car at a distance.

Augie drove just across the Maryland border into Chevy Chase, the area where the swanky ladies shop on those days they are not shopping in Georgetown. He pulled into a parking lot and took Melinda into one of those Hamburger Hamlet places for lunch. My stomach begged me to follow them inside. But I didn't think that that was the best strategy. I needed to get to her when she was alone. I still didn't want Augie to know that I was after his lady.

I did leave my car long enough to buy a few slices of pizza at a takeout place, then returned to my car to eat and wait. After about an hour, Augie and Melinda came out of the restaurant and walked across the street into Lord & Taylor, where I did follow them. I trailed them into the dress department, the shoe department, the lingerie department, the perfume department, always hiding out behind racks of clothes or around corners. I tell you the man bought the lady enough clothes to outfit all three of Charlie's Angels and the Bionic Woman. And he didn't leave her side for a second, not even to take a leak. Guy had great bladder control for someone his age. He said Melinda made him younger, and I was starting to believe him.

They left the store, each carrying boxes and bags in their hands and under their arms. They got back in the car and drove right on back to Augie's place. Man, was I disgusted. I'd wasted my entire Saturday afternoon chasing them around like an idiot, and the lady didn't even know I was in the vicinity. I had no choice but to go home and try to find a way to talk with her at the game that evening.

During the game, I sat out in the bullpen wondering what I would do if Melinda did not visit the clubhouse. I was getting so desperate I even considered kidnapping her.

It was a nasty, drizzly night and there weren't too many people in the stands, which was too bad, since both teams put on a good show. The weather made it difficult for the pitchers to get a good grip on the ball, and so the hitters on both clubs—and that includes ours—got on base with as little difficulty as it takes to get on a bus. The two starting pitchers were both in the showers before the first inning ended, and they were soon joined by their immediate successors. By the third inning, the score was already 7–7 and it was developing into the kind of slugfest fans love to see. One of the stranger things about baseball is that we pitchers get paid to keep the score low, but the fans who pay our salaries would rather see a high-scoring contest anytime. It's as if they come out to see us fail. I remember after the Reds and Red Sox finished that exciting 1975 World Series—best Series I've ever seen—Gus, my dry cleaner, said to me that all you need for a great Series is two teams with lousy pitching. I bet most fans would agree. Fact is, the fans would like baseball better if they got rid of pitchers all together and used the iron mike during games.

While the fans thrived on the high-scoring action that evening, the guys out in the bullpen with me ignored it, as usual. They were emotionally involved in a good game of "Thigh Spy." They took turns playing navigator, standing at the bullpen fence with a pair of high-powered binoculars that belonged to our pitching coach, Puff Sweet, and combed the stands in search of exposed beavers. Soon as the navigator spotted one, everyone else ran over to take a peek. That particular game of "Thigh Spy" was continually interrupted by the phone ringing to give Puff orders to get another pitcher up and throwing, which didn't please the relievers at all.

In the fourth inning, Sticky Thomas was the navigator, and he shouted, "Hey, where's the old man's bitch tonight?"

"She's gotta be there next to him," I said. "Maybe she left her seat for a few minutes."

"Uh-uh," Sticky said. "Every seat in the box is filled, and her tight little ass ain't in any one of them."

"Give me those," I said, grabbing the binoculars. Sure enough, all five seats around Augie were filled with men, none of whom could be mistaken for Melinda.

I handed the field glasses back to Sticky. I had to get to a phone. I turned to Puff and said, "Hey, coach, you think I'm running a fever?"

"Why, ain't you feeling good?" he asked.

"Nah, I'm awfully chilly and I feel kind of flushed. I think I oughta be in bed."

"Well, I'll tell you, Gather," Puff said, spitting out a mouthful of sunflower-seed shells, "I'm already on my fourth pitcher and we ain't even gone halfway. I might have to call on you as a last resort."

"Ah, come on, Puff," I said. "I threw nine innings yesterday. You still got five guys left out here. It would be a major emergency if you had to use me."

"Well," he said. "Never can tell about those things. Crazy game, this baseball is. Why don't you go into the clubhouse and get yourself warm, and if I need you, I'll know where to find you."

"Good idea, Puff," I said. And I headed under the stands to the clubhouse. I stopped at the pay phone just outside the clubhouse door and dialed Augie's home number. Melinda answered.

"Why aren't you here?" I asked.

"I didn't want to sit outside in the rain," she said.

"What are you doing?"

"Drinking some wine. Listening to some music."

The setup was too perfect for me to resist. "I'll be right over," I said, and I hung up.

While I speeded crosstown in my Stingray, I kept track of the ball game on my radio. Balls just kept dropping into empty spaces like they had eyes. And in the top of the sixth, when I was ringing Augie's doorbell, the score was already 11–11.

"I can't believe you," Melinda said, standing at the door in a green oriental-type dressing gown.

"What can't you believe?" I said.

"Your team's in the middle of a big game, and you're here."

"I pitched yesterday," I said. "Today's my day of rest. And besides, I'd rather be with you anytime."

I could tell she was amused and flattered. "You're a crazy man, Gather Morse," she said. "Come on in."

She went into the kitchen to fetch another wineglass, and I switched the radio from music to our game. It was a convenient situation. Not only was I alone with Melinda, but I could also keep tabs on when Augie would be leaving the ball park and heading to where we were.

She came back into the living room, poured me some red wine, and we lay down opposite each other on the August-auburn carpet, the same damn rug we had in the clubhouse. Augie must have got himself a bargain on the stuff.

"You're not only a romantic," Melinda said to me as we clinked glasses, "but you also have a real sense of adventure, coming into this house like this."

"You have a sense of adventure too," I said. "You let me in."

We both laughed, naughty-type laughs, and we sipped at our wine. The lights were low, and so were our voices. The wine was full-bodied, and so was Melinda. It was a real romantic setting, except of course for the ball game on the radio. But that just sort of reminded us of the suspense and intrigue surrounding us. We were bad little kids making mischief behind Daddy's back. And that turned us both on.

"I had a nice time with you yesterday," I said. "You're very mysterious and I like that."

She pulled her sleeve across her face like one of those Arabian-type princesses. "I'm so mysterious," she said in a deep voice. "No one knows what danger lurks behind my veil."

I pulled that there veil away from her face and put my lips where it was. We did a little gentle, friendly-type kissing for a warm-up, then got into the heavy stuff. She rolled on top of me and rubbed every inch of her body against every inch of mine. If we were wood, we would have started a fire. As it was, the temperature in the room shot way up.

I kept my hands on the carpet and let her make all the moves. This one was on her, as they say. She rolled off me and reached for my fly. But before she could unzip it and find the big fella, I turned away from her.

"What's the matter?" she said. "Are you shy all of a sudden?"

"Not shy," I said. "Just cautious."

"Don't worry," she said. "I'm on the pill."

"That's not what I'm cautious about," I said.

"What is it, then?" she asked, and her face was confused.

I knew I had her set up perfectly. She was ready for the kill. "I like you, Melinda," I said.

"Well, that's encouraging," she said.

"No, I mean, I could like you a lot. A real lot. And I'm afraid I could get hurt."

"That's a woman's line, not a man's," she said. "I'll bet you're the first jock who ever used that one on a lady."

She might have been calling my bluff, but I didn't let on. I took to the defensive approach. "Well, that's how I feel," I said. "If you don't believe me, there's nothing I can do about it."

She went along with my act. "I wasn't doubting you, Gather," she said. "I'm sorry. But how can I hurt you?"

"Well, here I am liking you and on the verge of risking liking you even more. Meanwhile, you're living here in a house with another man. You're sleeping in his bed."

She looked away from me and sighed. "I am," she said. "But he's not."

"Don't bullshit me," I said.

"He's not. Really," she said. "I sleep in the master bedroom in the tower in front of the house, and Augie sleeps in a guest room in the back."

"Are you trying to tell me that the old man has someone fine as you in this house and he doesn't even take advantage of the convenience?"

"I'm sure he'd like to," she said. "But he can't."

I thought I understood what she was telling me, but I wasn't sure. I didn't know what to say, so I said nothing.

"Augie can't fuck," Melinda said.

"That's surprising," I said. "He sure fucked me plenty."

She didn't respond to that. I guess the remark was in poor taste at that moment.

I'd said many times that the old man was no man at all, but I never really meant it. You never like to think that kind of thing about anyone. It made me a little sad to hear it about Augie.

We both lay on our backs on the carpet looking up at the wood beam ceiling. The only noise in the room was the radio, but I didn't pay attention to it.

"Does the setup here bother you?" I asked softly.

She laughed, a sad laugh. "It's funny," she said. "I spent most of my life with men who fucked me but wouldn't love me. Now I'm with someone who loves me but can't fuck me. Oh, it's much better this way. I didn't know that when I was younger, but I know it now. Yeah, it's better this way. But it's still not perfect. It's also not permanent."

"Does the old man know that?" I asked.

She sighed again. "I've told him, kind of. He's really like a father to me, which I like and I think he likes. But little girls don't stay home forever."

"You might have told him," I said. "But I doubt that he heard."

"You sound concerned for him," she said behind a sly little smile.

I guess I did sound that way, too. I still hated him and wanted out. But I could sympathize with his situation—being in love with a lady who thought of him only as her father. That's a situation I sure wouldn't fancy myself.

"Don't worry about Augie," she said. "He's a big boy. Now, let's see how big you are."

"I better check the score first," I said.

"The score!" she blurted.

"Shhh! I just want to make sure that Augie's not gonna walk in on us. That's all."

We lay there silently as Mushmouth Jones, the Dudes' radio announcer, filled us in on the doings at RFK. "So the Dudes will take an eighteen-to-seventeen lead into the ninth inning," Mushmouth said. "And we're gonna see Bert Smith come on to pitch. He's the only man skipper Jack Shaw's got left besides Gather Morse, who went nine innings yesterday."

"Holy shit," I shrieked.

"What's the matter?" Melinda asked.

"Did you hear that? I'm the only pitcher left. If Smith gets in trouble, I gotta go in."

"It's a long walk from here to the mound."

"Hey, this isn't funny, Melinda," I said.

She started in kissing my neck, but I pushed her away. "Stop it," I said. "I gotta listen."

"What are you, a fag?" she said. And she had this angry look in her eyes. Well, I couldn't stand for that kind of talk. So I grabbed her waist and rolled over on top of her. I kissed her furiously and pulled off her dressing gown. As I undressed her, she undressed me. We were like two kids in a hurry to fuck before the parents got home.

"Oh, there's my old friend," she said as she pulled my pants off. She lay on her back and I sat over her waist. She took Fellini in her hands and started rolling him softly between her palms. I reached my hand down behind my back and between her legs.

She played with me and I played with her and I also tried to keep an ear tuned to the play-by-play of the game.

Larry Bowa hit a single and Melinda started moving her hips up and down. The fans were cheering and I felt like I was riding a bucking bronco. Melinda started moving faster, Mike Schmidt walked, Bert Smith fell behind on Luzinski, Melinda started moaning. It was a tense moment on all fronts.

"And here's the pitch to Luzinski," Mushmouth said.

There was a brief silence in the room and on the radio. Melinda froze. I froze. I heard the crack of the bat. Then, all at once, Melinda let out a cry of pleasure, I started writhing and leaving a deposit all over her breasts, and Mushmouth was screaming, "Gabby Smith bobbled the ball. All hands are safe. The bases are loaded."

"Oh, God," Melinda said.

"Oh, shit," I said.

"Manager Jack Shaw's walking out to the mound," Mushmouth said.

"Oh, Gather Morse," Melinda said.

"We're going to see Gather Morse," Mushmouth said.

"Going to see Gather Morse," I shrieked.

I jumped up off Melinda and started pulling on my clothes.

"What's going on?" Melinda said.

"Hurry, Melinda, call an ambulance," I said.

"An ambulance? What's wrong, Gather?"

"Nothing's wrong. I gotta go in the game. Hurry. Call the fucking ambulance."

Melinda jumped up and ran to the phone. I finished pulling my clothes on.

"It's on the way," she said.

"Oh, it better get here fast," I said.

"When will I see you again?" she said.

"Later, soon, sometime. I don't know, Melinda."

I started to run out the door.

"Hold it," she said. She ran to me. "Kiss me," she said.

I kissed her and flew out the door, zipping up my fly along the way. The ambulance pulled up in front of the house. A young guy in a white coat got out. "Get back in there," I said.

"Hey, you're Gather Morse," he said. "I saw you—"

"Never mind," I said. "Get me to the stadium. Fast."

I jumped in the back of the ambulance. The driver turned on the siren and tore ass out of there. Along the way, as we wove around cars and went the wrong way up one-way streets, I explained my predicament as best I could. The driver had a good sense of humor and was a diehard Dudes fan. He was glad to help me.

As the ambulance raced down Massachusetts Avenue, I undressed in the back. I still had to pull on my uniform, and by undressing there I saved some time. We arrived at the stadium, usually a twenty-minute trip, in about seven minutes. I directed the driver down the driveway and through the garage door beside the players' entrance. I jumped out of the back, thanked the driver and ran down the hall, naked, toward the clubhouse.

I pulled on my uniform without putting on any underwear. Then I ran down the tunnel to the dugout, buttoning my shirt along the way. When I got there, I saw that Chi Chi was out on the mound taking some warm-ups.

"What the fuck is he doing out there?" I shouted. "Get a pitcher in there."

"Morse," Skip shouted. "Puff said you went home sick."

"I did, but I'm back," I said. "Put me in there, Skip."

"Morse, I love you," Skip said, and he trotted out to the mound.

In the excitement, Skip had forgotten the rules. But the ump came out and told him that Chi Chi had to throw one pitch before he was taken out.

Skip trotted back to the dugout. "I have to let him throw one pitch," Skip said.

"Did you tell him to throw a pitch that can't be hit?" I asked.

"Shit, I forgot," Skip said.

We were in trouble. Well, everyone in the dugout stood up, climbed to the top step, and started yelling at Chi Chi. "Throw it way outside, Chi Chi." "Don't let him hit it, Chi Chi." "Roll it to him, Chi Chi."

Chi Chi looked at us. His face was swollen with confusion. We were all yelling different things and he didn't understand a word we said.

Richie Hebner, the Phillies' first baseman, stepped in. Chi Chi went into his imitation of a pitcher's windup and delivered. As the pitch traveled to the plate, we all held our breaths. All of us except Hebner, that is. The ball was coming right at his strength and must have looked like a grapefruit to him. He lashed at it and sent it into the cheap seats in centerfield. As four Phillies trotted nonchalantly around the bases, all the guys in our dugout collapsed onto the bench.

We were behind 21–18 now, so Skip didn't bother to put me in. We didn't score in our half of the inning and our winning streak was snapped. It was all my fault.

Well, I figured I broke even that afternoon. I had let down my team, but I had helped myself with Melinda. I had teased her, taunted her, given her a little taste of my medicine, but saved some of my best stuff. Running out on her, suddenly like that, was good strategy. Now she would be dying for more.

In bed by myself Saturday night, I dreamed up a clutch play. The clincher. It was the oldest trick in the game between the sexes—the old jealousy play—but I had a feeling it would work. Melinda was all set up for it. And if it didn't work, I still had three days left to think of something else.

Sunday morning I called up Mary Zachary, my stew friend and some of the most mouth-watering dressing that ever sat beside any turkey. I woke her up, but I made it sound urgent. I asked her to accompany me to the game that afternoon and then to dinner. Fortunately, she wasn't flying and was happy to tag along.

She sat in the wives' section behind home plate as we beat the Phillies 3–1 to start a new winning streak. From the dugout, I could see all the guys' wives staring her down, wondering who she belonged to, hoping it wasn't their husbands. That wives' section is a mean place to watch a game if you're not one of them. Those ladies give intruders stares that could freeze the Potomac. But Mary was used to that kind of treatment. She was the kind of fox that men hated to love and ladies loved to hate.

Anyway, for my plan to be effective, Melinda had to catch me and Mary together. But that wasn't too difficult to arrange. Soon as the game ended, I ran from the bullpen to the clubhouse, so that by the time Augie came in to congratulate his boys, I was dressed and ready to split.

I left the clubhouse at the same time as Augie. He went to fetch Melinda and I met Mary at the players' entrance. We walked over to my Stingray but didn't get in. Augie's car was beside mine, and I knew in a matter of minutes he and Melinda would be where they couldn't help but see me and Mary.

"I just have to wait here for a friend," I told Mary, and we stood leaning against my car and talking.

Wasn't more than a few minutes when the old man and Melinda approached his Mercedes hand-in-hand. Soon as I saw them, I leaned off my car, moved in front of Mary, pressed against her, and started kissing her with vigor. I acted as passionate as I could with my eyes still open.

Augie was the first one to spot me like that. And then Melinda spotted me too. I could tell she didn't take kindly to what she was witnessing. And when I winked at her, she got in Augie's car and slammed the door so hard I thought it was gonna fall off. It was all working just like I had planned.

Well, when Augie pulled away, me and Mary got in my car and headed downtown. I asked her to feel my head and tell me if it seemed warm to her. It didn't, but I insisted I had some disease coming on.

"Oh, Gather," she said. "I hope you're all right. I read where you got sick at yesterday's game. You gotta take care of yourself."

"I guess I ain't fully recovered from yesterday," I said. "Will you be angry if we skip dinner?"

"I can have my dinner right here," she said.

I looked into her green eyes, which were visibly hungry, but not for food. I pulled off Massachusetts Avenue onto a side street in the rundown part of town. I didn't see anybody on the block. "Hurry up," I said, "before we have an audience."

"Thanks, Gather," Mary said. I slid over away from the steering wheel. She unzipped my fly, reached her tiny hand inside, and took Fellini out.

"All right," she said. "Outtasight." And the big fella wasn't even hard yet.

'Course, Mary had him that way real quick. She massaged my cubes gently with her fingertips and explored every inch of Fellini with her tongue. Lady sure knew what head was all about. Never did a tooth touch my soft skin. She was all tongue and cheek, which is the way I like it to be.

As she ate, I tried to keep my eyes on the street to make sure no one saw us. But the vibrations that started in Fellini ran through my whole body and removed my attention from anything but myself. I leaned my head back on the seat, closed my eyes, rubbed my fingers through Mary's hair, and enjoyed the alternating chills and warmth, the tingling sensation that was covering my body like a blanket. She felt my excitement increasing and, like the old pro she is, froze her head at the exact right moment, held it steady as a statue as Fellini erupted like a geyser in her mouth.

Fellini stopped, started again, stopped, started, stopped again. Mary lifted up her head and tucked it in against my neck, kissing me softly. I opened my eyes to look at her. As I did, I heard clapping. I looked beyond her blond head and saw a dozen young black folks standing with their noses pressed against my car window, clapping and slapping their hands.

"Let's get out of here," I said. I tucked Fellini back inside my drawers and headed for Mary's place, where I left her.

Sweet girl, that Mary. Gonna miss her now. But that evening, I promised her a rain check and raced back home alone. I had this funny feeling that I was gonna receive a frantic phone call from another lady, one who was hurt and jealous.

Well, I was wrong about that one. Never did get that call. But what I did get was better.

About nine o'clock, my doorbell started ringing, I answered it, and sure enough, it was Melinda Towers in the flesh. She was not put together as carefully as usual. Her blond hair was disheveled, she wore no makeup, and her face was worried, like she expected to walk in and find something that she didn't want to see.

"Are you alone?" she said.

"Was before you got here," I said. "Come on in."

Lady didn't just walk in, she flew in. Flung her arms around my neck, tucked her head against my shoulder, and started sobbing like a newborn child. "Oh, Gather," she said, sniffing to keep her nose from running down my shirt. "I'm sorry I came here like this. But I just had to see you."

"Just calm down, you sweet little thing," I said, patting her on the head. "I'm glad you came."

Hearing that, she stepped back, and the worry disappeared from her eyes. "Are you really?" she said.

I just smiled and shook my head.

"Oh, I'm so glad, Gather," she said. "I know it's crazy, but when I saw you with that woman in the parking lot, I felt this hollow pit in my stomach. I mean, there I was going home with this man I didn't desire, and the man I did desire was with another woman."

Well, folks, it was as if I had written the script myself, which I guess you could say I had done. It seemed so strange, though, working out that way, since all my previous plans had backfired on me. It was as if I was this lousy Little League pitcher who woke up one day with Koufax's curve ball. I tried to disguise my jubilation the best I could.

"Melinda, honey," I said. "You know how much I want you. But I can't sit around waiting until you have time to see me. You're usually busy with someone else."

She sighed, stood there doing some deep-type thinking for a minute or two. "Can we sit down?" she said.

We walked to the couch and sat with some space between us. I could see she was struggling with herself. But finally she said, "Gather, do you really want me? I mean, really."

"Well, I think I do," I said.

"That's good enough, then," she said. "Because I think I want you too. I can't explain it, it's just this feeling I have that we can be right for each other. There's no explanation for these things. It's just . . . It's just . . ."

"Passion?" I said.

"Oh, yeah, Gather. That's what it is. You always know just how to put things." She sat there thinking some more. Slowly, her troubled face grew determined. "Gather, I'm going back to Augie's—in fact, I should hurry. He thinks I went for milk—but I'm going back there and telling Augie that I'm leaving him."

"Are you sure you want to do this?" I said, and immediately regretted saying it.

"Oh, yes, yes, I'm sure," she said. "I think I'm sure."

"Well, sure," I said.

She looked down at her hands. "Look at me. I'm shaking," she said. "The big, tough lady is shaking."

I took her hands in mine, pulled her to me, and squeezed her tight. At that moment, I tell you, I loved her for what she was going to do. I didn't consider what it all meant, but a good pitcher doesn't plan too far ahead. He just concentrates on one pitch at a time.

She got up to leave, and I kissed her softly. "What should I do?" I said.

"Nothing. Just wait," she said. "I have to take care of this my way. I'll talk to you as soon as I can."

I kissed her through the door, closed it, counted to fifty to give her time to get away, then let out a war whoop so loud that I must've awakened all my neighbors.

"You're a fucking genius, Gather Morse," I said to myself. I paced around my apartment nervously, not even conscious of where I was walking. If all went well, my freedom was just a day away. What could I do to make sure it happens? Nothing. There was nothing I could do but wait. I'd waited this long, I could wait another day. No, I couldn't. But I had to.

I went into my bedroom, pulled out eleven T-shirts, and drew a logo of a National League team—every one but the Dudes and Reds—on each shirt. Then I stood in front of the bathroom mirror and tried them on one at a time. They all looked good to me.

"Gather Morse, you did it," I said to myself when I was wearing the eleventh shirt with "Dodgers" written across the chest. Then all of a sudden, my excitement disappeared. I looked into my own brown eyes and asked myself, "What the hell are you going to do with Melinda?"

10

Okay.

I know.

You don't have to tell me.

You're sitting there right now listening to me complain about Augie and defend myself, and you're thinking this Gather Morse character is nothing but a nasty, rotten, no-good sumbitch himself. He's as evil and conniving as the next guy, playing with that nice lady's feelings like that.

Well, you're absolutely right. And the reason you don't have to tell me about it is that that's exactly the way I was feeling about myself that there Sunday night.

I admit it. I was using Melinda Towers to help me get what I wanted, with no concern for what she wanted. I was leading her down a blind path in the woods and intending to leave her there, lost, by herself. I was making her promises that I was not about to keep. Fact is, I wasn't treating her any better than Augie August had treated me. It was as if I was an owner and she was my ballplayer. She existed only to help me to get the success I desired, and once that was achieved, I could discard her at my whim.

The only difference between me and a major-league owner was that I knew I was doing wrong by my player and felt guilty about it. Augie August didn't know that guilt existed. It was another one of those terms, along with reliability, trust, and renegotiation, that never got past the bouncer guarding the door to his mind. Oh, sure, sometimes he pretended to be plagued by his cruelty, like that time in his office when he apologized for hurting me and begged me to sign a new contract. But he was just spitting wooden nickels. His guilt was counterfeit, just another one of his manipulative con games. To feel guilt, you have to have some concept of right and wrong, and Augie didn't. I take that back. He did. Everything he did was right, and everything anyone else did was wrong.

Well, I sure hope that that's not the way I am. If the only way to succeed is at other people's expense, then success is not of any value to me.

So I didn't like myself that night after Melinda had confessed some genuine feelings to me and I'd spit my own wooden nickels back at her. Near as I was to accomplishing my goal, I felt like pulling the plug on my plan. I felt like calling her up and telling her that I only wanted her because having her would get me traded.

I sat up by myself in the living room in the middle of the night, sipping at a beer and thinking: How can you hurt a sweet girl like that? She doesn't mean to hurt anyone. She doesn't want anything more than to be loved—in all ways—which isn't an unfair request in my book. Sure, she's journeyed from man to man, which isn't something you tell Mom about, but it was always in search of the same things. And you can't blame her for traveling on when she couldn't find them.

Lot of guys wouldn't accept her with her background. Guys spend their young life chasing after the veteran girls, then expect the one they marry to be a rookie. But not me. I was realistic about that. I didn't expect any ladies to be saving it for me. How's anyone supposed to know if they like Chinese food unless they try it?

'Course, I was just another guy from column A that Melinda wanted to try. But I know what she meant about those feelings you can't explain. I'd had those feelings myself for Bernadine.

Melinda wasn't just suggesting another roll in the hay like most of the ladies I met up with. She was offering to care for me and asking to be cared for back. That wasn't a request I heard too often, and it kind of touched me at that point in my life. Still touches me today, thinking about it. Everyone you meet claims they're looking for a relationship, but with most people it only lasts from dinner until breakfast. It just ain't laid back and cool enough these days to admit you have feelings for someone. I never even hear the guys on the club admit they have feelings for their own wives. Only time they mention them is when they say, "My old lady'll kill me." Sounds like they're in prison, not in love.

As the sun came up Monday morning, I was still sitting in my living room thinking, and I realized that something was happening to me that wasn't in my plan. I thought about looking in Melinda's worried little eyes when she was at my place. And holding her close to me. And smelling her hair. And touching her soft skin. My heart was pounding away and I had a shit eating grin on my puss. I felt better than I'd felt in a long time. I knew then that that lady meant something to me. I wanted her. I could feel it in my body. I'd gone out looking to be traded, and I'd found passion along the way.

I sat in my apartment all day Monday with the tube on and the paper on my lap, anxious for Melinda to call. By the afternoon, I couldn't wait any longer, so I called Augie's house myself. There was no answer.

I was a little worried that the old man had snowed her like he had done to me so many times, convinced her that she wanted to do what he wanted her to do. I dialed Augie's number again and again, but never got an answer. I tried not to panic. We were opening a three-game set with the Pirates that evening and I just hoped that Melinda would be at the game.

Our clubhouse was buzzing with excitement when I arrived at around 5:30. We were about to begin the most important series the Dudes had ever played. Actually, it was the only important series the Dudes had ever played. The Pirates were two games up on us in the loss column, and if we could win all three games, we'd move into first place. Gus—you know, my dry cleaner—he said that our being in first would just mean that the whole division stunk. But that didn't matter to our guys. You could feel the pressure in the room. Most of the folks were tight but pretending to be loose, which is the opposite of most ladies I know.

Chi Chi sat on the stool in front of his locker with his head bowed. "Why aren't you dancing?" Pinky asked him.

"No time," Chi Chi said. "I want to get full meaning of game, you know."

The Smiths were sitting around the domino table as usual, but none of them were concentrating on the game. As I walked by I noticed a lot of four-dot squares lined up next to five-dot squares, and no one pointed it out.

Bubba stood at his locker with one end of a bat resting on his stool and the other end resting on my stool. He was trying to break the stick with a karate chop. I went to pull my stool away, but Bubba grabbed me. "Don't do that," he said. "I ain't tough enough yet."

The tension in the room matched my personal mood. But it wasn't the upcoming game that was making my palms sweaty. All that the other guys were concerned with was first place, but my whole future was on the line. At least their fate was in their own gloves. But me, I was dependent on Melinda coming through.

Before the game, I ran my wind sprints with the other pitchers in the outfield. I kept an eye on Augie's box, waiting for the old man and Melinda to arrive.

At game time they still had not shown. I walked into the bullpen with the rest of the staff and volunteered to be the first navigator in the evening's game of "Thigh Spy." I grabbed the binoculars and stood at the fence with the lenses focused on Augie's box. His seats were still empty when we took the field and during the National Anthem and when Frank Taveras, the leadoff hitter, stepped up for the Pirates. I couldn't imagine where the old man was. He hadn't missed a home game in the four years he owned the club.

After Taveras popped up to Chi Chi in center, Phil Garner stepped up, and Cynthia, Augie's secretary, and her husband took the two empty seats in the old man's box. Now I knew I was in trouble. Augie wasn't showing up tonight. I had to find out where he was and where Melinda was. Cynthia would know. She always knew his schedule. I needed an excuse to get out of the bullpen and onto the field, where I could talk with her.

"Hey, Puff," I called to our pitching coach. "Catch me, will ya? I wanna see how the arm feels."

"Later, Gather," Puff said. "I wanna see how Layton's throwing tonight."

"Gotta do it now while I'm still warm from my sprints," I said. "Later it'll be chilly and I might pull something."

Puff reluctantly grabbed a catcher's mitt and stood with his back to the fence. I walked to the back of the bullpen and threw at him. I tossed my first ball high. He had to reach over his head to catch it. I threw the next one higher, and he just managed to knock it down. My third toss sailed over Puff's head, over the fence, and into foul territory outside first base.

"I'll retrieve it," I said. And I hopped the fence and ran toward the ball. I didn't glance at the game. My attention was focused on getting to Cynthia.

Just as I reached the ball, Garner popped up into foul territory outside first base. Aurelio Smith had a beat on the pop. His eyes were in the air, watching the ball descend. My eyes were on Cynthia. We banged into each other and both fell to the ground. So did the foul ball.

"You fucker," Aurelio shouted. "What are you doing here? You cost us an out."

"I had to retrieve the ball," I said.

The fans were booing as Aurelio walked back to his position. I picked up the bullpen ball. The ump called time out and waited for me to get off the field. But I wasn't ready to leave. I walked over to Augie's box, leaned over the fence, and spoke to Cynthia.

"Cynthia, where's Augie?" I said.

"Hey, Morse, get off the field," the ump yelled.

"Cynthia, I gotta see Augie. Where is he?" I said.

Skip was standing in the corner of the dugout shouting at me to get off the field. But I ignored him. I was frantic. I grabbed Cynthia's arm and started to shake her. "Where is he? Where is he?" I demanded. The fans were booing me. The plate ump and the first base ump walked toward me.

"He's out of town," Cynthia said.

"Out of town?" I shrieked. "Where?"

"I don't know. He's away for the week."

"The week? That no-good motherfucker. I gotta see him. Where is he? Where is he?"

I was shaking the poor little lady. Her husband got furious and pushed me away. Skip sent Bubba and Aurelio over, and they grabbed me and started dragging me off the field. I was kicking and screaming. "Where is he? Where is the sumbitch?" I shouted.

Three more of my teammates ran out and grabbed me. I kept yelling like a madman. The crowd kept booing. I was carried into the dugout, down the runway, and into the clubhouse. The guys tossed me in there like I was a sack of potatoes, then slammed the steel door behind me.

I sat on the floor of the empty clubhouse. I was dumbfounded. Augie had tricked me once again. He had disappeared for the week that included the trade deadline and had taken Melinda with him. I was so shocked that I was

numb. I couldn't move. I was still sitting there on the
floor by the door three hours later when the team came in
after scoring in the tenth, to win 4–3. I found out later
that we should have won in the ninth when Chi Chi hit a
home run with Chatsworth on first. But Chi Chi got so
excited that he ran right past the Soul Chink between second and third and one run was disallowed.

Skip was the last man through the clubhouse door. He
was hooting and hollering until he saw me sitting there on
the floor. "You all right, Gather?" he asked, bending
down to look at me.

"I guess so," I said.

He helped me up. "Come on into my office," he said,
guiding me with an arm around my shoulder. "We gotta
have ourselves a little chat."

I sat down in a chair and Skip closed the office door.
"You sure you're all right?" he asked.

"I'm all right," I said in a distant, zombie-type voice.
My eyes were glassy and I must've looked just like some
of the crazies I had seen at St. E.'s. You know, guys in a
permanent state of nowhere. Any idiot could tell I was
not all right. But not Skip.

"Well, I'm glad you're all right," he said. " 'Cause we're
right in it now, Gather. You're gonna throw for us
Wednesday night, and we need you."

I just sat there staring at nothing in particular. Skip
called in Benny the Nip and told him to help me to the
showers.

"He all right, Skip?" Benny said when he saw me.

"Sure he's all right," Skip said. "He's gotta pitch
Wednesday."

"Don't look all right," Benny said.

"He's all right," Skip said. "Aren't you, Gather?"

"I'm all right," I said.

So Benny dragged me through the clubhouse and
stopped at my locker to help me undress. I peeled my
uniform off out of habit. I wasn't conscious of what I was

doing. He's taken Melinda away, I kept thinking to myself. He's taken her away from me.

Terrorists could have raided the clubhouse and opened fire and I wouldn't have noticed. I was completely detached from my surroundings. Bubba helped Benny pull me into the showers. I dragged my feet along the ground like I'd just downed a few kegs of beer.

When the ice-cold water spread over my body, it startled me at first. Froze me back to my senses. "Holy shit," I shouted, shivering and shaking. But I got used to the cold water and stood under it for what must have been an hour, letting it massage my brain.

When I walked slowly back to my locker, everyone else was dressed and gone. I pulled on my civvies, then sat there on my stool in the empty room.

I was exhausted, mentally and physically, from my endless game of cat and mouse with Augie. This last move had drained me. I never expected it. I'd been operating on practically no sleep for nearly two weeks. And in that time my emotions had been through more peaks and valleys than a hiker in the Grand Canyon. I felt like a fighter who had gone through fourteen grueling rounds. My mind and my body couldn't function anymore. I had nothing left and knew it. But I couldn't quit yet. I had to go out for the fifteenth and hope that my instincts could carry me. I had to gut it out.

On Tuesday morning I called Cynthia at the office, told her I urgently needed to talk with Augie, and begged her to tell me where he was hiding out. She insisted she didn't know, which I didn't believe, but there was no way to force it out of her. I certainly had no idea in hell where the old man was. Could've been in hell for all I knew.

There were less than forty-eight hours left until the trade deadline, and no way that I could possibly find the old man and Melinda. My only hope was to try to force them to come back to Washington. But how?

Nasty thoughts that I don't even like to admit flowed

through my head that day. One was that if Augie had a wife and some kids, I could arrange for them to be kidnapped. Well, maybe I couldn't do that. But he didn't have any, so I didn't have to worry. Then I thought of burning his house down. Swear I did. But I'm afraid of lighting a match, so how could I play with real fire? Okay, that's just an excuse. Let's face it, I just didn't have it in me to do something that drastic.

I'd run out of plans. The man had beat me at my own game. I was a loser.

I was driving myself bananas sitting at home alone and thinking about all this. So I decided to pass the afternoon at the Circle Theater. Turned out, that was a brainstorm in itself.

You see, the dollar double feature that day was *The French Connection* and *French Connection II*. Two cop pictures, full of action, which is sometimes enough to relax my mind. Anyway, sitting alone in the dark, eerie old movie house, watching the coppers trying to bust a drug ring, I got myself a new idea. It was a nasty idea, but not as nasty as kidnapping or arson. I waited long enough to see the car-chase scene in *The French Connection*—I could watch that a hundred times—then left the theater and headed for Bernadine Green's apartment.

I didn't even know if she was still living where I had left her or if her friend Bill was still with her, but I went there to find out. I parked in front of the building and ran up the stairs to her place. I was a little hesitant, being that I wasn't a favorite in that section of town after my television interviews and being that the last time I'd seen Bernadine she was leading a rally to protest my existence. But I sucked in my gut and carried on.

I reached the fourth floor and knocked on the red apartment door. Sure enough, Bill opened it. Never imagined I'd be so glad to see that dude. He wasn't wearing a shirt and his arms looked like bricks. His eyes were glassy, like he was strung out or something, but he recognized me nonetheless.

"Hey, if it isn't the baseball bigot," he said, and he flashed a smile.

"I gotta talk to you, Bill," I said.

His face suddenly turned mean. "Bernadine ain't here," he said. "Ain't seen her in months, man. Bitch up and left me."

I got a certain pleasure out of hearing that. Certainly didn't want him to have what I couldn't. But I didn't show my true feelings. "It's you I wanna talk to," I said. "I think we can do some business together."

He let out a hearty laugh that echoed through the hallway. "Well, come on in," he said, and he stepped aside to let me pass.

There was a slim black lady in a slip standing in a doorway, but she disappeared as soon as she saw me. Dirty plates full of crumbs and bones and dirty glasses were all over the room. The couch and chairs were all ripped and the stuffing stuck out of the upholstery. Place needed a maid.

"Sit right down here," Bill said, pulling some dirty clothes off a chair and tossing them on the floor. "Now, tell me what I can do for you."

"Well, Bill," I said in a hesitant tone of voice. "How are you fixed for, uh, cocaine?"

He let out that chesty laugh again. "How am I fixed for cocaine? How am I fixed for cocaine?" He reached his hand down underneath the couch pillow he was sitting on and pulled out a plastic bag the size of a football. He tossed it on my lap. "That enough for you?" he said. "Or you be thinking you need more."

"No, no, no, no. This is fine," I said. "What's the damage on this stuff?"

"That there? Oh, I'd say about a buck and a half."

"Buck and a half? That all?"

"Yeah, hundred and fifty grand."

"Oh, golly," I said, which is something I don't think I ever said before. "Do you have a less expensive model?"

"How much you got on you, bro'?" he said.

"Well, in cash," I said, "I have about two hundred dollars. But I could write you a check."

"Check? You crazy," he said. He jumped up and swiped the bag off my lap. "Wait right here," he said, and he disappeared into the doorway where the lady in the slip was standing when I arrived.

I wasn't real comfortable sitting there in that dirty room without him. Place smelled like a window hadn't been open in a dog's age. And I fully expected, with my luck going the way it had been, that the door would fly open and the narcs would storm in to catch me in the act. That sure would've given Augie a cute new teaser ad to run before my next start. *Come see Gather Morse, the Junkball Junkie.*

Bill came back into the room and tossed me a plastic bag the size of a resin bag. Inside was a package of aluminum foil. "Two hundred," he said.

I wasn't getting much for my money, but I wasn't gonna question him. I just wanted to get out of there. I took the cash out of my pocket and put the bag in. He grabbed the money, made sure I stayed in my chair while he counted it, then showed me out. "You're gonna like that stuff," he said, standing at the door.

"Oh, it's not for me," I said, protecting my image. "It's a present."

He shook his head. "Always knew you were a sport, Morse," he said. "Later." He slammed the door and bolted it. I walked down the stairs and out of the building with my hand in my pocket clutching the bag.

When I reached the street, I looked all around me, like my head was a periscope, making sure there were no Smokeys on my trail. But it wasn't the Smokeys I should have been watching out for. Suddenly I felt this hard, sharp point sticking in my back.

"Put you hands in the air, motherfucker," this voice said.

Oh, shit, I thought to myself. I suspected that Bill had set me up. I couldn't put my hands up, or my two-

hundred-dollar stash would have vanished and my latest
plan would have failed before it began. I don't know
where I got the courage, but I spun around quickly on
one foot and planted my other foot right between the
black mugger's legs. He fell to the concrete, holding his
privates and groaning. I ran to my car and left tracks
peeling out of my parking space.

"Did you do that, Gather Morse?" I asked myself as I
tore ass out of the neighborhood. "Can't believe you did
that. You're really crazy."

It was a little past three and I knew I still had at least
an hour before any of the Dudes showed up at the
clubhouse for the night's game. I pulled my Stingray
down into a hidden driveway beside the stadium so that
anyone who might be in the parking lot would not see it.
Trouble with having a honey of a car like that is that it
announces your presence wherever you go. Sometimes
you crave the attention. But that day I wanted to be
anonymous.

I walked down the concrete corridor and found the
clubhouse door open, which indicated that Benny the Nip
was already there. I had suspected this and prepared
some strategy. I dropped a dime in the pay phone outside
the door, dialed the stadium office, and asked for the
clubhouse. I heard the phone ringing inside. Benny answered.

"Benny my man, this is Gather," I said, cupping my
hand over the phone so he wouldn't hear me through the
door. "Listen, I need a small favor from you. I had this
St. Christopher medal that my mom gave me, and I think
I dropped it when I was throwing in the bullpen last
night. I wondered if you'd be kind enough to run down
there and see if you could find it in the dirt."

He told me to hang on and I heard him leave the
clubhouse through the field entrance. The coast was clear.
I had ten minutes to accomplish my mission. I was so excited that my plan was working that I stupidly hung up
the pay phone. I had to waste some of my precious time

to run into the clubhouse, hang up Benny's phone, come back out, dial the stadium and ask for the clubhouse again, then go back inside and answer the phone there.

That done, I went about planting the criminal evidence. Each player on the team had a safety razor in a plastic case that the nice folks at Techmagic—you know, the folks who sponsor the all-star balloting—had handed out. Well, now the nice folk from Mantua, Ohio, was handing out a new freebie. I hurried from locker to locker and sprinkled a little bit of white powder into each plastic box. I even put some in my own locker. I couldn't leave myself out of this scheme or everyone would know just where to point the finger.

As I finished spreading the dope, I heard Benny coming back into the clubhouse. I ran into the corridor and picked up the dangling phone receiver.

"Gather," Benny said.

"Yeah, Benny. You find it?" I said.

"Nah, only thing there is fucking sunflower seed shells."

"That's too bad, Benny," I said. "I really treasure that medal. Well, thanks anyway. See you in a while."

Later in the evening, just before we went out to the field, I paid a return visit to that phone in the hall. This time I put a handkerchief over the receiver, dialed the D.C. police department, and asked for the narcotics division.

"Narcotics. Troll speaking," a raspy voice said.

"Yes, officer," I said in a deep voice. "I'm with the Pittsburgh *Post-Gazette* and I'm in town covering the Pirates."

"They're gonna get their asses wiped tonight, buddy," Officer Troll said.

"They may," I said. "But I have something to report to you. After last night's game I was doing some interviews in the Dudes' locker room and I noticed some unusual activity going on."

"You mean winning?" Troll said.

I laughed politely. "No, no, officer," I said. "I know this will surprise you and I hate to be the one to have to report it, but instead of facing the press, the Dudes' players were hiding in the trainer's room and, uh, snorting coke."

"Come on, buster," Troll said. "Is this a crank call?"

"I'm serious, officer," I said. "In fact, this information is going to appear in my column tomorrow morning, so I thought I'd give you the chance to do something about it before you get embarrassed."

"Ah, bullshit," Troll said. "You guys will do anything to keep your team in first place. It won't work."

"I'm a journalist, officer," I said. "I don't work for the team or root for them. I think it would be worth your while to visit the Dudes' clubhouse during the game this evening and peek inside the plastic shaving kits they all keep in their lockers. I think you'll find more than just Super Blues. Game's starting now. I gotta go to work."

I hung up the phone and headed to the bullpen to watch and wait. I got a little bit panicky in the third when Sticky Thomas, who was pitching that night, loaded the bases. Skip visited the mound, and I realized that if he sent Sticky to the showers, I'd have to run to the locker room and prevent him from shaving and blowing my plan. But Sticky got out of the inning after giving up only one run, and Skip let him continue.

More than thirty-five thousand fans came out that night to watch the Dudes battle for a share of first place, and they gave RFK a slight touch of pennant fever. 'Course, in any other town, pennant fever's not a June disease, but a September disease. But the fans in Washington had no reason to be aware of that. By September, the Dudes were usually so far out of the race that the fans acted like we had measles and stayed home so they wouldn't catch it.

There were banners draped all over the ball park that evening and the fans came to their feet cheering with every Pirate out. The stands were filled with Washington notables, and the only missing VIP was our owner, Augie August. But if I had anything to do with it, he'd be back for the next night's series finale.

Our ball club came through for the fans, though we waited until the last possible moment to do so. With two outs in the bottom of the ninth we were trailing 3–1 and Jim Rooker, the Pirate's starter, was still coasting easily like he was going downhill on a ten-speed bike. Seemed like he had a win wrapped up when Chi Chi rolled one at Phil Garner, the third baseman. But Garner nonchalanted, took his time, and tossed the ball over first baseman Willie Stargell's head. Chi Chi ended up on second and scored on a single by Tony Smith. The fans started stomping their feet so hard I thought the upper deck would tumble down and become part of the lower deck. Gabby walked to keep us alive, and then old Bubba Bassoon came to the plate representing the winning run. It was a breezy night and Bubba lifted a fast ball high to left field that sat on the wind like it was a train. Everyone in the stadium held their breath, except for Bill Robinson, the Pirate's left fielder. He charged at the wall. He probably could have caught it if he hadn't slipped in a hole on the warning track and tumbled into the Coca-Cola sign. But he ended up on his can and the ball ended up in the Pirates' bullpen. Gabby always said that with baseball and women, you take what you can get. And we gratefully accepted the win.

Our whole team was gathered at home plate to congratulate Bubba when the big fella returned from his trip around the bases. It looked like a Russian circus act out there. Everyone was lifting each other and hugging each other and patting each other on the rump, like ballplayers tend to do. There was more love out on that field than at one of those est seminars. Even I gotta admit it was a beautiful scene. The guys all ran off the field waving one finger in the air to indicate to the crowd that we were in first place. Chi Chi bent his finger, " 'Cause we only tied for first," he said.

The Dudes hooted and howled and celebrated their way down the runway to the clubhouse. But as soon as the door opened, the noise stopped like a radio when a fuse blows. The guys had expected to run in and find the chipmunks there anxious to ask them questions. 'Stead it was the men in blue who lined the room and had a few questions of their own to ask. One by one, the cops removed the gloves from the players' hands and replaced them with handcuffs.

"What's going on here?" Pinky said.

"You're all under arrest," said Officer Troll, who turned out to be a little bowling ball with a mouth.

"Under arrest?" Bubba barked. "We won fair and square."

"You're all under arrest," Troll repeated. "Every one of you."

All the guys looked at each other, trying to decide whether to laugh or cry.

"You want a pair for tomorrow night, officer?" Gabby said to Troll. "You got 'em."

Troll ignored the remark. "Read them their rights, sergeant," he said to this black folk at his side. So the cop took a piece of paper out of his cap and started reading.

"Hold everything," Skip said, walking over to Troll. The sergeant ignored Skip—like we all did—and kept on reading. "Officer, sir, I'm in charge of this outfit," Skip said. "Can you please tell me what is going on here?"

Troll took a shaving kit out of his pocket, opened it, and stuck it in Skip's kisser. "Sir, do you know what that powder is?" Troll said.

Skip dipped his finger into the box and tasted the stuff. "Oh, no," he said. "Not one of my boys."

"All your boys," Troll said. "Get them out of here, men."

"Oh, no, not my boys," Skip said, falling at the officer's feet and begging. "Not my boys. They're good kids. Every one of them. They're fine athletes. And they're in first place."

"Tied for first," Chi Chi shouted as a cop escorted him out the door.

The rest of us followed Chi Chi, each accompanied by our own Smokey. "I always wondered how I'd look in pinstripes," Gabby said. "But I meant Yankee pinstripes."

Skip hung from Troll and kept pleading. "It's gotta be a frame-up," he insisted. I didn't blink an eye at that one.

The chipmunks and some fans stood by in amazement as we were escorted down the hallway and out the players' entrance. It was a parade that no one had ever seen or expected to see, and even the chipmunks were speechless.

Finally, Bobby Ward of the *Star* shouted to Gabby, "What the hell is going on?"

"I got caught stealing," Gabby said, and all our players cracked up.

In the parking lot we were piled onto two paddy wagons. The guys still couldn't believe what was going on, so the mood remained jovial. Gabby asked a cop if there were any stews on the flight, but the cop wouldn't crack a smile.

As I look back now, it was a funny experience. I'm sure all the guys would agree with that. 'Course, they're all gonna be real surprised when they read this and see who set them up, but I don't think they'll mind. Like Gabby said as the paddy wagons pulled out of the parking lot, " 'Stead of celebrating our win at the bars, we'll just have to celebrate behind them."

11

You know how when you're waiting anxiously for something important to happen, all the things that can possibly go wrong and ruin it for you pop into your nervous head? Well, that's what happened to me that night in the slammer. I sat there drinking some mud they passed off as coffee, worrying that I had done some miscalculating. I had counted on Augie hearing about the bust, rushing home from his hideout, and bailing the team out of jail so that we were available to play for first place the next evening. But that might have been overestimating Augie's generosity. To bail out our entire twenty-five man-roster, it would have cost the old man fifty G's. Being as tight as he is, it occurred to me that Augie might cough up only enough bucks to release the nine players who would start the game. And maybe a reliever or two. Or, even worse, he could have gone out and signed up nine free agents to pose as the Dudes just so that the fans would have a game to pay to see. Most folks in the stands are so far away from the field that they can't see our faces anyway. Long as he puts the recognizable numbers on the players' backs, he could suit up nine chinks and the fans wouldn't know the difference. (Except of course for the fact that our uniforms would be too big on them.)

Anyway, as so often happens, my worried speculation proved to be unnecessary. Oh, I was right about Augie not dishing up the bread. But he found a way to avoid that. We weren't locked up for more than a few hours when the old man came walking into the joint, smoking his cigar and accompanied by the mayor of D.C., Walter Washington.

"Let these fellas out of here," the mayor said to Officer Troll as Augie stood by watching. "It's all been a big mistake."

"How do you know it's a mistake, Mayor?" Troll said.

"Because Mr. August told me," Washington said, patting our boss on the back. "And that's good enough for me."

Troll unlocked the cells and we started to pile out.

"Go home and get some sleep, fellas," the mayor said. "You got the biggest game of your lives tomorrow night and I want you to know that all of Washington is pulling for you."

We let out a big cheer for the mayor and walked out of the station house. Gabby walked up to Washington and said, "Is this gonna be in the papers, sir?"

"Well, we're gonna do our best to hush it up," the mayor said.

"Ah, please, don't do that," Gabby pleaded. "My old lady'll never believe that this is where I was till four A.M. unless she reads it in the papers."

I pulled Gabby along and walked outside. The paddy wagons were waiting to take us back to the stadium so we could change out of our uniforms and pick up our cars. But before I got on board, I stopped to talk with Augie.

"Have a nice vacation?" I asked him.

"Too short, son," the old man said, with no visible hostility toward me. "Way too short."

"Too bad about this," I said, testing him. "Wonder who would want to frame us?"

"Don't worry," Augie said, bouncing up and down on the balls of his feet. "I know who did it."

"Who?" I said, worried that he suspected me.

"The commissioner, of course," Augie said. "He doesn't want my team in first place. It's bad for baseball."

"Why's that?" I asked.

" 'Cause we stink, that's why," Augie said, twirling his cigar in his mouth. "Go home and rest up, son. You gotta pitch your heart out tomorrow."

"That's just what I was planning on doing," I said, and I climbed onto the paddy wagon.

'Course, that wasn't my plan at all. It wasn't my own home I was planning on visiting, but Augie's. I had gone to all this trouble just to get Melinda back in town, and I had to see her as soon as possible, even if it was four in the morning.

I got dressed in the clubhouse, got in my Stingray, and headed up to Augie's place. I assumed the old man had beaten me there since he had left directly from the precinct house and I had to stop at the stadium. His car must've been in the garage, but I couldn't tell for sure. I wasn't about to ring the doorbell and announce that I'd come to pick Melinda up for a late-night date. Actually, that might have been good strategy if I was sure she still wanted me as much as she did Sunday night. But she'd spent two days alone with Augie, and I didn't know what evil thoughts he had put in her impressionable, confused little mind. She might have forgotten about me already. So I left my car around the block and ran around the hedges into Augie's front yard.

I knew that Melinda slept in the master bedroom, which was in the round stone tower in the front of the Gothic-style house. And Augie supposedly slept in a guest room in the back. Least that's what the lady had told me. She could have been joshing, of course, since telling a prospective parker that someone else is parking there regularly sends him looking for more available spaces. But I had to take her word.

That cool summer breeze that had carried Bubba's blast out of the park rustled the branches on the husky oaks in Augie's front yard. I stood in the moonlit shadow of one of those trees and looked up at the window of Melinda's dark room. Fortunately, she'd left the window open to draw in a little of the comfortable breeze. Well, I can't do nothing if I can't toss a baseball through an open window like that. So I went back to my trunk, pulled out a Rawlings, pranced quietly back to the yard, and tossed the ball into her room. In an instant, Melinda appeared at the window in a see-through nightgown, holding the ball in her two hands.

"Melinda, it's me, Gather," I said in a loud whisper.

"Gather. Oh, Gather," she said. "What are you doing here?"

Standing there and talking like that, I felt like the prince in one of those fairy stories Mom used to read to me when I was a little bugger. I wished that Melinda could let down her hair for me to climb, like the folks did back in those days. 'Course, in those days the one fairy you never heard about was the hairdresser, so I guess those people just let their locks grow forever.

"I gotta see you, Melinda," I said.

"Not now, Gather," she said. "I . . ."

Then she turned away from the window. Someone must've come into the room, and that someone had to be Augie. I dived into the bushes beside the house. Then I saw Augie looking out the window. I knew right away that Melinda was telling the truth about the separate bedrooms, because the old man wasn't wearing his ridiculous rug.

Augie disappeared from my view, but I stayed in the bushes awhile longer for safe measure, which turned out to be a good idea. Next thing I knew, all the floodlights around the house went on, illuminating the place like the Vegas strip. And Augie came out of the house in his monogrammed robe, carrying a twelve-gauge shotgun. He walked around his property all ready to play Clint Eastwood and stick it to the prowlers. But he had left his front door open behind him.

When his back was turned, I sneaked out of the bushes and into the house. Sure, I was a crazy dude to do that when the old man was standing there holding buckshot in his mitts. But that's how urgent it was for me to see Melinda.

I ran up the carpeted wood staircase and found her standing in the doorway with her speakers peeking through her nightie. Her eyes opened wide when she saw me.

"Gather, get out of here. He'll kill you," she said.

"Melinda, I gotta talk to you," I said. "You gotta come with me now."

"I can't, Gather. I just can't," she said.

"Don't you want to?" I asked.

She looked down at the floor. "I'm not sure," she said.

I couldn't believe my ears. The lady had to be sure. The trade deadline was less than twenty-four hours away. But I didn't have time to persuade her right there. I heard the front door slam shut and footsteps on the stairs. If I didn't vanish, Augie might walk in the room and pull the trigger without realizing he was canceling his only annuity. I couldn't take that chance.

"Quick. The window," Melinda said.

Without considering what I was doing, I listened to her and climbed out. I was hanging on the ledge by my fingertips, getting ready to jump. But before I did, Melinda slammed the window shut on my fingers. I managed not to scream, both when the window hit me and when I fell into the thorny rosebushes below.

I climbed out of the bushes and scooted to my car, picking thorns out of my skin along the way. I sat in the car out of breath from the excitement. I was in serious trouble. My plan was in jeopardy, my heart was aching, and my fingers were numb. But I couldn't afford to sit there feeling sorry for myself. Pitching had taught me to keep concentrating under pressure no matter how bad I might feel, and that training was valuable now.

The most important thing was still for me to get alone with Melinda. If I could only see her, I was sure I could persuade her that she wanted me more than the old buzzard. I couldn't go back to the house. I'm sure Augie was sitting on the floor of her room like a watchdog. And there was no sense waiting for them to go out together, since I'd already tried that one with little success. My only alternative seemed to be to find a way to lure Augie out of the house alone. But how?

I sat up the block in my car, watching the sun come up and trying to think of someplace Augie might be summoned where he would not bring Melinda. He wasn't the kind of man who frequented any of those type places where ladies weren't welcomed. And he certainly didn't attend any of those smoker-type parties where only hired women were welcome. You don't jump in the water if you can't swim.

It must've been close to noon, I'd been sitting there for nearly eight hours, and my princess was still locked away in her tower. I guess I'd drifted into some kind of quiet hysteria, 'cause I came up with the most morbid-type idea I ever did think of in my life. You ain't gonna believe this one.

I drove out to Wisconsin Avenue and walked up to a pay phone in front of a People's Drugstore. Some graffiti freak had written "This is a bomb, not a phone. Call at your own risk" on the dialing-information card. But I took my chances and dialed Augie's number anyway. The old man answered. I tried to talk in a raspy voice that sounded like Officer Troll to my ears.

"Hello, Mr. August," I said. "This is Officer Troll. I'm afraid I have some bad news for you."

"Go ahead," Augie said.

"Well, sir, we just found one of your players, that Morse fellow, lying unconscious in the street up in the black part of town. He's been beat up pretty bad. Guess those folks didn't appreciate his remarks last week, and finally got a piece of him."

"Oh, my God," Augie said. "He's gotta pitch tonight."

"Oh, he won't be pitching tonight. Guarantee you that. He's in critical condition at D.C. General."

"Okay, I'm rushing right over there," Augie said.

"And, sir," I said. "I wouldn't bring any women or children along if I were you. He's not a pretty sight."

I didn't know what the reaction would be when Augie found out that this was a hoax. But I didn't have time to worry about it. I got back in my car, drove to Augie's, and parked around the corner. I sat in my car waiting for him to drive by and for me to have Melinda to myself.

Well, the man was genuinely concerned about me. Wasn't ten minutes after the phone call when his Mercedes shot by me on the way to the hospital. Unfortunately, Melinda was real concerned also. She was sitting there next to him in the passenger seat. Augie never listens to other people's suggestions. And I was foiled again.

Well, I don't know what they found when they got down to the hospital. But I know what they didn't find— me. I still had a few hours to waste before I had to be at the stadium, so I drove over to Duke Ziebert's restaurant and ordered myself your basic steak and baked potato. It wasn't the kind of pregame meal I was accustomed to. But that was all right. I didn't have time that day to start worrying about the free-swinging Pirate hitters. My thoughts were concentrated instead on my lingering plan of escape. I only had one opportunity left to get to Melinda—at the game that night. 'Course, my spare time would be limited, since I was obligated to spend a good portion of the evening on the mound, and I couldn't possibly talk to her from that location. But I was still determined to find some way to make Augie feel that his relationship was threatened in the little time I had left. Like Yogi says, "It's never over till it's over."

In the clubhouse before the game, Chi Chi ran around

with a palm full of talcum powder yelling, "Cocaine. See. I have cocaine."

"Hey, Chi Chi," Bubba bellowed. "Lemme see that stuff." Chi Chi mischievously scampered over and held his hand up for Bubba to see. Bubba took a deep breath and blew the powder right into the Latino's face. Well, Chi Chi started sneezing like he had a French tickler up his nose. Benny the Nip had to give the poor fella an antihistamine so he was able to play.

That incident shows what the mood was in our clubhouse before the biggest game the Dudes ever played. Since we had beaten the Bucs two straight, the guys were pretty confident we could beat them once more. Pinky wore his good-luck Jockeys—a pair painted like a hot dog stand that said "Open for business" above the fly. Other than that, no one did anything peculiar just 'cause a win that night would give us solo possession of first place.

Me, I felt like I'd just flown the red-eye in from the coast. I hadn't slept all night and the fingers of my pitching hand were throbbing like my heart does when I look at Suzanne Somers wrapped in a towel. Feeling the way I was, I probably should have begged out of my pitching turn. But I didn't want teams that might still be interested in acquiring me to get thinking that I might be injured.

Just before I went out to throw, Bubba pulled his stool up next to mine to go over the hitters in the Pirates' lineup. He talked about jamming Al Oliver and keeping the ball away from Dave Parker, and I thought about jamming my fist down Augie's throat and keeping Melinda away from him. I certainly wasn't thinking about the Pirates, which meant I was ready to go out and play ball.

"All set," Bubba said when he was finished.

"We're gonna find out," I said.

Bubba stood up on his stool, pounded his fist in his mitt, and yelled, "Let's go after these guys like they're good pussy," and we all trotted out to the field to warm up.

The stands were packed that evening, mostly with black folk. Not only was it a crucial game, but it was also our third annual Hubcap Night. That's right. Like Augie always said, you gotta give the folks what they want. 'Course, he didn't just give his premium items away gratis like other teams did. No chance of that. But any fan who bought ham hocks or grits got them served up on a shiny new hubcap.

With the way the black folk felt about me, I figured they would use those hubcaps like Odd Job in the James Bond flicks used his hat. Try to decapitate the Baseball Bigot. But I figured wrong. The game meant too much to the fans to try to interrupt it. And besides, they all knew they could get a good price for their souvenirs at the local hock shop. So when I took the mound, I was actually received with a rousing cheer.

As I stood listening to the National Anthem, I felt an evening breeze rustling my uniform. It was blowing out to right, which gave an advantage to Dave Parker and Willie Stargell, the Pirates' left-handed power. I had to pitch low and away on them.

After the song, I turned toward the plate to take my final warm-up tosses and noticed Augie and Melinda taking their seats in the first row. Yes sir, there she was, just where I wanted her and needed her. She was wearing dark glasses so that I couldn't make any eye contact. But I was gonna pick my spot and get to her, even if it meant walking off the mound with the bases loaded. I left half a mind on her and focused the other half on the Pirates' hitters.

The crowd started buzzing with my first pitch, a low curve that Frank Taveras foul-tipped. And they kept buzzing with each successive pitch. There was a constant hum in the background, like the static on a distant FM radio station. From the first batter, it was a real tense-type game, which was something no one on our club was used to. I probably would have been pissing in my plastic cup if I didn't have to keep one eye on Melinda in between pitches.

I got through the first inning easily enough, ending it in a flurry by striking out Dave Parker, the league's leading hitter. After throwing four pitches away from him, I messed up his head by coming with a screwball that broke at his fists. He swung and missed by so much that if he was white he would have blushed.

Al Oliver led off the second with a crisp single to left, and Bill Robinson followed with a hot grounder in the hole between the shortstop and the third baseman. Gabby went deep in that hole, made a backhand grab, got rid of the ball like it was a hot coal, and started a slick double play. Still don't know how that lard-ass got to that ball.

So I was pretty much in control of the Pirate hitters. Only trouble was, our guys weren't kissing any of John Candelaria's pitches either. Candy Man kept coming in with the express, and our guys didn't swing until the train went by the station. Gabby hit a bloop single in the first and Chi Chi beat out a little nibbler in the third, but neither of them got past first base.

It was me and the Candy Man going at each other like two cowboy sharpshooters showing off their best tricks. I'd get out of my half inning in six pitches and he'd come right back and strike out the side. With nothing on the line, this kind of pitchers' duel could be a real yawner for the fans. But with first place waiting for the winner, every pitch, every swing, every play in the field was crucial and exciting. It seemed like one misplay and one run would decide the contest. The crowd cheered each time one of our guys managed to lift a fly to the outfield, and gasped each time one of their guys did the same.

Though I didn't start out caring much about that particular contest, I got swept up by its intensity. My adrenaline must've been running nine hundred miles per hour. I was both nervous and confident on every pitch. The sweat on my uniform could've ended the drought in California. But I tell you, I loved the feeling of pitching in that game. Loved every minute of it.

'Course, every minute brought me closer to the trade

deadline. So I was torn between the excitement of that tight, critical game and the need to get off the field and alone with Melinda.

Pitchers' battles like that one usually move along quickly, so I didn't get too concerned with the time early on. But when we finished the ninth inning at 10:05 without either team even threatening to score a run, I knew that I either had to end the game fast or make sure that I got taken out.

In the bottom of the eleventh Aurelio Smith led off with a single and Rod Smith followed with another. Bill Robinson retrieved the ball quickly in left, so Aurelio had to put on his brakes at second. It was only 10:35, and with two on and no out, I was confident my guys would come through and leave me a little breathing space. Chuck Tanner, the Pirates' manager, wasted some precious time by removing Candelaria from the game. I was kind of sorry to see him leave after he had thrown his heart out for eleven innings. But with the way he fires that goose egg, it was amazing that he could last as long as he did. He must've had to soak that elbow in ice for three days after throwing so much smoke for so long.

Bruce "the Goose" Gossage, the league leader in ERA, came on and picked up right where the Candy Man had left off. He got Pinky to bounce into a third-to-first double play, which left Rod Smith at second with two outs. Chatsworth was up next and then I was scheduled to hit. I was sure they'd walk Chatsworth to set up the force and pitch to the light-hitting pitcher. In that case, Skip would've pinch-hit for me, which would have taken me out of the game. Considering all this, I was both sad and glad. I hated to walk away from that game without a win, and if the pinch hitter made out, I'd be in the showers without a decision. On the other hand, I'd be able to rush over to Melinda's seat and try to pry her away from Augie.

As usual, all this forethought went to waste. Gossage is a mean mother on the mound, and he had no intention of giving Chatsworth a free pass. He battled Soul Chink to a full count, then came in with a blazer that Chatsworth hit off the top of the bat. The ball went straight up in the air and fell into Duffy Dyer's catcher's mitt.

So I went back out and pitched the twelfth. And the thirteenth. Skip kept suggesting that I quit, and I kept begging him for one more inning. He was probably wrong to let me continue, but he had trouble saying no to people, so I stayed in the game. That was one night when I was lucky that I couldn't throw a fastball. If I could, my arm would have been like wet ziti by the ninth or certainly by the tenth. But when you keep coming with the local like I do, you can throw from sundown to dawn without feeling too much pain.

It was 11:30 already when I took the mound for the fourteenth. My time was running low. Melinda was still sitting patiently beside Augie, where I could keep an eye on her, but even so, I was still worried that I wouldn't have time to do everything that had to be done by that three A.M. trade deadline.

Frank Taveras led off that inning by poking a drop pitch to right for a bloop single. Taveras is a weasel on the base paths. Blink, and he'll steal on you. So his leadoff hit put me in immediate danger.

Phil Garner stepped in next, and Taveras took a four-step lead. Garner is the ideal second hitter, since he makes frequent contact and is a good hit-and-run man. I had to watch Taveras, be careful with Garner, and keep glancing at Melinda. I went into my stretch and stopped with the ball at my waist. I checked Taveras, looked at Garner, looked back at Taveras. As I swung my head back toward the plate, I caught a quick glimpse of Melinda getting out of her seat and heading up the aisle. Augie stayed put to watch the action. Melinda was finally alone. This was my chance. Maybe my last chance.

It pains me to admit this even now, but you know all about what I'd been through so you'll understand. I was left with no choice. I had to get out of that game at that very instant or spend the rest of my life with Augie August.

I kicked my leg high in the air and released the ball. It wasn't a curve. It was a screwball. It wasn't a greaser. Fact is, I put nothing on the ball at all except an invitation for Garner to knock it out of the park and me out of the game. His eyes opened wide and he lashed out at it. The meat of his bat met the meat of the ball.

Next thing I knew, the baseball was coming right at my skull. My nightmare had come true. It must've been traveling one hundred miles per hour, but it looked like slow motion to me. The ball would've killed me if I gave it the chance. But I didn't. Instead, I fainted.

Well, I couldn't have been seeing birdies for more than a few seconds. I opened my eyes and saw all my teammates standing around me looking at me like I was a dead man.

Skip was leaning over me and barking at me through his tobacco breath. "Can you hear me, Gather?" he said. "Can you hear me?"

I looked him in the eyes. I realized where I was. I remembered what had happened.

"Melinda," I shouted. And I jumped to my feet and ran off the field.

I ran through the clubhouse, down the hall, and up the ramp to the field box level. I found section eleven, where Augie's box was located, then found the ladies room closest to the section. Melinda had to be in there.

The place was SRO and there was a line of ladies in the hall waiting for an empty seat. But I couldn't wait my turn.

"Excuse me. Excuse me," I said, bobbing and weaving my way past the ladies in line. And I walked right on into that ladies' room. It was packed like Clyde's on a Friday night. Foxes were all lined up waiting to get a peek at themselves in the mirrors.

"There's a man in here," a lady shrieked, and everyone started giggling like schoolgirls looking at a *Playgirl* centerfold. Soon as they realized who I was, which wasn't difficult, since I was in uniform, they all started pulling lipstick out of their purses and begging me for autographs. But I didn't have time to oblige my fans. I had to find Melinda.

I couldn't find her in the crowd, so I knew she had to be doing her thing behind one of the closed doors. I walked from john to john, pulling myself up on each door to glance inside. All the ladies with their dropped drawers screamed when they saw me. But sure enough, in the fourth stall, I found myself face to face with Melinda.

"Psst," I said.

"Oh, lordy," she said when she looked up and saw me hanging on the door.

"Melinda, I love you. I want you," I said.

"You sure know how to be romantic, Gather," she said as she flushed and pulled up her drawers.

"Oh, Melinda, I want to be with you forever," I said.

"You gotta let me outta here first," she said.

I fell off the door and she came out of the john. I grabbed her arms and held her in front of me. All the other ladies gathered around us like we were playing a love scene for them. There were even some heads peeking out over the stall doors to see us.

"Gather, can't we talk someplace else?" she said, looking around embarrassed.

"No, Melinda," I said. "I won't let you get away from me ever again. I love you and I'm not walking out of here till you promise to come home with me."

She stared into my begging eyes. I don't know if she was touched or humiliated. But she took my hand and said, "Let's go."

As we ran out of the ladies' room hand-in-hand, one woman said, "Isn't that the most beautiful thing you've ever seen?"

We left the stadium, ran through the parking lot, and got into my Stingray. As I pulled out of the parking lot, I stopped and told the attendant, "If anyone's looking for us, we'll be at my place."

My hunch was that when Melinda did not come back to her seat, Augie would go looking for her. And I wanted him to find her.

As we hurried home, I questioned Melinda about the past few days and discovered that she was one very confused lady. She had left my place Sunday night, gone back to Augie, and told him that she wanted to leave him. She didn't say that there was a third party involved and that I was that third party. She just couldn't hurt him like that.

Well, he begged her to stay and pleaded with her and promised her the world on a silver plate and conned her into going away with him to Virginia Beach. She wasn't sure if she wanted to go and she wasn't sure if she didn't want to go, so she went, 'cause that was easier. Augie was too good to leave, but not good enough to stay with. I was too good to pass up, but . . . But nothing. She wanted to be with him and she wanted to be with me. If all this sounds confusing to you, how do you think I felt hearing it? Melinda had no idea what she wanted, except for everything, which she couldn't have. But me and Fellini were gonna help her make her decision.

I pulled up in front of my building and we ran together into my apartment. I closed the door behind me, but made sure it wasn't locked, just in case Augie intended on paying us a little visit. Then I pulled Melinda into my bedroom and started going at her like a hungry bear.

I kissed her all over her face and her neck and rubbed my hands all over her breasts and ass. She knew right off that I meant business, and she was a good customer. She ran her fingers furiously through my hair and swirled her golden hair around as I continued to shower her soft skin with my kisses. She pulled my mouth to hers and when I arrived, her lips were spread wide as the Mississippi. Our tongues flitted around frantically like butterflies on uppers. Soon we began to peel off each other's clothes and fling them around the room. Our tongues continued to flutter as I ran my fingers lightly down her waist, through her hair, around her thighs, and into her cunt. She touched Fellini softly and moved her cold fingertips slowly around the tip, sending chills all through my body. We were working each other into a wild frenzy. It was so exciting it was almost unbearable. Our tongues stopped and we started biting each other's lips.

She fell back onto my bed and pulled me with her. Fellini slid into her easily as skiing downhill. She threw her legs around my neck, clasped her ankles, and reached for the sky. I put my hands under her ass and pulled her up higher. I was never as excited with a woman before. I felt as if my whole body was going to explode, and I wanted it to.

We were both moaning and groaning and gasping and swaying. It was as if we were both delirious with delight. And then, all of a sudden, there was this loud scream that seemed to shake the walls of the room. Melinda and I froze. Her legs bounced on the mattress. She opened her eyes and looked over my shoulder, and her face filled with horror. Augie August was standing there in the doorway. He had ripped his toupee off his head, thrown it to the floor, and he was jumping up and down on it and shouting like a madman. When he stopped, he lost his balance and fell against the wall. His skin was ashen. One tear slid slowly down his cheek.

I rolled off Melinda. She threw her arms over her eyes. It was the moment I had been waiting for, though I didn't expect it to happen quite like that. I felt pride in my accomplishment and pity for the old man. I didn't know what to say, so said nothing.

Augie peeled himself off the wall. He seemed calmer now. He tugged at his blazer and straightened his collar. He cleared his throat and said, "Can I use your phone?"

I pointed to the phone on the night table. Augie walked to it, lifted the receiver, and dialed. He looked at the window instead of at our naked bodies.

"Hi there, buddy. This is Augie August," he said into the phone in his jolly salesman's voice. "Tell me. Are you still interested in Morse?"

He listened for a second. "Well, you got him," he said. "Let's talk tomorrow and work out the details."

He hung up and stood there with his hands in his pockets and his head bowed.

"Who is it, Augie?" I said. "The Reds?"

"The Reds?" he said, looking at me like I was crazy. "What do the Reds need you for? They traded for Tom Seaver this evening. Nah, Morse, it's not the Reds. You are now the property of the New York Mets."

Epilogue

If You Look Hard Enough, You'll Find a Moral in Here Someplace

I haven't had a chance to tell you yet that the Dudes came up with two runs in the bottom of the fourteenth to beat the Pirates, 2–1, and become the temporary front-runners in the National League East. So I'm sure all of my former teammates got a lot of yuks the next morning when they heard that I'd been traded to the Mets and gone from first place to last overnight. 'Course, I ain't exactly sitting here now and crying over the fact that they've lost eight in a row since I left, and fallen back into the pack.

The Dudes are still ahead of my new team in the standings. But I don't have any complaints about the deal. How can I, after all my crazy-ass scheming? All I wanted was to get away from Augie August, and I guess you can say that's all I got. 'Course, now I'm stuck with Mr. M. Donald Grant, which might seem like going from the cesspool to the sewer. But I'm gonna forget what I've heard about the man and give my new boss a chance. Maybe it'll be different for me than it was for Tom Seaver and Jon Matlack and Rusty Staub and Jerry Grote and all the other fine players who left the Mets unhappy.

Fact is, all the major-league baseball teams are the

same. They're great when you're winning and drawing and uncomfortable when you're losing and dying at the gate. It's always been that way. Today, there's one additional factor. They're great when you've got a signed contract and uncomfortable when you're negotiating. I guess all players' emotions go up and down like a pop fly.

As for the rest of my story—Melinda ended up going home with Augie from my place that evening he caught us. The old man put his foot down and demanded it. He acted just like her father, which I guess he was, and she acted just like a naughty little girl, which I guess she was. I was too busy enjoying the trade to concern myself with Melinda leaving. Sure, I wanted the lady, but I didn't need to be in a hurry to have her anymore.

The next morning, I was awakened by a phone call from Joe Torre, the Mets' new manager, who said he was glad to have me aboard. I told him I was happy to be aboard, even though the ship was sinking. He said his G.M. was on the other phone with Payton working out the details of transferring my contract. I know that having Payton represent my interests is like having George Wallace representing Martin Luther King in court. And once I settle down up here, I plan to get myself a new agent. Gabby Smith once said to me that changing agents is like a beggar changing cups, but sometimes even a new cup'll make you happy. For a short while anyway.

After talking to Joe, I packed up all my belongings and put them in my Stingray. My furniture was rented, so I didn't have to worry about it. Still, the car is small and it was crowded and the only place I could fit my case of Scrubble Bubbles was on the seat next to me. From there I went to the stadium to clean out my locker. Only things I needed were my gloves and my spikes. I gave Benny the Nip a few bucks and told him to say good-bye to the guys for me.

There was no one in town that I needed to say good-bye to, and that made me a little bit sad. I'd succeeded on the field in Washington, but I'd failed off it. I hadn't really made any genuine friends. But I was starting all over and there was no premium in looking back. So I headed out to the Baltimore–Washington Parkway and pointed the nose of my Stingray toward Big Apple Town.

Driving along the highway, I had to laugh out loud thinking about all the insane things I'd done the past two weeks. If anyone else saw me laughing alone in my car like that, they would have sent me back to St. E.'s.

Oh, lord, St. E.'s. I couldn't believe I actually spent a night in that place. I still can't. And I can't believe that the black folks had that rally to protest me and that I walked out to the mound in the altogether and that I bought the cocaine and that I got the whole team arrested. Shoot, all that just to get myself traded. All most guys have to do is hit .220 or lose more games than they win. But not ol' Gather Morse, Baseball Bigot, Nude on the Mound, Junkball Junkie.

And then there was Melinda. Ah, beautiful, soft, sweet-smelling Melinda. With the greatest set of speakers since sound was invented. As I drove along, pictures of her flashed through my mind. Her standing there in the shower room. And in the dressing room at Ruby's. Sitting in Augie's box licking her lips. And sitting across from me at the restaurant in Georgetown. Standing in her bedroom in her see-through nightie. And lying underneath me. Clinging to me. Loving me.

I was already at the toll gate for the Baltimore Harbor Tunnel when I said to myself, "Gather Morse, you ain't going nowhere without that lady."

It wasn't an easy place for me to turn back, the tunnel wasn't. I told the toll collector that I had left my wallet back in my Washington hotel room. The parkway police had to stop the traffic in both directions just so that I could turn around. And I had to pay a toll going each way. But it was worth it. And it was also worth the twenty-five dollars I had to cough up when a Smokey caught me going one hundred on the way back to Washington.

Funny thing is, I didn't realize I was going that fast. I swear it. I was too busy worrying about the scene that would take place when I arrived at Augie's. I was sure it was gonna be one of those teary-eyed confrontations with me begging Melinda to come and Augie begging her to stay and her trying to figure out how to do both at once. But I wasn't gonna leave that house without her. No way. 'Less, of course, Augie pulled out his twelve-gauge.

This time, when I got to Augie's neighborhood, I didn't see no reason to leave my Stingray around the block. I just pulled it right up onto his driveway, walked to the front door, and rang the bell. I'm not sure what I would have said if Augie had opened the door. But he didn't. Melinda did.

"Melinda," I said. "You gotta come with me. I won't take no for an answer. I'm not leaving without you."

"Just wait one minute," she said. She disappeared behind the door, and I didn't know what was coming. Next thing I knew, she came walking on out of the house carrying two large suitcases. Lady's as smart as a whipsaw. She knew all along that I wasn't leaving town without her next to me. 'Course, I didn't tell her that I almost had.

"Did you tell Augie you were leaving?" I asked as I tied her suitcases on the roof of my car.

"Yeah," she said.

"Well, what'd he say?"

"You were right about him," she said. "He didn't hear me. But what else can I do, Gather?"

Her face was real troubled. I tried to think of the right thing to say. "Get in the car," was all I could come up with.

She picked my carton of Scrubble Bubbles off the seat and held them on her lap, since there was no place else to put them. "What is this stuff for?" she asked, holding a can in the air.

Well, I'd never shared the secret of my success with anyone before, and I didn't even know if I should tell her. "Can't say," I said.

"Tell me or I'll shoot," she said, aiming the nozzle at my face.

"I can't, Melinda. It's a secret I wouldn't even share with my wife if I had one."

That got her onto a new topic. "You want one?" she said.

"Well, someday maybe," I said.

"How 'bout today?" she said.

That sure took me by surprise. I stared into her baby-blues and could see that she wasn't just joshing me.

Well, as I told you, at that point in my life I was no longer too happy with the casual-type relationships I usually got involved in. Oh, sure, there were a few tough foxes I met that it was worth having any kind of relationship with, casual or even less. But none were any finer than the sweet thing sitting next to me. And like Yogi says, "When you got the guns, you gotta go with them."

Maybe he didn't say that one. But I know I heard it someplace.

"How can we possibly get married today?" I said.

She had it all planned. "We'll stop in Elkton, Maryland," she said. "It's on the way."

So about two hours out of Washington, we pulled off the Maryland Pike when we got to Elkton. It's no more than a hitching post of the town. Fact is, it's no more than a hitching post. They marry you up just like you make instant coffee. All you need is a pair of witnesses, and they got them sitting around the place for hire.

Just like that, Gather Morse became an old married man and Melinda Towers became an old lady. 'Course, I swore to myself that I wouldn't call her that, being that I didn't like it when my teammates said it 'bout their old ladies.

From there, we continued on up to the big city and checked right in here at the Plaza Hotel, where we've been ever since. We're about to start looking for a little place to set up like home. I don't mind the hotel, except that I was surprised when we first got here and I found two toilets in the john. I guess you call that class. So far, we haven't left the room at all, except to go to the ball park. And that brings me to the sad part of the ending.

First night I went out to Shea, must've been Friday, June 17, I walked into Joe Torre's office and he said to me, "Too bad about your old boss, isn't it?"

"What're you telling me?" I said.

"Oh, I'm sorry, Gather. I thought you already knew," Joe said. "They found Augie dead in his house last night."

I felt like I'd just been punched in the gut. My ten-dollar New York lunch started working its way up out of my stomach.

"How'd it happen?" I asked.

"Heart failure is what they say," Torre told me.

'Course, I knew that the old man had had a heart attack just four years ago, which was no surprise after eating his own greasy junk food all those years. And he didn't take the best care of himself, smoking those cigars like they were part of his face. But me and Melinda, we couldn't help but feel a little bit responsible for the final blow. We didn't kill him or nothing like that, and I resent folks implying that we did. We're real sad about what happened, and I guess it's just something we're gonna have to live with for the rest of our lives.

The saddest part is that it didn't have to happen like this. All the man had to do was treat me like a fella human being instead of a piece of merchandise. And even if he didn't wanna do that, he could have been straight with me 'stead of deceiving me. But that just ain't the way it goes down between baseball players and their bosses these days.

I guess the only consolation I could get now would be for the other owners, and the players too, to hear this whole story like I told it here, and learn a little lesson about how to live with each other. 'Course, there's as much chance of that happening as there is of Tom Seaver coming back to the Mets.

Anyway, Augie August left his mark on this game in a lot of ways. And they ought to put up one of those plaques in the Hall of Fame to memorialize the old man. He's the only owner I know of who sacrificed his life trying to hold on to a great baseball player. And if what he tried to do ain't just downright smart baseball, well then, my name ain't Gather Morse.

About the Author

Marty Bell was formerly senior editor at *New Times* magazine and *Sport Magazine*. He is the author of CARNIVAL AT FOREST HILLS and THE LEGEND OF DR. J. BREAKING BALLS is his first novel.